***How long had it been since a woman
felt this good in his arms?
Rio wondered.***

Too long. Way too long. Holding Maggie was like holding a piece of heaven. Why was it that whenever she looked at him or touched him or did a hundred other little things, he felt no one had ever done it before? What was it about her that made him feel not quite so used up and worn-out? When in his life had he ever known such peace, such hope, except when he was with her? And she was so soft, her body yielding to his perfectly, causing him to remember he was a man with needs.

***How long had it been since she had
been held in a man's arms like this?
Maggie wondered.***

Too long. Rio's embrace was fiercely protective and overwhelmingly seductive at the same time. He held her pressed against him, as if he had no plans to turn her loose until the end of the century. Delicious sensations moved across her body, as if prompted by a misbegotten whirlwind, touching her here, there, everywhere, enticing, exciting, making her feel more alive than she had in oh, so long. Making her remember that she was a woman with needs.

D0041126

Sandy Steen is acknowledged as the author of this work.

Special thanks and acknowledgment to Sutton Press Inc. for its contribution to the concept for the Crystal Creek series.

ISBN 0-373-82529-3

SHAMELESS

Printed in U.S.A.

Sandy Steen

SHAMELESS

Harlequin Books

TORONTO • NEW YORK • LONDON
AMSTERDAM • PARIS • SYDNEY • HAMBURG
STOCKHOLM • ATHENS • TOKYO • MILAN
MADRID • WARSAW • BUDAPEST • AUCKLAND

Dear Reader,

Reviewers and readers alike can't seem to get enough of Crystal Creek!

"The McKinney family just gets more and more fascinating. I have read every book in the collection.... Just when I think the next one can't be as good as the previous, I am surprised to find it is just as—if not more—satisfying than the last."

—Melissa Barnes,
South Carolina

"The continuing saga of Crystal Creek is so enjoyable because piece by piece you are learning to know the entire town. It almost makes you want to move there and be part of it. What a great way to spend a lazy afternoon!"

—*Affaire de Coeur*

This month, Sandy Steen makes her Crystal Creek debut with a heartwarming tale of reunion, of belonging, and of the power of love to break down insurmountable barriers. In *Shameless,* an infant manages to touch the desperate lives of a lonely rancher, a Houston power broker, an empathetic social worker and a well-to-do college student. You'll find it a great addition to the series!

And next month, author Barbara Kaye, who first introduced you to Crystal Creek, will weave the tale Crystal Creek fans have long been waiting for, the decades-long story of the irrepressible Hank Travis—from his humble origins as a peanut farmer's son, to his astonishing rise to fortune in the booming oil fields! Watch for *Let's Turn Back the Years,* available wherever Harlequin books are sold. And stick around in Crystal Creek—home of sultry Texas drawls, smooth Texas charm and tall, sexy Texans!

Marsha Zinberg
Coordinator, Crystal Creek

A Note from the Author

As a Texan, born and bred, I lay claim to a certain Bill of Boasts, similar to the Bill of Rights, but wearing cowboy boots, a Stetson and a cocky attitude. So, forgive my braggadocio, but it's in the genes.

From the Rio Grande to the Red River, from boot scootin' to bull shootin', Texas has been, and probably always will be, thought of as larger than life. We claim our women are the prettiest, our oilmen the richest and our tales the tallest. We brag, swagger and reinvent the language to suit ourselves. We come complete with longhorns and long necks, cowboys and Indians, famous outlaws and lawmen...and enough love in our hearts to fill our high, wide and handsome state.

It's this love that has flowed from Crystal Creek and all its characters since the beginning and makes it such a special place to visit, both as a writer and a reader. So special, I can tell you that if the lovingly created Hill Country town really did exist outside the imaginations of its authors, several of us, myself included, would be receiving our mail there.

With *Shameless*, I've introduced two characters who have this special kind of love, for each other and for a baby. I hope you'll take them to your hearts as you have the rest of the citizens of Crystal Creek. Enjoy your visit and c'mon back anytime.

Sandy Steen

Who's Who in Crystal Creek

Have you missed the story of one of your favorite Crystal Creek characters? Here's a quick guide to help you easily locate the titles and story lines:

DEEP IN THE HEART   J. T. McKinney and Cynthia
COWBOYS AND CABERNET   Tyler McKinney and Ruth
AMARILLO BY MORNING   Cal McKinney and Serena
WHITE LIGHTNING   Lynn McKinney and Sam
EVEN THE NIGHTS ARE BETTER   Carolyn Townsend and Vernon
AFTER THE LIGHTS GO OUT   Scott Harris and Val
HEARTS AGAINST THE WIND   Jeff Harris and Beverly
THE THUNDER ROLLS   Ken Slattery and Nora
GUITARS, CADILLACS   Wayne Jackson and Jessica
STAND BY YOUR MAN   Manny Hernandez and Tracey
NEW WAY TO FLY   Brock Munroe and Amanda
EVERYBODY'S TALKIN'   Cody Hendricks and Lori
MUSTANG HEART   Sara Gibson and Warren
PASSIONATE KISSES   J. T. McKinney and Pauline
RHINESTONE COWBOY   Liz Babcock and Guy
SOUTHERN NIGHTS   Lisa Croft and Tony

Available at your local bookseller, or see the Crystal Creek back-page ad for reorder information.

For Marsha,

Thanks for inviting me to the party. I've had a ball.

CHAPTER ONE

TESS HOLLOWAY didn't believe in coincidence. It wasn't coincidence that had brought Rio Langley into her life just when she needed him. Just when she so desperately needed a hero. From what little she knew of the tall, somber cowboy, he would probably laugh out loud to know she thought of him as heroic. But she did.

Standing in the moonlight across the narrow dirt road that wound past the Langley ranch house, Tess hugged her precious burden more tightly against the unseasonably chilly wind. This was the hardest thing she had ever done in her young, but not untroubled life. She hoped and prayed that God understood. Surely He did. Didn't they say that He watched out for fools and little children? She had never been much of a churchgoer, but that didn't mean her faith was weak. Lord knew, if that had been the case she could never have come to this point. To this decision. Yes, she was sure that God understood and maybe even forgave. That, too, was part of her prayers.

Praying was just about all Tess had done since she'd arrived in Crystal Creek two days ago and dis-

covered that Delora Langley, the woman she had
come to see, had died nearly a month ago. She had
almost decided that her prayers were falling on deaf
ears until yesterday, when she overheard Delora's son
offer his opinion about families. She would never
forget the hushed, almost reverent tone in Rio Langley's voice when he said that he had learned the hard
way that family was *the* most important thing in the
world. And how, now that he was alone, if he had a
chance, he would do *anything* to have even a small
part of his family again.

Call it luck, fate, or divine Providence, but at that
moment, Tess knew she had been right to come to
Crystal Creek, and an idea born out of her emotional fatigue and desperation had taken root.

As discreetly as possible, she had asked around and
found out that Rio had just returned to claim his inheritance, a two-hundred-and-seventy-five-acre ranch
located a few miles outside the town limits. Even
though he was considered a loner by most of the
townspeople, he was respected, particularly among
the men. Only yesterday afternoon at the café, Cal
McKinney had told his pretty wife that Rio was one
of the best judges of horseflesh he had ever known.
Nora Slattery, the owner of the Longhorn Coffee
Shop, allowed as how her husband, Ken, would
wholeheartedly agree. Another customer, a pleasant-
looking woman Nora Slattery had called Mary, said
that it was a shame Delora hadn't lived long enough

to see what a fine, hardworking man her son had become.

Tess had been in town for only two days, but it was clear the Longhorn was *the* gathering place. At any given time in the day, one could get the finest chicken-fried steak in Claro County and the latest gossip and news, both good and bad, all at the same time. It didn't take her long to figure out which customers made the news and which ones reported it. As far as she could tell, Rio Langley fit neither category, which made him just the man she needed.

Last night she had agonized over her decision, and now the time had come to do what she was convinced, despite her weariness and confusion, was the right thing to do. She had parked the aged Volkswagen, which had doubled as transportation and living quarters for her and her baby the past week, far enough down the road not to be seen, but close enough to easily walk to the Langley property. And she had waited and watched until she saw Rio Langley come out of the barn and walk to the house. That had been almost fifteen minutes ago, and still no lights blazed in the front of the house, which probably meant he was fixing himself something to eat in the kitchen. But he *was* there, and that was all she really needed to know.

Carefully lifting the blanket-wrapped bundle in her arms, she placed a whisper-soft kiss on a baby-soft cheek. Then she wiped at the tears that streamed down her cheeks and over her lips as she murmured goodbye.

No, she didn't believe in coincidence, but she did believe in the power of prayer. And Rio Langley was heaven-sent.

Tapping the last reserves of her strength, Tess gently, ever so gently, nestled her sweet burden in the downy blanket carefully arranged inside the pillow-stuffed wicker basket that served as a bassinet. She pulled the strap of the overstuffed duffel bag higher on her shoulder, picked up the basket, then walked across the dirt road, up the narrow, cracked sidewalk and onto the front porch of the old house. There, she set the basket down, then placed the bag nearby and proceeded to pull up the edges of the blanket over the basket's rim to form a makeshift hood, telling herself it was to block the wind and not a tactic to delay the final leaving. At last, the arrangement suited her. She had delayed as long as she could, as long as she dared.

Her hands trembling, her heart breaking, she reached inside the pocket of her worn jacket and withdrew a folded piece of paper. She tucked the note into the creases of the blanket, and gave the basket a quick shake.

Just enough to wake the occupant who now protested loudly.

Tess turned and ran out of the yard, across the dirt road and into a stand of trees. Hidden in the shadows, she felt her heart hammer in her chest, blood pound in her ears, but she barely noticed.

All she could hear was the sound of her baby crying.

It tore at her heart, shredded her soul, but she forced herself not to respond. As the moon coasted toward a cloud playing hide-and-seek with shadows, she waited for Rio Langley to discover her treasure. She waited. And prayed.

AT THE BACK of the Langley ranch house, Rio stared out into the Texas night. Maybe it was time to pray, he thought. Prayer was just about the only thing he hadn't tried. A dust-covered, booted foot resting on the rail of the screened-in porch, his cane-bottom chair tilted precariously on two legs, Rio watched the moon slip behind a cloud and felt his own hopes and dreams sliding from his grasp. The cold, crisp moonlight cast shadows as dark as his outlook.

If he had any sense at all he would leave town on the next thing smoking. *Yeah, by train, plane or Greyhound I should just get the hell out of Dodge. Get the hell away from this run-down ranch and these holier-than-thou citizens who think where a man's been is more important than where he's going.* He had busted his butt for the past ten days, trying to turn this sow's ear of a ranch into a silk purse of a decent piece of property. And for what? Time, money and even the weather had worked against him every step of the way. He was beating his head against a brick

wall and didn't even have sense enough to know when
to quit.

But quitting wasn't in his blood.

Then again, Rio thought, as he used his thumb to
shove his cowboy hat back on his head, his blood,
actually his lack of bloodline, was part of the reason
he didn't have—and probably stood a snowball's
chance in hell of getting—the kind of money he
needed to clean up and fix up this miserable excuse
for a ranch in order to get the asking price he needed.
The second bank in as many days had rejected his request for a home-improvement loan. Now what? In
its present condition, the place wasn't worth the
powder to blow it to hell. He never should have come
back to Crystal Creek.

*Dammit! Why didn't I call Vernon Trent and tell
him to get what he could for this godforsaken place
and forget it?*

For that matter, why hadn't he told Trent, when
he'd finally reached him with news of his mother's
death, that he didn't want his inheritance? The answer to both questions stood out in Rio's mind with
startling clarity.

Guilt and shame.

Guilt. He had been chasing mustangs in the Montana back country when the only person who had ever
truly loved him had needed him . . . and had died vir-
tually alone.

Shame. He couldn't bring himself to throw away
the only thing his mother had been proud of—her

land. God knew, her son had never been a source of pride.

So, here he was, a ramblin' man stuck with roots he didn't want and a load of guilt and shame he didn't need. So far, nothing had turned out the way he'd expected since he got home.

Home.

After having been away for twelve years, he was only mildly surprised that he still harbored warm thoughts of Crystal Creek. After all, he had grown up here and it *was* the only real home he had ever known. Thanks to his mother.

Delora Langley had loved this land as passionately as she had loved her son, and had never so much as entertained a passing thought of living anywhere else, despite the fact that she had suffered at the hands of the town gossips. Raising a child alone was difficult in the best of conditions, but a Kiowa woman's raising her half-breed, illegitimate son was not only defying convention; it was, some thought, defying reason. Delora had never thought it was anything but gratifying. Hard, but gratifying.

Rio's deep sigh rose and mingled with the chilly night breeze as a faint keening sound reached his ears. He absently wondered if the wind was picking up, then hoped it wasn't. The front legs of his chair came down hard on the weathered planks of the porch. *Damn. If it blows too hard, those new fence posts won't stay even with the stakes. And there's a whole day's work down the drain.*

The sound came again, and Rio realized it wasn't the wind. In fact, the sound was coming from the front of the house and it was almost like the mewing of a lost kitten. Must be the stray mama cat that had whelped the day he arrived, Rio decided. The whole litter was probably stuck in that wisteria bush he had been intending to cut back. *Aw, hell.* If he didn't take care of the situation, he would be up half the night listening to them yowl. Reluctantly, he dragged his weary body out of the chair, settled his hat firmly on his head, shrugged into his jacket and went to investigate.

Expecting to see the mama cat when he rounded the side of the house, he was surprised when he didn't spot her on guard near the shrub, as he had for the past couple of nights. If the cats weren't yowling, then . . . The sound came again. Rio turned the corner, stepped up onto the front porch . . . and came to a dead stop.

What the hell?

At first he didn't believe his own eyes. But he couldn't deny his ears. A baby!

He took a step closer. Not only was it a baby, but a baby at full volume.

What the hell's a baby doing on my doorstep?

Rio glanced around, but didn't see a soul. This was the only house for at least a mile and a half, and as far as he knew, he was totally alone. "How'd you get here?" he asked the squalling infant. "Where's your folks?"

Judging from the decibel level of his crying and the way he was waving his arms in the air, the infant didn't appear to be in the mood for polite conversation, but Rio didn't have the foggiest idea what to do next.

"Hush now, baby. Hush." He hunkered down beside the basket. "Everything's going to be all right." He wasn't sure who needed reassurance more, he or the child. "Don't cry now, okay?" He reached out and gently rocked the basket, but the movement, meant to have a calming effect, failed miserably.

"Aw, hell." He was going to have to pick him up.

The sum total of Rio's experience with anything this small and helpless was zero, and he suddenly wished he had paid more attention to the kids of some of his married rodeo buddies. "Day late and a dollar short, cowboy," he whispered to himself as he tried to gauge the best way to go about this.

The problem, as he saw it, was that the baby was too small and his hands were too big. And there wasn't a damned thing he could do about either one. He would just have to bite the bullet. *And for God's sake, be careful.* By the time he had worked his wide, rough hands beneath the tiny head and under the tiny bottom, Rio was sweating.

"All right now, partner. Just hang on," he said, trying first one way, then another, to hold the child with some security. Finally, he put the baby up on his left shoulder and gently patted his little back. The crying stopped almost instantly, leaving only a smacking noise as the baby crammed his own fist into his mouth and sucked. *His?* Rio realized that he had automatically tagged the kid a boy. Standing on his front porch, holding a baby that appeared to be abandoned, he decided it didn't make any difference as long as the kid was quiet.

"Attaboy," he said, carefully pulling his jacket over the infant's body to shield him from the night air. Rio's gaze scanned the yard, the road, for the person or persons responsible for his unexpected visitor. But there was no one. Not a soul.

Now what?

Several loud smacks inches away from his left ear warned him another problem was imminent. Rio was a good ten seconds into a full panic before he noticed the duffel bag....

And the note.

Cautiously, so as not to disturb the hard-earned balance between broad shoulder and tiny body, he squatted, retrieved the note, flipped it open and read:

This is Emily. Please take care of her as if she were part of your own family.

Her? Rio glanced down at the baby nestled comfortably in the folds of his jacket. "Sorry, Emily."

In a totally accepting gesture, Emily laid her head on Rio's shoulder and snuggled against the warmth of his big body.

Rio swallowed hard. Suddenly his chest felt constricted and he fought an unexpected urge to smile.

Then a tight, hard knot of anger twisted in his gut. *What kind of idiot would dump a helpless baby on a stranger's porch, then just walk away?* A worthless idiot was the only answer Rio could give. The sheer callousness of the act of abandonment made him hope he would get the opportunity to give the jerk a piece of his mind. And his fist.

But what if the jerk was the mother?

Feeling dumbfounded and totally out of his depth, the only thing Rio knew for certain was that any minute the kid—Emily, he corrected himself—was going to kick up another fuss. It was a question of standing on the porch in the chilly breeze or going inside and trying to put together the puzzle of the baby's appearance. Emily chose that moment to voice her opinion. Long and loud. Inside won, hands down. Quickly, Rio crammed the note into the hip pocket of his jeans and one-handedly tossed the duffel bag into the basket, then carried baby, basket and bag into the ramshackle old ranch house.

From her position hidden among the trees and shadows, Tess wiped more tears from her eyes and offered a silent prayer of thanks. She watched for several more long, lonely minutes before she slipped away and started back to the spot where she had parked her beat-up Volkswagen. Her feet felt as if they weighed a ton, and her heart was at least ten times as heavy. She had no one, no money, no future and no hope. Her child deserved better, and regardless of how much it hurt, she *had* done the right thing. Emily was safe now; she was with family. Tess's step didn't falter. One glance back and she would be lost.

ONCE INSIDE the house, Rio was lost in indecision as he struggled out of his jacket, shifting Emily from the crook of one arm to the other. *What do I do now? Who do I call?*

Surely there would be a state agency he could contact that could take her and hopefully find her parents. As far as that went, Doc Purdy could probably help him out. In this day and age everyone was listed on a computer somewhere. There had to be a record of Emily's birth. It was just a matter of tracking a paper trail.

But a state agency would probably take her away.

Maybe he shouldn't be so quick to call anybody. Maybe the parents just left the baby for a few minutes and intended to come right back? *Naw, that's crazy. Who would come this far from town, then walk off?*

Not satisfied with divided attention, Emily screwed up her little face in a prelude to more crying, so Rio quickly hoisted her back up on his shoulder. Absently, he patted her back, still trying to fit together the puzzle pieces of this unusual situation.

The way tongues wagged in Crystal Creek, by now at least half the county knew he was back and working on his mother's property. But it wasn't as if the

Langley ranch was the center of social activity. In fact, since his return, Cal McKinney and Ken Slattery had been his only visitors. The only other person he saw regularly was Elena Morales, the woman who had been his mother's housekeeper, friend and companion since he'd been in diapers. So, why would someone randomly pick *his* doorstep to abandon a baby, unless...

Unless the choice wasn't random.

Unless the child was his.

Rio's hand stilled. Frantically, he racked his brain trying to figure out if the possibility was indeed... possible.

Could she be mine? Not likely, he assured himself, since he hadn't had an ongoing, intimate relationship with a woman in over a year. Of course, there was a brief encounter seven or eight months ago with that lively nurse in Billings, Montana. But no, he had seen her at a local watering hole about six weeks before he received word of his mother's death, and the dress she was wearing that night left little room for breathing, much less a pregnancy.

Then there was Tami with an "i," the sexiest little barrel racer it had ever been his pleasure to meet. Rio smiled at the memory of their time together. Tami, whose last name he couldn't even remember now, had been hell-bent on taming him and she'd almost succeeded for a while. He had to admit he liked the idea of having someone to be with at the end of a hard day, but only the idea. Tami had been everything a man could want between the sheets, but she was young and had demanded all of his attention. Rio resumed stroking the baby's back. No, Tami was too selfish; besides, he'd last seen her almost a year ago.

And how long does it take to make a baby? Two minutes and nine months.

Rio couldn't even begin to guess how old Emily was. She could easily be two weeks or two months old. In which case...

In which case you're in trouble, cowboy.

But was he really? Something, call it instinct, intuition or the kind of sixth sense most people thought Indians, even half-breeds, were born with, told him this baby wasn't his. God knew, he had sowed enough wild oats in his time to get caught, but so far as he knew—and he had always been extremely careful—he was the only illegitimate Langley progeny running around loose. Long ago, Rio had sworn he would never put a child of his through the kind of hell he had known growing up without a father.

Still, he wasn't certain, and until he was, Emily wasn't going to suffer if he could help it. When Elena showed up tomorrow morning, they would figure out what to do, but for tonight at least, he intended to make sure this baby was safe and protected.

Right, cowboy. All you've got to do is make it through the night.

BY THE TIME the sun peeked over a few clouds and streaked across the floor of the big old kitchen and onto Rio's exhausted face, he had decided he might not survive until the next sunrise. One thing was for sure—his knowledge of babies had doubled since sunset yesterday. That is to say, he knew twice as much as nothing. And that was just about equal to the amount of sleep he had gotten last night.

He glanced over at Emily sleeping contentedly in her basket. Now he knew what people meant when they said someone "slept like a baby." When she slept, which was scarcely more than two hours at a time, little Emily slept deeply, totally relaxed. Rio, on the other hand, hadn't had a wink of sleep. Not because Emily had cried the night through. Actually, she had been much more pleasant than he had expected. Once, around three o'clock in the morning, she had even stayed awake for a while, gurgling and playfully waving her little arms around like a punch-drunk prizefighter. Rio had laughed out loud. Then Emily jumped at the sound, her blue eyes wide, watching. Instantly, he stopped laughing, leaned over her and softly asked, "You okay, sunshine?"

Rio had expected her to cry, but instead he got a smile. He had received a lot of smiles in his time, but none had ever affected him like that gentle curling of Emily's tiny rosebud mouth.

His chest had suddenly felt too small to hold his heart. Even now, the memory brought a flood of emotions and warmth. Whenever he looked at Emily, he felt warm clear through to his soul.

No, Rio thought, he had gone without sleep, not because the baby was a disturbance. At least, not in the way he had expected. He hadn't slept because he was scared. Scared to even close his eyes for a second.

He had faced some junkyard-dog-mean bulls in his time and some even nastier cowboys, but nothing had ever scared him half as much as this helpless little pink-cheeked baby and the way she made him feel. He remembered staring at the almost imperceptible rise and fall of her tiny chest to make sure she was still breathing. He had even gone so far—on several occasions—as to place his index finger up to her nose in order to test for tiny puffs of air. And Lord, but his heart had skipped a few beats waiting. Thank goodness the night was over. And thank goodness, Elena would be here any minute.

Practically before he could finish the thought, Elena Morales's dilapidated Chevy station wagon rattled to a stop in the driveway. The noise woke Emily, and she started to fret.

Elena Morales got out of her station wagon, walked around to the back, lowered the tailgate and hauled out two full sacks of groceries. She stood for a moment staring at the house, wondering why Rio didn't come out to help her as he usually did. She'd say one thing for the boy, he hadn't forgotten the manners his mama had worked so hard to teach him. So where was he? With a sigh she grasped the bags, then lifted her knee, raising the tailgate just enough for her to use the determined sway of her ample hips to finish closing it. She hefted the sacks in her arms and walked up to the screened-in back porch.

"Rio, you in there?"

"Just a sec," he called from the kitchen. "I've got my hands full."

"So do I. Come get this door, sonny."

Rio appeared in the doorway, then walked across the porch, a bundle of some sort held in the crook of one arm. As he pushed open the outside door with the other hand, Elena noticed he was unshaved, haggard and, judging from the look in his eyes, right glad to see her.

"You're just about the best-lookin' thing I've ever laid eyes on," Rio said, his voice sounding as if he had been out all night in wild company.

From the moment she'd first set eyes on sullen, brown-eyed Rio, almost two years old, clinging to the hem of his mother's dress, Elena had loved him. As the years passed and she and Delora grew almost as close as sisters, there were times when she felt as if he were one of her own. She and Delora Langley had shared triumphs and heartaches. Rio was both.

"Well, I can't say the same for you. You look like you've been rode hard and put away wet." Eyeing him closely, she noticed a white smear on his right temple, as though something had clung to his fingers, and he'd then raked them through his hair. "What have you been up to..." The sound coming from the bundle he held brought her up short. She pointed to the bundle. "What's in there?"

"A baby."

Elena grinned. "You're mighty feisty, tryin' to fool me so early in the morning."

"I'm not fooling."

She looked at him for a second or two, then her grin widened. "Go on with you."

He raised his left hand in a solemn gesture as he gently bounced his burden with his right hand. "I swear. Take a look for yourself."

Her grin faded and she was about to tell him he ought to be ashamed for teasing an old woman, when he leaned forward enough for her to get a good look into the blankets. Elena's eyes grew as round as half dollars and her mouth dropped open. "It's a baby! What in the world are you doin' with a..." Suddenly the look of astonishment changed to one of admonition. "Rio Langley, is this baby yours?"

"No! At least I don't think it is."

"What do you mean, you don't *think?*"

"Someone left this baby on my front porch last night, then just walked away."

"That still don't answer my question. Are you this baby's daddy or ain't you?"

"I could be."

The woman who had been his mother's closest friend and had helped to raise him looked Rio in the eye. She pointed an accusing finger at him. "Now you listen to me, sonny. Your mama must be lookin' down from heaven, hangin' her head in shame. If this child is your flesh, you stand up like a man and own your responsibilities, you hear me?"

Rio almost smiled at the intensity in Elena's manner and voice as she gazed up from her barely five feet of height to his six feet plus, but he didn't. He knew she was scolding him out of love.

"Believe me, Elena, I've racked my brain for most of the night, trying to decide if there was even a possibility this baby might be mine."

"And?"

"It depends."

"On what?"

"On how old the baby is."

Elena looked at the infant for several seconds before replying. "My bet is somewheres around two, maybe three months."

Rio thought again of Tami with the forgotten last name. The time frame might be applicable, but the young barrel racer had been adamant about wanting only good times and no strings. So much so, she had all but admitted to a previous abortion; so why would she hesitate a second time? In fact, if he were honest with himself, their relationship had cooled quickly after the night she told him she had made one "mistake" and didn't ever intend to make another.

So, who had he been with before that? No one.

With the fingers of his free hand, Rio raked again through the existing furrows in his dark hair. "I'm almost certain she's not mine," he said at last.

"Almost ain't good enough, Rio."

"I know."

Emily started to fret in earnest. Bone-tired and not exactly eager to admit that he had spent most of the night scared right down to his toes that his inept handling might do some harm to the infant, Rio quickly hustled Elena inside.

"I—I don't understand," she said.

"That makes two of us." A long, weary sigh slipped from Rio's lips. "But I haven't had enough sleep for squat, so don't depend on me for much understanding."

"Kept you up all night bawlin', huh?"

"Actually, she wasn't that bad."

"Did you say 'she'?"

"Yeah. And she didn't cry all that much. A couple of times she even smiled at me." Rio looked down at Emily and smiled himself. "Didn't you, sunshine?"

"You want me to take her now?" Elena held out her arms.

"Yeah."

But he didn't hand over the baby immediately. In fact, now that he could turn her over to someone else, he seemed almost reluctant to do it. "She's real wiggly. And she's a strong little thing. Last night she stiff-armed herself off my shoulder." He swallowed hard with the memory. "Nearly scared me out of ten years' growth."

"After raisin' four of my own and helpin' raise two grandbabies, I think I can handle this young'un."

Elena took the baby and followed Rio across the porch and through the kitchen doorway. And came to an abrupt halt. If she thought Rio looked bad, he couldn't hold a candle to the kitchen.

Half of the cabinets stood open, the top of the stove was littered with pans of various sizes all filled with water, and several lumps of used disposable diapers dotted the area around the trash container, as if he had tossed them and missed. The whole kitchen looked as though it had been hit by a fair-sized Texas twister. Or a very frantic man.

Rio glanced away, embarrassed. "I uh, got kinda desperate when I couldn't find what I was looking for."

"What were you lookin' for, the keys to Fort Knox?"

"Cornstarch."

"Cornstarch?"

"Yeah, well, Emily—"

"Emily?"

"Her name's Emily. Anyway, uh, I had to change her and... I, uh, remembered Mama saying once that cornstarch helped keep babies dry. And I figured the drier she was, the less she would cry. But I couldn't find any. Then later I discovered this..." He reached over to the table and held up a tube of diaper rash cream.

That would account for the white smear on his temple, Elena thought, a mental picture of Rio coping with diaper, ointment and baby causing her to grin from ear to ear. "That musta been a sight."

Rio rubbed the back of his neck. "You don't know the half of it. What is that stuff anyway? It's thick as axle grease and stinks to high heaven."

"An ointment made out of cod liver oil and zinc." She waited for her description to hit home and didn't have long to wait.

He wrinkled his nose in disgust. "No wonder I had to wash my hands a dozen times before I got that smell off," he said, following her into the bedroom.

"It's great for babies' bottoms, but it don't do much for you."

"Is she all right?" He peered over Elena's shoulder as she started to change Emily. "I mean, I didn't do anything to hurt her . . . or anything?"

"Seems perfectly fine, or at least she will be soon as she gets her tummy full." She propped Emily up on her shoulder and returned to the kitchen.

"There's a bottle warming in that pan." Rio gestured toward the stove without taking his eyes off Emily. "She doesn't like it too warm and she takes her own sweet time with it. You sure she's okay?"

"Fit as a fiddle. Is that bottle glass?"

"Plastic."

"Rio, you can't heat a plastic bottle on the stove."

"I know that," he said as if she had just reminded him how to tie his shoelaces. "There were some instructions written on a piece of paper. You just set the bottle in some hot water until it gets warm." He went to the stove, removed the bottle, then proceeded to test the temperature of the liquid on the inside of his forearm like a pro. He glanced up and caught Elena staring at him. "Uh, the instructions told how to test the milk."

For the first time she noticed that only the left sleeve of his shirt was rolled up past his elbow. She grinned. Sometime during the night Rio had become an expert tester.

"Here you go, sunshine." Leaning over Elena's shoulder, he poked the nipple into Emily's mouth. She latched on, sucking loudly. For a reason he didn't understand, the suckling noise made him smile. "Attagirl."

Elena took over the feeding while Rio put on some coffee, and in no time, it seemed, the bottle was empty.

"She likes to be high on your shoulder when she's burped. And she takes her sweet time about that, too."

Elena watched Rio watch Emily. *Sometime during the night Rio got more than a bottle-testing and baby-burping lesson. He got attached.* This little bundle of sugar and spice had a hold on the world-weary cowboy, and it looked like a solid connection.

When Elena finished the feeding, she placed Emily on her tummy in the wicker basket, gave the child a reassuring pat on her little rump, then turned back to what she considered to be the real problem at hand.

"I gotta make a phone call. You keep an eye on her for a minute," she ordered Rio and left the room.

When she came back five minutes later, Rio was sitting at the table, gazing down on the sleeping baby.

"I called a woman I know who works for county welfare. Lives in town but I caught her before she left for work, so she's comin' right over—"

Rio's head snapped up. "They'll take her away, won't they?"

"I reckon so."

He had waited hours for Elena to arrive so he could hand over his responsibility to someone else. Now the idea of doing so permanently wasn't as comforting as he had thought it would be. And handing Emily over to a perfect stranger didn't sit well at all. "What... what do they do with kids like this?"

"Put them in a foster home, I reckon."

Even though he knew there were lots of good foster parents, eager and willing to give love and care to abandoned children, he also knew there were those more interested in the state's monthly check. Just the thought of Emily in one of the not-so-caring homes sent a cold chill down Rio's spine. Thank God, his mother had been a strong, determined woman, or he might have ended up in just such a place, or worse.

"It isn't fair," he said, more to himself than to Elena.

Uh-oh, she thought. The attachment between man and child was going to be difficult to break even after such a short time. Rio was like his mother when it came to commitment. He didn't give it lightly, but when he did, it took an act of God to break it. "Well," she said with a sigh, pulling a wooden chair away from the kitchen table and settling her wide, compact frame on its seat, "not much in life is."

"I guess I was lucky."

"Luckier than most. Your mama woulda died before she'd give you up. Though, Lord knows, there was probably times when it would have been better for her and you if she had. You weren't much more than a year older than this—" she gestured to the sleeping baby "—little bit of fluff when Delora first showed up in Crystal Creek. She was scared to death...."

"Then she met you."

"Yeah." Elena's voice was soft, her eyes distant, as though she was remembering the early days when she and Delora had found in each other a friendship so rare, so close, it had lasted almost thirty-two years.

Rio rose from the table, crossed to the stove and poured himself another cup of coffee. "Maybe that's why Emily's mama gave up. She didn't have anyone to help."

"Maybe. We'll probably never know." At the sound of a car turning into the driveway, Elena pushed herself out of her chair and headed for the back door. "That's probably Margaret. Don't take her but ten minutes to get here from town."

"Who?"

"Margaret Blake."

In the process of taking a sip of piping-hot coffee, Rio almost choked. "Who . . . who did you say?"

"Well, actually," Elena said, as she walked to the back door, opened it and waved to their visitor, "her name's Conway now. Her husband died, you know, couple of years back."

Several seconds later a young woman with auburn hair and a dazzling smile stepped through the doorway.

"You remember Margaret, don't you?" Elena said. "Hello, Rio."

Did he remember Maggie? Sweet Maggie. Oh yeah, he definitely remembered her. And the thing he remembered most was that she had the sweetest, softest lips he had ever kissed.

CHAPTER TWO

WHY THAT KISS HAD LIVED so long and vividly in his memory, he didn't know. But it had, perhaps because her kiss had been tentative, tender and filled with an innocence he hadn't known since. Whatever the reason, Rio found himself staring at Maggie's mouth, wondering if her lips were still as soft and sweet.

"Hello, Maggie."

He had never called her Margaret, even when she was a long-legged filly of a girl, her nose covered with freckles and invariably stuck in a book. Well, the freckles were gone, the rest of her body had caught up with her legs, and there was absolutely nothing coltish or girlish about Maggie Conway. The shy teenager was gone and in her place stood a woman. A very attractive woman.

"Good to see you again, Rio."

She had forgotten how big he was. Not just his size, but his presence. He filled up the room the way sunlight fills up the day, the intensity, *his* intensity, reaching into every corner. And no one else called her Maggie. No one ever had. In fact, she had always insisted she didn't like the abbreviation of her given name. Yet she had never objected to Rio's use of the nickname; not when they were younger and not now. It was something only the two of them shared. As a girl, hearing him use her nickname had sent a thrill scooting through her. It still did. Only as a woman, she knew the thrill was decidedly sensual. And sexual.

Of course, she had known he was back in town almost since the first day he arrived. Nothing much happened around here that didn't get telegraphed far and wide on the ever-active grapevine. On several occasions she had almost gotten up enough nerve to call him or come by, but always, at the last minute, her courage faded. Now, it seemed fate had made the decision for her.

"Yeah. You too." His curt nod betrayed nothing of his surprise at seeing her. Surprise? Shock was more like it. This wasn't the shy little Maggie Blake he remembered.

Pigtails had given way to thick auburn curls that fell softly around her shoulders, framing an oval face. The freckles—if he looked closely he could still see a smattering across the bridge of her nose—had been replaced by a glowing ivory complexion. From the crown of her auburn hair to the tips of her dainty high heels, this was a woman. He was dead wrong when he thought nothing had changed in Crystal Creek since he left.

"I understand you had an unexpected visitor last night."

"Just wait till you see her," Elena said, urging Maggie through the kitchen door. "She's a little Kewpie doll."

When Maggie walked past him, Rio caught a whiff of her perfume. If he had needed anything else to remind him that she was no longer the girl he remembered, the fragrance did the trick. Seductive was the first word that popped into his mind. The unmistakable fragrance of a mature woman.

"There." Elena pointed to the sleeping infant. "What did I tell you? Ain't she just the sweetest little thing you ever laid eyes on?"

"Yes, she is. Where did you find her?" Maggie was increasingly aware of Rio standing behind her. His rugged good looks hadn't changed, except that now his face had a history written in the fine lines around his eyes and mouth. His hair was still black as night except for a few, very few—was that gray?—highlights here and there. And he still wore it too long for the conservative folks in town—straight and just curling over his collar. Otherwise, he looked exactly the same. He looked great. Clearly, Rio had left Crystal Creek a boy and returned a man.

"Actually, Rio found her on his doorstep," Elena told her.

Maggie looked up at Rio. "Really?"

He downed the last of his coffee, then set the empty cup on the table, his gaze never leaving her face.

"Literally. I heard a noise, went to investigate and found her and a note on my front porch."

"Could I see it?" Maggie asked. Rio pulled the folded piece of paper from his back pocket and handed it to her. After reading the note, she looked directly at him.

He didn't need to be clairvoyant to read the question in her eyes. "No, I'm not the father."

"At least he don't think so," Elena added.

With Elena listening, Rio proceeded to give Maggie all the reasons why he thought Emily might be his, but probably wasn't. "In short," he concluded. "I can't be positive, and until I am, *I'm* not abandoning this baby."

"Doing the right thing for little Emily doesn't mean you're abandoning her."

"You're going to put her in a foster home, aren't you?"

"Well, that's the general—"

"I don't want her with strangers."

Maggie wondered if he had any idea how absurd his statement sounded given the circumstances. "She'll be well taken care of."

"Can you guarantee that?"

"As much as humanly possible—"

Rio wasn't looking at her anymore. He was looking at Emily. "Can you positively guarantee that whoever takes care of her will love her like their own?"

"The system is designed to ensure babies like Emily are placed with families that know how, and are willing, to care for infants. I can't give you an ironclad guarantee, Rio. At the moment the state and county systems are vastly overcrowded and—"

"Pardon me for puttin' in my two cents' worth," Elena interjected. "But there's not much you can do about it, sonny. Now, Margaret here is gonna do the best she can for Emily. Aren't you, Margaret?"

"I'll select the family myself, Rio. And she'll be placed just as soon as the necessary forms have been filled out. Probably in a day or two."

Now it was Elena's turn to be concerned. "You mean she won't go to somebody today?"

These situations were never easy for Margaret, and dealing with people she knew made it that much harder. "No. Claro County is short on foster parents, but it's only temporary," she assured them. "I'll push the paperwork through as fast as I can, but she will stay at the county facility until a family becomes available."

"How long's that gonna be?"

Maggie sighed. "It could be anywhere from a day to a week."

"A week!"

Rio listened to both women, while focusing his attention on Emily as she slept, blissfully unaware her future was being decided.

Maggie felt as if she had been cast as a silent-screen villain about to foreclose on the mortgage. She hated this part of her job. Only knowing the end results were gratifying made this part bearable. Obviously, Rio and Elena were both concerned, but sugarcoating the situation wouldn't be a kindness. The truth, no matter how unpleasant, was always best. "I know both of you mean well, and I wish I could tell you everything will be peaches and cream for this little girl, but I can't."

Rio turned to face Maggie. "What if she *was* mine?"

As if the object of their conversation had suddenly decided she didn't appreciate being verbally tossed about, Emily started to cry. All three people responded, but Rio got to the baby first.

"Hey there, sunshine," he said softly, his wide hands, less unsteady than they had been the night before, cradling Emily's tiny body. "Bet you're wet." He turned to Maggie. "She hates having a wet diaper. The minute she gets dry, she gets happy. Don't you, sunshine?" His full attention was back on Emily. "Hang on, darlin'."

"I'll change her," Elena offered. She plucked a disposable diaper from the duffel bag, took Emily and disappeared into the bedroom.

Rio watched them go, then frowned, snatched up his empty cup, crossed the kitchen to the stove, jerked up the pot and poured himself more coffee.

He didn't offer Maggie a cup, but when he turned to face her, she saw clearly that he was in no mood to be hospitable. Standing with one hip cocked, a thumb hooked in the front pocket of his jeans, he looked ready to take on all comers.

"Is she yours, Rio?"

When he didn't answer for a moment, Maggie realized she was holding her breath. What difference could it possibly make if Rio was the father? Why should she care? They hadn't seen each in years, had lived totally different lives and shared nothing in common except a hometown and a . . .

A kiss?

The result of a silly, schoolgirl crush. Kid stuff. She doubted he even remembered.

If Rio was little Emily's father, so be it. But Maggie couldn't help but wonder about the mother.

"Could she stay here if I said yes?"

"If it was the truth."

"And if not?"

"Then Emily will have to go into a foster home."

"Why?"

"Why?" She couldn't believe he was asking such an obvious question. "Because that's the way the system works. That's my job. And even if it wasn't, I can't turn my back on an abandoned baby. She has to be placed—"

"Then to hell with the system. And to hell with you." He turned and stormed out of the house, leaving an astonished Maggie in his wake.

"Go talk to him, Margaret."

She turned to find Elena with Emily in her arms, standing in the bedroom doorway. "I don't think that's such a good—"

"He's been fightin' a passel of demons since he come home. Can't seem to do any good for himself. Then this baby drops outta nowhere—darnedest thing I ever saw—and he sorta connected to her. You shoulda seen him when I got here. He wanted me to take her, but didn't wanna let her go. Then when I took her, he kept hoverin' over me, tellin' me she liked to be burped this way and held that way. Darnedest thing I ever saw."

Clearly, even though Emily had "dropped outta nowhere" only the night before, Rio had formed an attachment to the baby girl. And just as clearly, he had strong feelings about putting her in a foster home. And Maggie didn't have to guess why. Considering his background, such strong feelings were more than reasonable; they were predictable.

She left the house and went looking for Rio. She didn't have to look far. He was in the barn throwing pitchforks of hay to the horses. "I'm sorry if I was blunt before," she said.

He didn't stop his work. "Like you said, it's your job."

"It's more than a job to me. I genuinely want to help these children. I want to make sure they're given the best possible care the county can provide."

Now he stopped. Turning to face her, he jabbed the pitchfork into the dirt floor of the barn and rested one elbow on the handle. "I guess that's where you and I part company. You keep talking about the *system*, and I'm talking about a helpless little baby."

"Rio, I don't want to fight with you over Emily. You and I are friends, or least we were." She glanced away from his intense gaze, again thinking of their one and only kiss. A kiss she had years ago convinced herself meant nothing.

Good grief, she had only been a kid then, tagging after her big brother's friend. Incredibly shy, she had lived for her brief encounters with the tall, dark-haired quarterback of the Crystal Creek Cougars. And those encounters had undoubtedly been harmless to Rio, but not to Maggie. At the impressionable age of fourteen, she had fancied herself in love with the dangerously handsome young man.

Rio looked down at his boots and said, "I guess I shot my mouth off back there. I don't have so many friends I can afford to lose one, so... I apologize."

"So do I."

Maggie smiled and Rio felt a surge of hope. For Emily. Maybe even for himself.

The old barn fell silent except for the occasional swish of a horse's tail. Rio and Maggie simply stared at each other. Finally Maggie broke the quiet. "Have, uh, you seen Cal since you've been home?"

"He and Ken Slattery came by the day I arrived. I had dinner at the Double C that same night."

"That's nice. Did you meet Serena?"

He nodded. "And his dad's new wife, too."

"The Double C has been a busy place in the past year. Full of brides and grooms and new endeavors."

"Ken told me he and Nora Jones tied the knot. Sounds like everybody's doin' okay."

"And you, Rio? How have you been?"

He shrugged.

"I'm so sorry about your mother."

She watched a muscle tighten in his jaw and knew he was having difficulty with Delora's death. Probably more difficulty than he would care to admit. "She and Mom started working together on a project for the homeless a couple of years ago. They became good friends. Mom and Dad have missed her."

"Your folks were some of the few I remember going out of their way to be kind to her... to us when I was young."

"Your mother was one of the most honest, gentle women I ever knew. And so beautiful. I must admit, I envied her long hair, black as a raven's wing and so shiny. Once, when I was a kid, I told her I was going to dye my hair black when I grew up, so I could be pretty like her. She just smiled and told me that would be a shame because she liked the way the sunshine made my hair almost sparkle with light." Maggie smiled. "I never thought about dyeing my hair again."

Rio wasn't a man given to poetic phrases, but he could easily imagine sunlight dancing through Maggie's thick, auburn hair. He could easily imagine burying his hands up to the wrists in the silky strands, still warm from sunshine.

He was staring at her, and Maggie could feel the heat rise beneath the collar of her dress. "Did I...did you know that your mother was partly responsible for my doing social work?"

He shook his head and continued to stare at her. "When Dr. Purdy told Mom to slow down and cut back on her activities, Delora asked me to pinch-hit with their project, and I agreed. Reluctantly, I might add."

"Why?"

"Why reluctantly? Oh, that was right after I came back, and I was convinced Crystal Creek wasn't the kind of life I wanted. But your mother knew instinctively that I needed to be needed. Anyway, working with her and Mom on the homeless project led to my job with Social Services."

"Why did your mother have to slow down?"

"Her heart. Not that she's in any imminent danger of a coronary," she assured him. "But she does have a weak heart from a mild case of polio back in the fifties. And since she never does anything half measure, Dr. Purdy just put his foot down."

"But she's all right?"

"Yes."

"And your dad? He's okay, too?"

"Actually, for a man in his sixties, who gets very little exercise, he's in excellent shape."

Rio nodded. "That's good. It's important to keep your family together as long as you can."

"I couldn't agree more."

"Can I hold you to that?"

They were back to the heart of their disagreement, the heart of their problem. "Rio, Emily isn't part of your family."

He hefted the pitchfork and tossed another mound of hay into the horse's stall with so much force that bits and pieces of straw flew everywhere. One even settled on Maggie's shoulder.

"The Kiowas believe that all men are part of the same family. That we are all brothers."

This was tearing Maggie up inside. How could she protect Emily and still not hurt Rio? "It's too bad everyone doesn't subscribe to that same belief."

He stopped working again and faced her. He looked so long and so deeply into her eyes, the urge to fidget was overwhelming. She gnawed at her bottom lip.

"What happens after abandoned babies go into a foster home?" he said at last.

"To the babies or the parents?"

"Both."

"The babies are well cared for, as I told you. As for the parents, the state tries to locate them, or at least the closest relatives."

"What happens if you find the parents?"

"It depends. If the parent or parents left the child with good intentions, for instance being too poor to care for the child, then we do what we can to get them some help. If that doesn't work, then we urge them to give the child up for adoption legally. If it's clear the parents are negligent, then when they're found, they're arrested and charged with child endangerment."

"And?"

"If they're found guilty, the minimum sentence is two to ten years in the Texas Department of Corrections."

Rio thought for a moment before asking, "What would happen if someone left a baby, then changed her mind a few days later? What if, say, a teenage mother panicked, then realized she had made a mistake? What would happen to her?"

Maggie gnawed her lip again. "You must understand how the law looks at these situations, Rio. They have to protect the children. Even if your hypothetical case were true, the parent would have to go through the court system to get the baby back, and I have to tell you, her chances are slim. The law takes a dim view of anyone deliberately abandoning or abusing a child. No matter what the circumstances. I'm afraid your hypothetical parent would be up to her ears in a legal mess that might take months, possibly even longer, to untangle. And in the end, she could lose."

Rio's eyes widened momentarily, but he didn't respond. In fact, he was silent for so long this time, Maggie was beginning to wonder if she should go back into the house and leave him alone with his thoughts.

"I want to keep Emily."

The bolt-out-of-the-blue statement threw Maggie off guard. "Rio—"

"Not forever. I know that's not possible, but why couldn't I keep her for a few days? A week?"

"But you're—"

"A man?"

An understatement at best, as far as Maggie was concerned, but that didn't exactly help his problem. "Well, frankly—"

"What if Elena helped?"

After seeing the look in his eyes in response to what she'd just told him, Maggie had a good idea what prompted Rio to make his request.

"She's here most of the day anyway. She could look after Emily, then I could take over at night."

"After a hard day's work? Rio, be realistic."

"What if Elena stayed here? You said yourself, the system is overloaded. It might be days before you can place Emily. In the meantime, there's no reason she can't stay here."

"I'm not sure Elena would appreciate your volunteering her services."

The fact that she didn't give him a flat no was encouraging. "You know she'd do it in a New York minute." When Maggie still looked dubious and started to shake her head, Rio cut her off with "Please don't say no."

It was his voice more than his words that swayed Maggie. There was something so sincere and almost forlorn in his tone that she couldn't bring herself to end his hope. Her head knew what she *should* do, but her heart wasn't so sure.

"You know this is never going to work."

"It might."

"You think the mother of this baby is going to change her mind and come back, don't you?"

He glanced away, a little embarrassed that she could read him so easily. "Yeah. And if you take Emily, then her mother changes her mind in a couple of days and returns, you said yourself there would be one hell of a legal mess."

"Do you *honestly* think the parents might show up?"

"I don't know. It's tough raising a kid alone. Maybe all this mother needs is a friend. Maybe she panicked and didn't know what else to do. Maybe she thought leaving Emily on my doorstep was the best thing she could do for her baby. And if she changes her mind and Emily is in the *system*..."

He didn't have to finish the sentence. Maggie knew only too well that numerous such cases had been routed through the Texas courts, and in fact, through courts all across the country, not always with positive results. All too often, in an effort to protect the child, the courts took the unforgiving attitude that once a mother had abandoned her child, she was forever afterward irredeemable. In those cases everyone lost, particularly the child, separated permanently from its natural parent.

Maggie released a long, tortured sigh. "Oh, Rio, you put me in such a difficult position."

"Yeah, I know." He reached out and picked up the errant piece of hay still on her shoulder. "And I'm sorry, but I've got a gut feeling about this, Maggie."

The pressure of his hand on her shoulder was so slight that for a moment she thought she might have imagined it. Then he flicked the straw away and looked deep into her eyes, his own filled with a kind of pain a lesser man couldn't handle. "Most of us never realize what we've got until we lose it. What could a second chance hurt?" Without waiting for her answer, he turned back to the task of pitching forkfuls of hay.

Maggie had seen that look before. More than twelve years before, in fact, on a crisp November night after a punishing football game when the Cougars had suffered a humiliating defeat. As quarterback, Rio had taken the brunt of the disappointment of the fans and fellow players. That night Rio, her brother, Ronnie, and Cal McKinney had dragged their bruised, sagging egos onto her front porch. But when Cal and Ronnie decided to make a roaring trip to Austin and drink their troubles away, Rio had declined.

To this day Maggie didn't know why he had decided to stay; she only knew that a few moments after Cal and Ronnie left, she and Rio were talking.

Actually, she listened while Rio did most of the talking. Her memory choreographed images of that night as they danced into startling clarity. . . .

The air was crisp with the first snap of autumn and quiet now that Cal and Ronnie had roared off into the night hell-bent on God-knew-what sort of mischief. Margaret sat on the glider on her parents' front porch, staring at the back of Rio Langley's head—a head bent in abject defeat. He hadn't said a word since the others disappeared more than ten minutes ago, and Margaret wondered why he had stayed. Not that she wasn't glad. In fact, she was thrilled.

Who wouldn't be thrilled to have her very own secret fantasy come true?

She sighed, her eyes never leaving the boy seated a few feet in front on her on the porch steps. *Rio. Rio.* He was here. So close she could almost reach out and touch him. Rio was here. And he hadn't bolted from fear of being left in the company of a lowly junior high school girl. A girl with an overwhelming crush on him.

She waited, wanting him to speak and afraid that when he did his words would be "See ya', kid."

Finally, she couldn't stand not being as near to him as possible. Slowly, so as not to startle him, she slipped from the glider, crossed the porch and sat down on the same step. Not too close, but oh, it was heaven.

He looked so miserable, so alone that Margaret couldn't stop herself from trying to comfort him.

"I'm sorry," she whispered, not even aware she had spoken her thoughts until he glanced up.

"Yeah. Thanks."

Her heart was beating so hard and fast, it was frightening. And wonderful. "You shouldn't blame yourself."

"I was the only one throwin' the ball out there tonight. Who else is there to blame?"

"But you weren't the only one playing. And Cal said you were going great until the last . . ." Her voice trailed off, embarrassed at having mentioned the one part of tonight's game he was undoubtedly trying to forget.

"Until the last quarter. Then I don't know what the hell went wrong." He glanced over at Margaret's wide-eyed expression. "Scuse me, Maggie."

She loved the way he called her Maggie, but that, too, was part of her secret fantasy. She professed to her family that she didn't like the nickname, so they wouldn't use it. She didn't want anyone but Rio to call her by that special name.

"It's okay. You did your best. If you search your mind and heart, you'll know that and that's what matters in the end."

"I just can't figure out how everything went sour so quick." He pushed himself up from the porch and Margaret's heart beat even faster. *He was leaving!*

But he wasn't. Instead, he began to pace back and forth in front of her, recounting the last few plays of the ball game. And Margaret listened, barely comprehending the codes and abbreviated names for plays and players. But it didn't matter that she knew very little about the game of football. All that mattered was that Rio needed to talk out his frustration, and if she could fulfill that need by listening intently, then so be it. Besides, the sound of his voice was such sweet music to her ears.

When he had gone over every one of those last plays, and their outcomes, at least twice, he stopped pacing and faced Margaret. "You're right. I did my best. But that's not all that matters in the end, Maggie." He glanced down at the toes of his boots and mumbled, "Not when you've got as many strikes against you as I have."

"What did you say?"

"Nothin'." He looked at her briefly, then glanced away. "Sorry I chewed your ear off."

"I didn't mind."

"Sometimes I forget there's anything else but football."

"It's okay. Really, I didn't mind. And... and I thought you sorta needed to talk."

Now he looked at her, his gaze piercing hers. "What made you say that?"

Maggie shrugged. "Just the way you looked, I guess. My dad says most people can find the answers to their problems if they just talk them out. Mostly to God, but sometimes anybody will do." She couldn't believe this was really happening. Where had she ever found the courage to talk to him like this?

"You're pretty smart for a..." He almost said "kid," then changed his mind. "For a girl your age."

"No. I just know what it's like to be lonely and need someone to talk to."

Rio looked at her—really looked at her—and wondered when his friend's little sister had grown from a tag-along brat to a sweet young girl. And despite her age, into a budding wise woman. He sat down beside her on the porch steps. "Guess everybody gets that way sometimes." Strange, he thought, but he didn't feel the least bit uncomfortable sharing his thoughts with Maggie. She had a way about her that made him feel at ease.

"Do you?"

"Yeah."

"Who do you talk to?"

He shrugged.

"My dad says you can always talk to God."

"I don't go in much for that kind of stuff. Besides, I'm never sure which God a half-breed should pray to."

The last part of the sentence was delivered with such raw pain, Maggie's breath caught in her throat. She had never thought of Rio as anything other than just a human being. And wonderful. She was shocked to hear the resentment in his voice.

"I never think of you that way," she blurted out.

Rio turned his body to face her. "Some do."

"They're wrong. Don't pay them any mind."

He smiled. So simple. So sweet. She really was a remarkable girl. As he stared into her wide green eyes, he forgot she was his best friend's little sister. He forgot she was the preacher's daughter and he was not exactly the town's most respectable citizen. All he thought about was the way she had offered him comfort at a moment when he desperately needed it.

Sitting there under stars so bright they put diamonds to shame, he touched her cheek and whispered, "Thanks, Maggie."

And then he kissed her.

At first the kiss had been tentative. On both their parts. But it changed, subtly, then more dramatically. Rio put his arm around her shoulder and eased her to him. So tender and sweet. She tasted so good and felt so good in his arms. And she leaned into him with complete trust.

And for the first time in his life Rio felt as if he were in the right place at the right time. That he belonged. It was crazy. Unreal. Yet that was exactly how he felt. He deepened the kiss, needing more. Then suddenly, he realized he was on the verge of going too far, of needing too much. He ended the kiss, but couldn't resist the urge to touch her cheek again.

"Sweet Maggie."

With no more than those words he had left her sitting on the porch to ponder what had happened.

And ponder she had. In fact, Maggie had thought about that kiss for hours, days, even years afterward. That sweet, sad touching of lips and souls that seemed to last forever. Sweet because it had been her dream of dreams coming true. Sad because she had known, even then, that it was only a dream. And that was all it could ever be for them. Rio had been bound for College Station and his freshman year at Texas A & M, and she had barely begun junior high. Oh, but that kiss had been more than she had ever hoped for... and not enough. In Rio's embrace she had experienced the first stirrings of her own sensuality. As his mouth took hers, gently at first, then hungrily, she had experienced the first rush of desire. A desire that had shocked and thrilled her. And when the kiss ended, they both knew that nothing would ever be the same between them again. She had offered comfort and received her first lesson in passion. He had accepted solace and given a moment of pleasure so pure he would spent the next twelve years wondering if such moments only came along once in a lifetime.

That night he had needed a second chance and it wasn't in her power to give him one. But now she could, albeit vicariously. Still, she had some reservations.

"I thought you wanted to leave Crystal Creek as soon as possible," she said.

"Work on this place is going to take longer than I thought, to make it presentable. I've got some time."

"Rumor around town is that you plan to sell just as soon as it's 'presentable.'"

"Probably."

"Oh," she said softly.

"I plan on using the money to get a place in Colorado and raise rodeo stock."

"Why not do that here? You've got enough acreage, the barn, some equipment and a good start on the stock. Lord knows, with the economy the way it is, the county can always use new businesses. And you've certainly got the credentials and experience. Why not stay right here?"

He tossed the pitchfork to the barn floor. "And who's going to do business with an illegitimate, half-breed, has-been rodeo cowboy?"

"Anyone who knows anything about good horseflesh and a good horseman. And in this state that covers a lot of territory. I think you're missing the obvious."

The reason he gave was only half-true. Rio noted the sincerity in her eyes and knew he owed her the whole truth. "Too many bad memories."

"Of your mother?"

"Not the way you think. I wasn't a very good son, Maggie. I told myself I had to leave so I could be proud of myself and not some rich man's bastard. Hell, I didn't know what pride was. But she did. She stood up to the gossips and the stares. She was proud of her heritage and proud of me. God knows why. I took the easy way. I left."

"Rio, she knew why you left and she never blamed you. Not once."

"I blamed myself. It was part of the reason I didn't come back for so long. I was ashamed of abandoning my mother."

"Abandoning?" Maggie was shocked.

"Oh, I wrote. I called. I even sent her money regularly, to be sure she had all the physical comforts. But I wasn't here when it counted. I wasn't here when she needed me. I was so angry at the man who sired me for not owning up to his responsibility, for abandoning my mother, and then...then I did the very same thing. And it took her dying to make me see how wrong I was."

He was carrying such a burden of guilt, Maggie's heart almost broke. No wonder trying to reunite Emily with her parent or parents was so important to him. No wonder he was willing to rearrange his life for a while to make that happen. How could she deny him? "Rio—"

"I know you've got rules in your job, but aren't people more important than rules? Don't say no, Maggie."

She knew in her head that she should refuse, but she couldn't bring herself to do it. If she had learned one thing after losing her husband, after witnessing similar losses day in and day out on her job, Maggie knew that sometimes the rules had to be bent in order to do the right thing. The human thing. "If I...if I agree to this proposition, and I'm not saying I will, how are you going to know if the person who turns up, assuming someone does, is Emily's natural parent?''

Maggie could almost see the relief in his face. "Because I'm not going to wait for someone to show up. I'm going to go looking. There's a reason why Emily was left on *my* doorstep, and I intend to find that reason. Something tells me that when I do, I'll find her folks."

"I would have to check on Emily at least once a day and—"

"And make sure I'm taking good care of her," Rio finished for her.

"Yes. And to hold you to the time limit. A week, Rio. That's all I could give you."

"It's all I need."

Maggie shook her head, knowing she had lost the battle. "You're as cocky and self-assured as you were in high school."

"Is that a yes?"

"Someone needs to take her to see Dr. Purdy so we can make sure she's healthy."

"Is that a *yes?*"

"I probably need to have my head examined, but yes."

A smile curled the corners of his mouth, then flowed into a full-fledged grin. "You won't be sorry, Maggie."

"You're right, because I'm going to watch you like a hawk."

The grin slowly changed into something more sensual than satisfied. Something very sensual. "You won't hear any complaints from me."

CHAPTER THREE

MAGGIE GAZED out the window of her Austin office at one of those clear Hill Country autumn mornings that always made her glad just to be alive. The sun was a blazing jewel and the sky such a dazzling blue it almost hurt to look at it. If her father were here, he would say God was in his heaven and everything was right with the world.

Well, almost everything, Maggie thought, remembering the way she had caved in to Rio's request to keep little Emily. Temporarily, she reminded herself. And she intended to see the baby every day to be sure nothing went wrong. Of course, she'd also see Rio. She couldn't deny that seeing him again had stirred up feelings she had long ago convinced herself were merely fantasy. But, of course, that didn't mean anything between them could or would be more than friendship.

Friendship? For almost two years she had been alone, until recently had been perfectly content to confine her social life to occasional dinners with friends. But lately she had begun to think about how she wanted to spend the rest of her life and with whom. The one thing she knew for sure was that she wasn't willing to settle for anything less than what she and Greg had had—a good marriage.

Still, the question of whether she was ready for anything more than friendship with any man remained unanswered. Her husband, Greg, had been her best friend, and she still missed him. Their marriage had been solid, enjoyable and, with the exception of their not being able to have children, completely fulfilling. And if it hadn't been for the drunk driver who'd hit Greg's car head-on as he was coming home late one night, she wouldn't be in the position of weighing her future. The fact of the matter was, if Greg were still alive, she wouldn't even be involved in the social welfare of Crystal Creek. She wouldn't be working for Claro County. And she probably would never have seen Rio Langley again. Fate, Maggie thought, could deliver some strange twists and turns in life.

Her intercom buzzed. Maggie picked up the phone, listened for a second, then replied, "Of course. Send them right in." As Rosa Walters and her daughter, Teresa, entered her office, she realized fate had intervened ironically in their lives, too.

"Good morning, Rosa. And how are you, Teresa?"

"Fine, thank you," the child replied politely. The little girl before Maggie was a far cry from the frightened, silent child who had accompanied her mother to Crystal Creek from Fort Stockton. And a far cry from the child Maggie had interviewed the first time Rosa had brought her in for counseling.

Teresa's story was at once remarkably similar to that of most abused children, yet chillingly different. Unknown to her mother, Teresa had been abused by Rosa's boyfriend. One night, when Rosa walked in on the man while he was brutally beating her child, she picked up a gun and shot him. The trial was long and the publicity lurid, but the worst result was that Teresa had been so traumatized that she refused to speak. To anyone, even her mother.

After Rosa moved to Crystal Creek, where she had secured a job on Carolyn Trent's Circle T Ranch, she'd tried to get help for her daughter, but until about eighteen months ago, nothing had worked. Maggie vividly remembered Teresa's hair-raising rescue by Vernon Trent on the night the Claro River had risen to a dangerous level. Since then, the girl had talked to anyone who would listen. Through social services with Maggie acting as her caseworker, she had received therapy to deal with her fears. Teresa was one of Maggie's success stories, and she was always pleased to see the beautiful, dark-eyed little girl.

"So, how is Bluebonnet?" Maggie asked, knowing the dog was Teresa's favorite subject. The creature that had started out as an injured stray had played a major role in the child's willing return to the speaking world.

Teresa's eyes lit up. "He's fine, too. Gloriana says he's the ranch mascot."

Maggie looked at Rosa. "Gloriana?"

"It's what she calls Carolyn."

"I give special names to all my friends." The child ducked her head shyly. "I call you Maid Marion."

Maggie smiled. "Thank you. I'm very flattered. Are you ready for the session with your therapist?"

"Yes." Teresa turned to her mother.

"Why don't you go ahead, sweetheart? I'd like to talk to Mrs. Conway for a minute." Smiling, the girl waved goodbye and headed to the office next door. When she closed the door behind her, Rosa turned to Maggie. They had become friends during the time Teresa had been coming for help, and now it was Rosa who needed some assistance.

"I received some money recently. Sort of what you might call a windfall."

"That's wonderful," Maggie said, thrilled for her friend.

"Yes. A great-uncle I had almost forgotten about left my sister and me ten thousand dollars. Each."

"That *is* wonderful."

"And I want to invest my money so it will make more money for me. I want to send Teresa to college someday, and that takes a lot of money."

"Yes, it does," Maggie responded, not quite sure where the conversation was headed.

"Well, you know Mrs. Slattery who owns the Longhorn, don't you?"

"I've known Nora for many years," Maggie replied.

"After Dottie Jones died, you know she sold off the motel. Now they say she wants to sell the café."

"Nora *is* looking for a buyer, but so far she hasn't found anyone."

At this, Rosa smiled. "I'm glad." Then her smile drooped slightly. "Do you think she's asking more than ten thousand dollars?"

"I don't know, Rosa."

"Do you think she would take what money I have and let me pay her the rest later?"

"I really can't answer that, Rosa. What does Karl think?"

Blushing like the recent bride she was, Rosa said softly, "He says whatever I want is okay with him."

Maggie thought for a moment. "Well, I do know Nora is eager to spend more of her time taking care of *her* new husband. And she's gone back to school to get her teaching certificate. Frankly, I don't have any idea what she's asking for the Longhorn, but Nora's a realist, and I think she might be interested in your proposition. Why don't I give her a call and set up a meeting between the two of you?"

Rosa sighed with relief. "Would you? Thanks, Margaret."

AFTER ROSA and Teresa left her office, Maggie reflected on how good it felt to be able to help a friend. Rosa and Nora had set a time to meet and, unless Maggie was mistaken, Nora was definitely interested in selling the Longhorn to Rosa. It was no secret that

Rosa's skill in the kitchen was responsible for the smiling ranch hands at the Circle T. And with her determination and her head for business, the Longhorn couldn't be in better hands.

This was what Maggie had missed in California. Being able to make a difference, to help people change their lives for the better. It was one of the reasons she had decided to remain in Crystal Creek when she had originally only intended to visit.

After the first few weeks of grief over Greg's death had settled into a dull ache, she had taken up a friend's offer to stay in a beach house not far from Carmel. For almost a month she had walked the beach, watched the stars and gotten in touch with not only her grief, but her love of life. Finally, she'd come to the conclusion that death had cheated her out of a good man and a good life with him, but *she* was still alive, and life was short.

She'd decided she couldn't waste it with maybes and could-have-beens. And she wasn't going to wait for it to hand her happiness all tied up in satin ribbons.

All her life she had been shy and retiring, content to "go long and get along," as her dad always said. Not that she was directionless, but she did tend to choose the course of least resistance. No more. Greg's death had taught her to speak out for the things she wanted in life and not to settle for anything less. It was a different Margaret Blake Conway who returned to her hometown. There was nothing passive about this Margaret.

It didn't take Maggie long to realize that some of her old school friends and some of the people she had known all her life preferred the old Margaret to the new and improved version. Several had commented that living in California had made her view life from the fast lane. A few had dismissed the changes as the effects of widowhood; others just ignored them.

At first she had tried to explain her transformation, but eventually she had stopped, deciding that those who really cared for and about her not only noticed the changes, but understood and applauded them. Her parents understood, but that was hardly surprising, since helping others and making a difference, no matter how small, had been the cornerstone of their family. And now, looking back over the time since her return to Crystal Creek, she was satisfied with everything she had accomplished. But it was time to move on to the next phase of her life.

Precisely what that phase was, she wasn't sure. Maybe it *was* time to start thinking about a new relationship. Maybe it was time to do something about her loneliness.

The problem was that the unattached males in Crystal Creek were few in number. Of course, that number had recently risen by one.

Rio Langley had made no secret of the fact that he planned to stay in town only long enough to fix up his mother's property, and then he would be gone. Rio wasn't a long-term possibility.

Then why does your heart do a little two-step every time you think about him?

"I shouldn't think about him," she said out loud.

"Think about who?"

Maggie turned to find her father, Reverend Howard Blake, standing in the doorway to her office. "Dad," she exclaimed, moving into his open arms. "What are you doing here?"

"Your mother is attending a seminar on How to Make Your Vacation Bible School More Fun...or some such. Anyway, she's tied up until two o'clock, so I came by to take my favorite daughter to lunch."

"I'm your only daughter."

Reverend Blake's eyes twinkled. "You're still my favorite. Now how about that lunch?"

"My treat."

"Absolutely not," he insisted. "Besides, I thought I might run some of my ideas about Sunday's sermon by you."

"So that's it. Some free lunch. You're going to make me work."

"Only a smidgen, and I promise not to belabor my thoughts. After all, an unbiased opinion like yours is too valuable to abuse."

"Unbiased, my foot. You know I think every one of your sermons has a message worth hearing."

"I know," he said as she grabbed her purse and he held the office door open for her. "That's why I'm taking you to lunch instead of your mother. After more than forty years of sermons, I've worn her out.''

A half hour later they were enjoying a delicious meal at a nearby Italian restaurant.

''Dad, can I ask you a hypothetical question regarding right and wrong?''

Reverend Blake glanced up from spreading garlic butter on his sourdough roll. ''Only if you allow me a hypothetical answer.''

Maggie smiled. ''Well, say...'' She stopped, looked her father in the eyes, then sighed. ''This is silly. Besides Mom, you know me better than any person in the world, and you'll see through my hypothetical smoke screen in a minute.''

He put down his roll. ''Well, now that we've gotten that out of the way, what's on your mind?''

''Did you know Rio Langley is back in town?''

''So, that's the *him* you shouldn't think about, huh?''

''What do you mean?''

''When I came into your office you were muttering something about not thinking about somebody.''

''Oh,'' she replied, annoyed with herself for allowing Rio to dominate her thoughts so completely. ''Guess I was thinking out loud.''

''I see,'' Howard said, carefully eyeing his daughter. ''Well, to answer your question, I heard that Rio had come back to take care of Delora's property.''

''Yes, he's trying to fix the place up. You should see what he's done already, Dad,'' she said, her eyes sparkling with something that—from Howard Blake's viewpoint—looked like pride. "He's repaired the barn and set new fence posts. And you remember that one spot in Delora's parlor where the roof leaked? He fixed that, too."

"That's great, honey. I didn't know you'd been seeing Rio," he said.

"Oh, I haven't. He—uh—he called me. Or rather, Elena Morales called me for him. He found a baby on his front porch last night. A little girl about two or three months old." Maggie smiled, remembering Emily's sweet face. "She's an absolute doll. I can't imagine how anyone could look at her and even think of abandoning her, but someone did."

"Why in the world would anyone go all the way to the Langley place to leave a baby, for goodness' sake?"

"We don't know, Dad. There was a note asking Rio to take care of her as if she were family, and not much else except some clothes, bottles, blankets and the like."

"Poor little thing," her father said. "I suppose you'll have to find her a foster home."

Maggie toyed with her fettuccine as her appetite waned. "Well…that's my problem. At present, there aren't any available, so she'll have to stay at a state facility. I tried to explain the system to Rio, but he wasn't exactly thrilled. And it's phenomenal how attached he is to Emily—that's her name, Emily. She really is the sweetest thing you've ever seen, Dad.

Then he got this crazy idea, and before you know it, I said yes." She took a deep breath. "And now I think I've made a mistake."

"What sort of crazy idea?"

"Rio wants to keep the baby—"

"Good heavens! By himself?"

"Not the way you think. Not permanently. Elena Morales is helping out. Anyway, he wants to try and find the parent or parents. He thinks the mother simply panicked and might come back."

"Any possibility he's right?"

"Well…yes, but frankly, Dad, I think the chances of that happening are remote."

"But Rio doesn't."

"No. And he's afraid if the baby is put into a foster home and then the mother changes her mind and returns, she might never get her baby back."

"Yes, well, he's right about that, of course. The courts aren't likely to give a baby back to a mother who's gone off and left it."

"We both know that, Dad."

"And you agreed to help Rio?"

"I agreed to give him a few days to see if the mother comes back or if he can find her."

Howard Blake studied his daughter and was deeply troubled. It wasn't like Margaret to step outside of the well-constructed procedures concerning the children that came under the state's care. But rule breaking or even bending aside, he was more concerned with the fact that Rio Langley was involved. Not that he had anything against Rio. Quite the contrary. From what Delora had told him and his wife, Eva, the boy had grown into an honest, hardworking man. No, it wasn't Rio that worried Howard, it was the look in his daughter's eyes when she talked about him.

"I think I see your problem." He couldn't help but remember Margaret as a teenager with a painful crush on the star quarterback. Neither could he forget that his daughter had carried a torch for her hero long after he had left town. It was the one time in her young life that Howard had felt absolutely powerless to help his child.

Maggie sighed again. Having given up on the fettuccine, she had moved on to pushing her parsley garnish absently around her plate. "I want to help Rio, but I...I'm scared about how all of this may turn out."

"I think you've got good reason to be scared, honey."

Glancing up from the parsley, her hand stilled. "You do?"

"Margaret, have you given any thought to what's going to happen if this baby's mother doesn't return in a week? *You* are going to have to go out there and take that baby away from Rio."

"I know."

"You've always been a stickler for the rules, or at least you used to be. Mind if I ask what brought on this urge to look the other way?"

"It's just that this time..."

"This time, what?"

"I don't know, Dad. If you could see the way Rio has connected with this baby, you might understand. And the uncanny thing is, she seems to respond to him, too. I...I couldn't bring myself to snatch her out of his arms and whisk her off. Maybe it's because of Delora's death." She shrugged. "Maybe I'm just a sucker for big brown eyes."

"The baby's?"

She shook her head. "Rio's."

Now Howard was more worried than ever, but he didn't want to add to his daughter's problems. "Well, I can't tell you how to do your job, honey, but it seems to me that after a week, Rio will be even more attached to this child and it will be even harder for him to give her up. Looks like you're between a rock and a hard place."

"Tell me about it."

Howard reached across the table and patted his daughter's hand. "You'll do the right thing. You always have."

"Thanks for the vote of confidence. I wish I was as sure of me as you seem to be."

He smiled. "A father's instinct, honey. My money's always on you."

Maggie glanced at her watch. "I'm sorry, Dad. We were going to talk about your sermon, and I've taken up the whole lunch whining over my problems."

"Not to worry." He winked. "There's always your mother."

A SHORT TIME LATER, Howard dropped Maggie back at her office, then drove several miles to pick up his wife.

The minute Eva Blake got into the car, she knew something was wrong. "Did you have lunch with Margaret?"

"Yes."

"Where did you go?"

"Some restaurant. I don't remember the name."

Now Eva *was sure* something was wrong. As much as he loved her cooking, there was nothing Howard Blake loved more than a leisurely meal with excellent food, good service and fine company. He always referred to restaurant dining as his only vice, and it was one of his very favorite pursuits in life. For him not even to remember the name of the restaurant meant something important was on his mind.

"All right, out with it," Eva said in a knowing tone of voice.

"Out with what?"

"With whatever has got you so preoccupied. It's Margaret, isn't it?"

"Now, why would you automatically think that there's a problem with Margaret?"

Eva smiled in satisfaction. "Because you said 'problem.' And because I know you've been concerned about Margaret ever since Rio Langley came back to town."

Howard glanced at his wife. "Do the ladies in your Bible study know you've got a crystal ball?" he said, trying to tease her into switching tracks.

"Don't try to change the subject. You think Margaret is going to get involved with Rio and—"

"I'm afraid she's already involved."

Eva knew her daughter too well to jump to any conclusions, but she also knew that the shy Margaret who had married and moved to California years earlier was not the same woman who had returned to Crystal Creek. And since her return and subsequent decision to stay, both Eva and Howard had talked several times about the changes in their daughter. She was more self-assured and certainly much more outspoken than either of her parents expected. She had, on occasion, even given them pause with some of her new attitudes and outlooks. So, just to be certain she and Howard were talking about the same thing, Eva asked hesitantly, "What do you mean, involved?"

"Someone abandoned a baby out at the Langley place and it seems Rio is determined to find the baby's parents. He's talked Elena into taking care of it and talked Margaret into *not* reporting the child for a week to give him a chance to look for the mother."

"Oh," Eva replied, only slightly relieved. Not that she was a prude. Far from it. But Eva, perhaps more than most, knew how people could gossip, could twist and distort facts into the kind of juicy fiction that labeled a woman as shameless. She knew what disastrous results could come from the wrong kind of involvement. But then, she thought, gazing at her husband's still-handsome profile, some wonderful things could come from the kind of involvements that provoked gossip. "Oh, dear," she said, the full implications suddenly hitting her. "And if he doesn't find the mother..."

"Exactly," Howard finished.

"Margaret will be crushed if she has to go out there after a week and collect that baby."

"She'll get her heart broken." Reverend Blake shook his head. "You know I'm proud of her, but I told you she was too tenderhearted for this kind of work. From the time she was big enough to walk she's brought home every stray animal within miles. The only difference now is that she's graduated from animals to people." He glanced at his wife of more than forty years and had to smile. She was every bit as lovely as the day he'd married her. No one on earth understood him as she did. "She's just like her mother."

Her eyes twinkling with pleasure, Eva looked at him. "I learned from you, my love." Instinctively they reached across the seat of the car to hold hands. "Margaret is a grown woman, Howard. You have to trust her to make her own decisions."

"I do," he insisted. "But—"

"But you would feel better if you could size up the situation firsthand."

"Well—"

"And you're her father and you're always going to worry about her."

He gave her hand a gentle squeeze. "Count on it."

"I do." After a moment or two of silence, Eva said casually, "You know, we haven't been very neighborly since Rio came home. I intended to bake an apple pie this afternoon. No trouble to bake two and take one out to the Langley place after supper."

Howard looked over at Eva and grinned. "I think that's a fine idea, sweetheart. A right fine idea."

YOU SHOULD BE ASHAMED of yourself, Maggie. The admonition, however well intended, obviously fell on deaf ears. Her desk was cluttered with files that needed her attention, but she hadn't been able to keep her thoughts from continually straying to Rio, Emily and her own ambiguous feelings over agreeing to Rio's plan. On one hand, she knew legally they were on thin ice. On the other, she couldn't help but feel her decision had been the right one. *Oh, stop gnawing on it like a dog with a bone. Face it—you're not going to rest until you can get to the Langley ranch and see Emily. And Rio.*

She hadn't been able to stop thinking about him. He was—what was the word the romance novels always used?—ruggedly handsome. Rugged. A good word for Rio. He had that kind of self-assured, nofrills, what-you-see-is-what-you-get attitude that men envied and women admired. He also had a body that had seen hard work, sunshine and hot-eyed glances

from probably every woman who looked. As bodies
went, Rio's certainly was one of the finest she had
ever seen. Not that she made it a habit to check out
men's physiques, but living in California had given
her the opportunity to view hard bodies galore at the
beach. And those men with their perfect tans and well
developed muscles could take lessons from a man like
Rio Langley. A man whose muscle power came from
working out on the land rather than in a gym. A man
who knew the sun as nature's life-giving centerpiece
rather than as a cosmetic image enhancer.

Realizing the direction of her thoughts, Maggie
tried again to concentrate on the files on her desk, but
finally gave up. She glanced at the clock and decided
she could afford to leave the office ten minutes early.
She told herself it was to get a jump on the traffic. She
told herself she was only anxious to hear the report of
Dr. Purdy's examination of Emily. She told herself
several things that fell into the category of viable ex-
cuses. The truth, when she felt brave enough to admit it, was that she *did* want to check on Emily. And
she wanted to see Rio again. Without further hesitat-
ing she picked up the phone, dialed her home and left
a message for her parents on the answering machine.

By the time Maggie pulled into the gravel driveway
at the Langley ranch, the sun was hanging low in the
Texas sky like a blazing orange polka dot painted on
a pale blue canvas. There was a slight chill in the air,
brought on by the autumn breeze.

"Hi," she said when Elena opened the back door.

"Hi yourself. How about a glass of iced tea after that drive out from Austin?"

"Sounds wonderful, thanks."

"Make yourself at home." Elena motioned toward a chair at the kitchen table. She poured two glasses of iced tea, and set one down in front of Maggie. "Rio's in the barn and little Miss Blue Eyes is fast asleep."

"How did the visit go with Dr. Purdy?"

"Smooth as silk. That baby's mama took real good care of her all right. Nate says she's healthy as all get out and bright as a new penny."

"That's good news."

"I seen a lot of babies in my time, but I swear, that child is just about the sweetest little thing I've ever come across. And good as gold. Not a peep outta her the whole time Nate was checkin' her over."

It appeared Emily had added Elena's heart to her list of conquests along with Rio's and Maggie's. "I called Dr. Purdy's office this morning and requested they take a set of Emily's footprints while she was there. Was that done?"

"Yeah. And I want you to know I might never have got that stuff off her feet. What do they use anyway, boot polish?"

Maggie grinned, wrinkling her nose a bit. "Yucky, huh?"

"And then some," Elena said. "You wanna stay for supper?"

"No, thanks. I just dropped by to see how the baby was getting along. No problems, huh?"

"Not with Emily."

"Does that mean you had problems with someone else?"

"Maybe."

"Who?"

Elena stared at Maggie for a moment, as if trying to decide how to answer. "Don't make no never mind. Let it be."

"Did someone say something to Rio, or about Rio?"

"You know how folks around here are. Nothin' they love better than gossip, and they sure as hell don't waste time. A juicy piece of news moves faster than a travelin' salesman with a shotgun-totin' daddy right behind."

"Yes, I know. So, tell me, what are they saying about Rio?"

"More like Rio and you."

"I see," Maggie said.

"Don't let it worry you none. Rio set every one to buzzin' when he came back, and now with you visitin' they see a chance to add fuel to the fire. Somebody probably passed by and saw your car parked in the driveway, and that's all it took to get the busybodies goin'. It'll all die down soon as they find someone else to flap their jaws over."

Maggie nodded, not certain that she wanted to know the extent of the gossip about her and Rio.

"So," she said, changing the subject, "how's Rio adjusting to having a baby in the house?"

"You wouldn't believe it, Margaret. I showed up 'long about sunup and, when I walked in the door, the two of them was in that big old bed together. Rio had her tucked in the crook of his arm, both of them wrapped in the quilt, sound asleep. Beats all I ever saw."

The mental image of Emily's delicate body cradled against Rio's powerful frame almost brought tears to Maggie's eyes. What had she done, allowing Rio to keep this child? The longer they were together, the more difficult the parting would be. She had to go back on her agreement with Rio... for his own good. And there was no point prolonging the agony.

Maggie took a long drink of the iced tea. "I uh, think I'll peek in on Emily, then go talk to Rio," she announced.

"Suit yourself. I've got potatoes to mash and corn bread to bake. Sure you won't stay for supper?" Elena cut Maggie a sly look. "Bet Rio wouldn't mind havin' a pretty face to look at across the table for a change. And I'm gonna serve it up, then get on home."

Elena's offer sounded casual enough, but the way she waited for a response, particularly to the last part, made Maggie think of how perfectly romantic such an evening could be...and how perfectly foolish she was to entertain such thoughts. "Uh, thanks for the invitation, but Mom and Dad are expecting me for dinner."

It was a lie, and not even a good lie at that. Somewhere in the back of her mind she remembered something about her parents attending a potluck supper. The lie came so easily Maggie was shocked and embarrassed, because she doubted she had fooled Elena. "Well, I'll, uh, just go check on Emily." She smiled awkwardly, tiptoed into the bedroom, then a few minutes later slipped outside to find Rio.

Elena stood at the screen door, watching Margaret cross the yard to the barn. "Dinner," she said, wiping her hands on the towel slung over her shoulder. In this part of the world, breakfast, dinner and supper were the three meals of the day. Only city folks referred to the evening meal as dinner. "Sweet girl, but she's gone and got too citified, if you ask me." Elena closed the screen door and went back to her corn bread preparations.

The last rays of the late-afternoon sun, filled with dust motes and bits of hay, streamed in between the aged barn's wooden siding like gold dust through a sieve. The air inside smelled of hay, horses and a hardworking man, dirt floors and old wood. Not an altogether unpleasant mixture. In fact, Maggie decided it was an aroma she could even grow to appreciate. Rio was near the back, filling a feed trough with crimped oats from a bucket.

As she approached, her shoes scarcely made a sound on the dirt floor, yet he turned before she reached him. "I saw you drive up."

"Oh," Maggie said, slightly startled. Oh, indeed, she thought, with her first good look at Rio. At fourteen, Maggie had thought he was the best-looking boy in Crystal Creek. Now, twelve years later, she didn't see a thing that would make her change her mind.

He wore jeans and a T-shirt. Two simple, ordinary items of clothing she had seen in one form or another probably every day of her life, but she had never seen them worn better. Or sexier, for that matter. The jeans . . . well, nobody looked better in worn jeans than Texas men; that was just all there was to say. But Rio looked exceptional. And the T-shirt—tight and faded to the point that she could barely make out the print proclaiming Cheyenne Frontier Days—molded, outlined and defined the muscles in his arms, shoulders and narrow rib cage. *Good heavens. The man is absolutely gorgeous.* Maggie's lips tilted in an almost smile. Rio would probably cringe to hear her describe him as gorgeous.

"What's so amusing?"

"Nothing," she lied, the smile flowing into a full-fledged grin.

Rio shrugged. "Did you see Emily?" he asked, turning back to finish filling the trough.

"Yes."

"Dr. Purdy says she looks good."

"So Elena told me." Every minute she was with him, her resolve to do what her head insisted she must do slipped farther and farther away. Her heart simply wasn't listening.

Rio wondered if Elena had told her about anything else, such as the gossip that was already floating around Crystal Creek about the two of them. It sure hadn't taken long.

"I've been thinking about how to find the mother." Rio put the lid to the oat container back in place and set it aside. "Elena said they took a set of the baby's footprints at the doctor's. Why couldn't we use those like fingerprints to help get information about Emily?"

"*We* can't, but I can."

"No," he said. "You've already risked your job. *And your reputation.* I won't ask you to use the state's time and money as well. This is my idea. I should do the work."

"I mean to do it on my own time. Besides, you *can't* walk into a hospital and ask them to check a set of footprints. They'll toss you out on your ear."

"Thanks for the vote of confidence."

"No, I simply meant that, coming from a civilian, so to speak, that kind of request would be ignored. Whereas, if I called and talked to a couple of friends, I could get the information with a minimum of hassle."

"You've done so much, I can't ask that of you, Maggie."

"I'm offering."

"What happens if you don't turn up a match for the footprints?"

"We check blood types and get a list of all the babies born with that blood type, say, within the past three months."

"Then what?"

"Then you *will* get your chance to do the work, because someone must check to be sure all the parents on the list have their babies, and that may mean physically checking to be sure."

"And if that fails?"

"If that fails, Rio, the time will probably be used up and Emily will have to be placed with Child Protective Services. They'll retrace all the ground we cover, plus run a story in the *Austin American Statesman* and whatever Austin TV stations will pick up the story. The story will probably be picked up by newspapers from the surrounding area, including the *Crystal Creek Record-Chronicle*." She paused before adding, "If they don't get a response, they'll petition for custody and Emily will become a ward of the state."

"I can't let that happen," he said quietly, firmly.

"Rio, you can only do so much, and after that, you may not have a choice. Remember, you've only got a few days."

He gazed into her eyes, remembering, searching for the same kind of understanding she had once given so generously. The same kind of understanding that still lived in his dreams. A young man's dreams full of desire and...hope. The missing ingredient. Hope for the good life, whatever that meant. Rio realized it meant a hell of a lot more to him now than it had back when his dreams were cheap and abundant. The man he had been had wanted so much, hoped for so much. And the man he had become? Was there so little left of that hopeful Rio?

"Then it will have to be enough," he said finally.

But it wouldn't be enough. None of it would, because Maggie knew she would have to take Emily...wouldn't she? Of course, she would. That was best for all concerned...wasn't it? *Then why can't you tell him? Why can't you do it?*

Because the look in Rio's eyes was breaking her heart. That look that said what he would probably never say, could never say...that he cared. Deeply. That this baby had somehow become a symbol to him. A symbol of family. A symbol of hope.

And she couldn't take away his hope.

"All right," she whispered. And with those words, something intangible settled in Maggie's heart and mind, a reconnection with Rio that was more solid than memory or a dream. It was real.

The day was sliding rapidly toward dusk as they walked across the yard and onto the wooden back porch a few moments later. Instead of opening the door, Rio took Maggie's hand and pulled her down to sit on the steps beside him. "Can you stay for a minute?"

"Of . . . of course."

"I didn't mean to be abrupt before." Unable to look at her and say the things he wanted to say, Rio gazed out over the yard for several seconds. He reached down and plucked a wide blade of Johnson grass from a clump growing beside the steps. "It's just that I'm not used to dealing with anything softer than an ornery Brahma bull fresh out of the chute. My social skills never were exactly polished."

"I didn't notice."

"Yes, you did, but you're too much of a lady to mention it. You always were. That's one of the things I remember most about you, Maggie. You were, and are, a lady, from the tips of your toes to the top of that beautiful head. Too much lady for this beat-up ol' cowboy."

Without considering her actions, Maggie put her hand on his arm. "Rio—"

"What I'm trying to say—" he swallowed, finally finding the courage to speak his mind "—is thank you." Slowly, he turned and looked at her. "Thanks, sweet Maggie."

They stared at each other, both wondering if the other remembered the words that called to mind another time, another need.

Timeless, Maggie thought, her eyes misting. *Some feelings are timeless.* She wondered if she had stepped through some invisible time warp, as the past swept over the present, washing the moment with memories. Once before they had sat like this, talked like this. Then the scene had played out on her front porch; now it was his back porch. She had comforted him then as she longed to do now. She had kissed him then as she longed to do now.

Rio, too, felt as if he had taken a step back in time. Back to that moment when Maggie had offered him comfort and the sweet innocence of her lips. He had accepted and lived with both regret and pleasure since that night. Regret for so quickly taking what she'd so sweetly offered. Pleasure for the memory of her sweetness. Now, facing the same decision, he knew he would kiss her again.

Without her realizing it, Maggie's body swayed toward his, her lips parted in anticipation as she lifted her head.

"Maggie?" Rio's heart was hammering in his chest as his head lowered to hers.

"Margaret?"

Maggie blinked, her lips mere inches from Rio's. Was he calling her name?

"Margaret, dear, where are you?" It wasn't Rio. The voice was coming from around the side of the house.

Maggie and Rio sprang apart just as Eva and Howard Blake rounded the corner and stepped into the backyard. "We called out but no one answered," Eva said.

"Mom, Dad, what are you doing here?" Suddenly Maggie was more nervous than she had been saying good-night under the porch light on her first date.

Rio rose from the steps and helped Maggie up. "Reverend Blake, Mrs. Blake."

Howard exchanged a quick look with Eva that said, *See, what did I tell you?*

"Hello, Rio." Eva shot a look back that said, *Don't jump to conclusions.* "My, I'd forgotten how much land you have back here. That big ol' pecan tree is so lovely."

"Thanks." Rio shook hands with Howard, then took a step back as Mrs. Blake greeted Maggie with a kiss on the cheek.

"We're a mite embarrassed at not coming sooner to pay our respects, Rio," Howard said. "Your mother was a fine woman. Eva and I were proud to call her a friend."

"Thank you, sir."

"Mom, I, uh, thought you and Dad had something to do at the church tonight."

"That's tomorrow night, honey. Potluck supper for the building fund," Howard added as an explanation to Rio.

At that moment Elena stepped onto the back porch. "Thought I heard voices out here. How you doin', Reverend, Eva?"

"Fine, thanks, Elena." Howard smiled and shook her hand.

"Good to see you again," Eva said. "We wanted to come over, say hello to Rio." Eva held out a luscious looking apple pie.

"You shouldn't have."

Maggie looked up at Rio and smiled. "You haven't tasted one of my mother's apple pies or you wouldn't say that."

Rio smiled down at her.

Howard and Eva exchanged another look.

Elena took the pie. "Mighty nice of you folks."

"Nonsense, happy to do it," Eva insisted.

"Why don't you folks stay to supper. We got plenty," Elena said.

"No, we couldn't," Howard said.

"But thanks anyway," Eva added. "We appreciate the invitation, but we better get on home. Howard wants to work on his message for Sunday."

"Yeah, I've got to figure out some way to keep everybody from falling asleep," Howard added, and they all laughed.

Thirty minutes later, after several invitations from Elena to prolong the visit, Rio stood on the front porch as the Blakes' car backed out of the driveway, followed by Maggie's. As he watched her taillights fade into the night, he recalled the seconds before they were interrupted. The seconds when their lips were so close he could feel her breath, almost taste her mouth.

Maybe it was just as well.

Rio had known a lot of women in his life, but none like Maggie. And she wasn't the kind of woman a man could know casually and then forget.

He knew her kind. Hell, he knew her. Not in the biblical sense, of course, but he had known her since she preferred pigtails and skinned knees to beg-a-man-to-touch curls and extremely shapely legs. That kind of longevity surely qualified him to speak with some authority. She wasn't the type of woman he was used to spending time with, but then, he probably wasn't the type of man she would list first on her hit parade either. She was the kind of woman a man took out to dinner and a movie, took home to meet Mother. A forever-and-ever kind of woman.

And if Rio knew nothing else about himself, he knew he was *not* a forever-and-ever kind of guy.

CHAPTER FOUR

STANDING in the ostentatiously masculine study of his exclusive Terrytown home, John Westlake was disgusted. Thoroughly disgusted with his son, Jeremy. "Dammit, son, you've got to get hold of yourself and snap out of it. You're well rid of that little piece of trash and her brat."

Jeremy Westlake wheeled on his father, his fists doubled. "Don't talk about Tess that way, Dad. No matter what she's done, I won't let you talk about her that way."

"I don't see how you can defend her after she took off and got rid of your baby." John watched for the look of gut-wrenching pain on his son's face. The boy was hurting. He knew that, but better to hurt now, this way, than to have his whole life ruined. And that was exactly what Tess Holloway would have done if John Westlake hadn't stepped in and taken matters into his own hands. He had worked too hard and waited too long to allow Jeremy's political future to go down the drain.

And to think that Jeremy had actually wanted to marry the girl!

"I still can't believe Tess could have an abortion," Jeremy said, so softly his father barely heard him.

"Well, she did. I'm just glad your mother isn't alive to see what the young women of today have become. She was too refined to even think about such things, much less have something like this in her own family."

"All right, Dad. You've made your point. As far as you're concerned, Tess is a selfish tramp out for her own pleasure and nothing else."

"You're damned right, and you're well rid of her." John stepped behind the massive oak desk that had belonged to three generations of Westlakes and picked up a file. "And the same goes for that worthless father of hers."

Jeremy couldn't argue with his father about Lee Holloway. Tess's father had chauffeured his father for the past ten years, and never in all that time had Jeremy seen him show any affection for his motherless daughter. Despite that drawback, or maybe because of it, Tess had grown into a generous, loving person.

And Jeremy had loved her with all his heart. He still loved her.

They had been friends long before they fell in love. Knowing that the chauffeur's daughter and the boss's son were light-years apart socially didn't matter. They were two lonely kids looking for something to hang on to, and they found it in each other. But their relationship was built on more than desperation and the need for love. From the moment they first saw each other, when Tess was seven and Jeremy was ten, they'd shared something special, almost as if they were two halves of the same person. What began as a bond of friendship had ripened into a deep and powerful love.

Or at least Jeremy had thought so.

Every time he thought about the events of the past six months, he wanted to cry, wanted to double up his fists and shake them at the heavens. How could he have been so wrong about Tess? How could she have betrayed him? How could she have said she loved him with such innocence in her eyes, then gotten rid of the child he thought they'd created out of their love?

"Jeremy?"

"Yes."

"Stop mulling it over and over in your mind. It's done, and there's nothing you can do about it."

Jeremy didn't answer. Normally he would have fought his father over this issue, but today he felt too emotionally battered to try. He had dreamed about Tess again last night. In the dream she had stood alone on a hill and called to him, crying, holding out her arms for him, but he couldn't reach her. There were dozens of paths leading up the hill, but he wasn't on the right one, and every step he took seemed to carry him farther away rather than closer. He knew she needed him, knew she was waiting for him to see the right path and take it. But he didn't. He woke up before he could find the path that would lead him straight into Tess's waiting arms.

The dream tortured him, partly because he wanted to believe it, and partly because he didn't. The dream didn't fit the reality that one day they had been happy, in love and expecting a baby, and the next, Tess had written a note and left. Since then, Jeremy's life had been colder and more lonely than he had thought possible.

"Jeremy, did you hear what I said?"

"Yes, I heard. Now, if you'll excuse me, Dad, I've got a killer final to study for." Without another word, Jeremy left the study.

John Westlake watched his son leave and knew a moment of regret for what he had done. The boy must never know he had used the one weapon Tess Holloway had no defense against—her love for his son—in order to get rid of her. John had skillfully convinced the painfully shy girl that a wife and a baby would not only ruin any political future Jeremy hoped for, but destroy anything he might feel for her. No matter how much Jeremy protested otherwise, his whole life had been aimed at a career in politics, a career that would never see the light of day after a shotgun wedding. And sooner or later he would know he had denied himself that future by marrying Tess, and he would blame her for his having to forfeit everything he had worked for.

It had taken more convincing than John had expected and less than he was prepared for. Finally, after a two-hour session that had all the earmarks of brainwashing, Tess had agreed to go away and qui-

etly get rid of the baby. But she had refused the
money he offered her. That had surprised him at first,
but in the long run it didn't matter, because Lee took
it for her. What mattered was that Tess Holloway was
out of their lives forever. His only son was safe.

Only son... only son... only son...

The phrase echoed in his mind like tin cans rat-
tling down an empty street. No, Jeremy wasn't his
only son, but he was the only one he would ever ac-
knowledge. He sat down at the desk, opened a drawer
and withdrew a locked box, then pulled out his keys,
selected one and turned the lock. Inside the box were
three documents, all legal, all signed by him, all copies of the originals. One was a copy of the deed to the
property in Crystal Creek he had bought for Delora
Langley; one was a copy of the birth certificate on
which he was named as the father of her son; and the
third was a duplicate passbook for a savings account
he had set up in the name of Delora Langley.

He supposed the passbook could be disposed of
now. Delora was the only one who knew of the account, and to be honest, she had rarely used the
money set aside for her and her son. Her son, not his;
certainly not *their* son. *Water under the bridge,* he
reminded himself, but still it was ironic that history
had more or less repeated itself with Jeremy and his
chauffeur's young daughter.

For John, it had been the dark-eyed young maid
hired by his wife. The memory of that time was faded,
but at least he was honest enough to admit that

Delora had been more than a passing fancy. He had known passionate women in his time, but never one like her. They had stolen kisses and embraces until finally they couldn't *not* have each other. Unfortunately, she was careless and became pregnant. To Delora's credit, she didn't beg or whine. When she asked him if he intended to leave his wife and he had replied, no, the proud young Kiowa woman had held her head up and walked out of John's life for good.

For the first time in a long time, John Westlake wondered what his other child looked like, wondered what kind of man he had become. Maybe the news of Delora's death had prompted this excursion down memory lane. Maybe it was this business with Jeremy and his young lover. Whatever the reason, John decided his thoughts were nonproductive. What difference did it make where Delora's son was? He wasn't part of his or Jeremy's life, and he never would be.

"HI, NORA, how are you?" Maggie leaned back in her office chair and cradled the telephone receiver between her ear and shoulder while she made notes regarding a case on a yellow pad.

"I'm fine, thanks. Or I should say, thanks to you. Rosa Walters and I talked on the phone for two hours last night, and this morning she came over to the café and met with Martin Avery and me to discuss the details. And this afternoon we'll finalize the sale of the Longhorn."

"That's great, Nora. You two didn't waste any time."

"Well, it seemed silly to play dickering games when we both knew what we wanted. I really appreciate your help, Margaret."

"I didn't do anything."

"Oh, yes, you did. I doubt Rosa ever would have called if she hadn't talked to you."

"Well, I'm glad for both of you." Maggie was especially glad to hear the happiness in Nora's voice. Lord knew, she had suffered enough over her first husband, Gordon. His tragic death had had tongues wagging in town for weeks. Only after the strong, silent foreman of the Double C had made her his wife, had the gossip died a natural death. And now it was obvious, just by the lilt in her voice, that Ken Slattery was doing his best to make her forget that dark part of her life.

"Rosa's gonna do fine, and I'm relieved to know the café is passing into good hands. I think Dottie would approve, too." Until her death, Nora's ex-mother-in-law, Dottie Jones, had owned the Longhorn for so long it was still difficult for the people in town to think of anyone but her running the landmark establishment.

"I'm sure she would."

"Rosa's got a good head on her shoulders, and she seems to have a real knack for dealing with people. I hired a new waitress the other day. She's a sweet girl and a hard worker, but she needs some guidance. Her name's Tess, and she got real nervous when I introduced Rosa as the new owner. But Rosa spent a few minutes with her, and when she left, I noticed Tess seemed relieved, even happy."

"Sounds like everybody is pleased all around."

"I think so. Listen," Nora said. "Ken has insisted we celebrate the sale and we've asked Rosa and Karl to join us tonight at the Lumber Yard in Austin. Cal and Serena will probably show up, too. Care to come along?"

"I don't think so, Nora. Besides, I'd feel like a fifth wheel."

"Oh, well, I thought . . ."

"You thought what?"

"Uh, Cal seemed to think . . . That is, rumor has it you've been out at the Langley place a lot, and I just thought . . . That is, everybody figures you and Rio are seeing each other." Nora wasn't one to gossip, but it was a much-talked-of subject at the café. "And I want you to know I think it's . . . nice."

In Crystal Creek, the phrase "seeing each other" defined a much more serious relationship than the face value of the words indicated. In fact, the word "courting" was a viable substitution. As Maggie had feared, her visits to the Langley ranch had not gone unnoticed or untalked about. The whole town was probably speculating on a wedding date. They would undoubtedly be shocked to learn the real reason for her visits. Well, this was as good a chance as any to set the record straight, she decided, then checked herself.

You can't set the record straight. At least, not yet.

Of course she couldn't.

If she revealed the reason for her trips to see Rio, then Emily would be gone in a heartbeat, and she would probably be unemployed. And Rio wouldn't have the time she had promised him. If she told the truth, she would break her word.

"Are we the topic of the week?"

"I'm sorry, Maggie."

"Don't be. It isn't your fault. You can't stop people from talking. And they *are* talking, aren't they?"

"Afraid so."

It was no more than Maggie would have expected if she had thought about it. Reports of famines in Africa or earthquakes in California might cause only a mild stir in the little Texas town. But the preacher's daughter openly visiting a man no one knew or understood anymore—now that was news. Big news. The kind of news that traveled too fast to cool off overnight.

Maggie thought for a moment, then made a decision, one based on instinct rather than logic. She reasoned that her choice was temporary and harmless. She reasoned that, in the long run, no one would be hurt. She reasoned that Rio would go along with her lie because, at least for the time being, it was the only way out.

"Word gets around fast, doesn't it?" she said, calmly giving credence to the rumor.

"Always has. So, what do you say? Think you and Rio can make it?"

Maggie hoped she didn't sound like the liar she was. "Let me check with Rio, and I'll give you a call."

"Sure thing. If you can't reach me at the Longhorn, try me at Ken's place—I mean, our place. I still have to remind myself it's *our* house. Sometimes I can't believe my good luck."

"You deserve it. I'll call you, and thanks for the invitation."

The instant Maggie hung up the phone, she broke out in a cold sweat. What in the world had she done? *Told a whopper, that's what.* And Rio? What would he do when he found out? What if he flatly refused to go along with her lie? *He wouldn't do that, would he?* What if he blamed her for the rumors? *No, he wasn't that kind of man.* What if he thought the whole idea was ridiculous and they would both come off looking like fools? *A likely prospect.* No matter what he thought, the die had been cast, and they could either go through with the charade or suffer the consequences.

She picked up the phone, punched out his number and was shocked to hear his voice at the other end. "I, uh...Rio?" she stammered after he answered.

"Maggie?"

"Uh, yes. How are you?"

"Fine."

There was a long pause.

"Maggie, is something wrong?"

"No. Well, not exactly. I, uh, got a call from Nora Slattery a while ago. She wanted to thank me for putting Rosa Martinez, er, Walters, in touch with her about buying the Longhorn. Did I mention that Rosa was interested in purchasing the café?" Maggie knew she was babbling like an idiot, but she couldn't stop herself.

"Anyway, she and Ken, Rosa and her husband Karl—they're all—I think Cal and Serena are coming along, too—going to the Lumber Yard for dinner and they invited us." Maggie took a deep breath, partly for air, partly to steady her nerves, and waited for his inevitable question.

"I can understand why they invited you, but why me?"

She took another deep breath. Several, in fact, gathering her courage. "Because they think...in fact, quite a few people seem to think that you and I are...well, that we're, uh—"

"A couple?"

"Yes."

"Because you've been coming out to the ranch." He didn't want to tell her that Cal had already called with the news. In fact, he had been downright nervous about how she might react.

"Yes."

"Does that bother you?"

"No. Does it bother you?"

"Let 'em think whatever they want to," he said casually, when in fact, he was relieved she wasn't upset. "They'll talk no matter what we say or do."

"I started to deny the rumor, then I realized that, if I did, I would have to tell Nora about Emily and..."

"And we can't do that."

"No, we can't."

"And I can't let you ruin your reputation over this. I'm still bad news in this town. You associate with me and no telling what people will—"

"I'm a big girl, Rio. I can take care of myself. Besides, we've done nothing to warrant the gossip. I refuse to bend and twist my life to suit wagging tongues."

"You sure?"

"Absolutely.

"You can back out. No one would blame you."

"No."

There was another one of his irritatingly long silences before he said, "All right. How's your acting?"

The question stunned her, coming out of left field as it did. If she didn't know better, and she was certain she did, Maggie could almost believe she heard a smile in Rio's voice. She could almost believe the idea wasn't completely objectionable to him. "My acting?

"Yeah. You think it runs in the family?"

"My mom, you mean?" Maggie said, referring to the fact that her mother had once courted a career on the stage. "I'm not sure."

"You think we can fool Cal, Ken and the rest?" Fooling Cal wouldn't be easy, since his old rodeo buddy had already voiced thoughts about how odd this pair appeared to be. Cal knew him probably better than any other man alive, and Rio wasn't certain he could get past his old friend.

"It's not as if we have to pretend to be madly, passionately in love. Definitely interested should be enough, don't you think?"

"Yeah. Definitely interested should do it."

Definitely interested. The two words kept stomping around in Rio's head like a drugstore cowboy in a new pair of boots. Could he act interested in Maggie? That was the problem. He wouldn't be acting.

You ought to have your butt kicked clear across the Red River for even considering the possibility. But he *had* been considering the possibility of him and Maggie together. Probably from the first minute she'd walked into his kitchen.

And it was no good.

They were no good together. At least, he was no good for Maggie. She deserved something better than a broken-down old cowboy with scarcely more than a couple of nickels in his jeans.

Forget it, cowboy. She was out of your reach twelve years ago and not one damned thing has changed.

But that wasn't entirely true. They had changed. Maggie was certainly not the wide-eyed, innocent little schoolgirl he had known, and he was certainly not the grab - the - world - by - the - tail - and - give - it - a - twist young man he had been all those years ago. He had mellowed.

Hell, who was he kidding? He hadn't mellowed, just gotten older. He had graduated cum laude from the school of hard knocks, then gone back for post-graduate work, only to discover that you never do get a degree in life. It's every day, any way you can, to do the best you can. He had left town with a Mount Everest–size chip on his shoulder, and over the years the chip hadn't been dislodged, only worn down. And, he had to admit, since he'd returned some of the old feelings of bitterness had worked their way back to the surface. Like the way Crystal Creek thrived on gossip and rumor.

It didn't surprise him in the least to learn that he and Maggie were the newest entry in the rumor sweepstakes. What did surprise him was the fact that he hadn't gotten nearly as upset as he used to. He should have been furious to have his name passed around like fried chicken at Sunday dinner. Lord knew he was familiar enough with the scenario; he had grown up with the knowledge that both he and his mother were frequently part of the rumor mill. Delora Langley had always ignored the whispers and sideways glances. And while he knew she considered it undignified to do otherwise, Rio couldn't take the same passive stance his mother had chosen. He had never been able to overlook the insults or the people who had delivered them.

Perhaps that was why Maggie's memory had stayed with him for so long. She, like her brother Ronnie, plus Cal, Ken and a few others, had never been deterred by his heritage or lack of a father.

Who are you fooling? Where Maggie's concerned, it's more than that, and you know it.

It was true. Over the years, any fond thoughts of his hometown were linked to Maggie. And not just because she had kissed him, but because of the way she'd made him feel with that kiss. That night, for the first and only time Rio could remember, with sweet young Maggie's lips pressed to his, he'd felt as if he belonged.

That was what Maggie had done for him all those years ago. And she was doing it again.

Every time she was near, an undeniable feeling of contentment flowed over him. He didn't want it, told himself he didn't need it, but there it was, nonetheless. All because of Maggie.

And then there were the other things she made him feel. Like desire. Like red-hot desire.

Maybe less has changed than you thought. Rio couldn't deny he had wanted Maggie all those years ago on her front porch. He'd known he was too old and experienced for her, but that hadn't stopped him from kissing her. And it sure as hell hadn't stopped him from wanting what he knew he couldn't have.

Then and now, no matter what name Rio put to the feeling, the fact of the matter was that he wanted her. And knowing he shouldn't didn't make one bit of difference. Tonight he would be able to hold her in his arms. She had asked if he could pretend to be definitely interested. Well, he could pretend, all right. For a little while he could pretend that it was real. That he and Maggie could be what the whole town was saying they were—a couple.

Get a grip on reality, cowboy. You won't be doing Maggie any favor by hooking up with her, pretend or otherwise. Rio knew the pretense made no difference to the gossip mongers. And he knew he was being selfish, only thinking of himself, of how much he wanted to be with Maggie. But it wasn't fair and he had to put an end to this before it got out of hand. Tonight, after their evening out, he would tell her the pretending had to stop. For her sake.

THE LUMBER YARD'S advertising promised a good time, and the place delivered with the kind of style Texans took for granted. It provided good country music and superior barbecue. The rest was BYOF— Bring Your Own Friends. The Crystal Creek crowd was only too happy to oblige.

"I'm done," Ken Slattery said, patting his stomach. "Those were good eats."

"Slats, you sure three helpings of ribs, beans, homemade bread and peach cobbler are going to be enough?" Cal McKinney asked, teasing his friend.

"Back off, boy. I didn't see your fork lying idle."

"And you're not likely to," Serena McKinney added, grinning at her spouse.

Cal grinned at his wife, then looked across the table at his old rodeo sidekick. "So, Rio, can you believe you're out on the town with a bunch of old married folks?"

Rio knew Cal's style, and unless he missed his guess, the question was the kickoff for some good-natured ribbing. "I think J.T. started an epidemic," Rio replied, the corners of his mouth tilting in a grin. "Remind me, Flash, to steer clear of the Double C in case it's contagious."

Cal glanced at Maggie. "Looks like you might already be exposed."

Serena McKinney could guess where her husband intended to direct the conversation, and decided that, before poor Maggie withered with embarrassment, she should head him off at the pass. "Why does Rio call you Flash?"

Cal, Rio and Ken exchanged glances. Rio and Ken smiled.

"Go on, Slick," Ken urged. "Tell your wife where you got such an unusual handle."

Nora glanced at her husband. "Y'all are terrible."

"Yeah, tell her," Rio chimed in.

"You guys are asking for it."

"Where *did* the name come from?" Serena wanted to know.

"You might as well tell," Nora said. "You know good and well these two aren't going to let up until you do."

A smiling Rosa and Karl waited, enjoying the bantering.

"Had something to do with kissing, if I recall," Ken said calmly.

"Slats—"

"Yeah, something about how fast he could—"

"Hey," Cal said, rising from the table. "C'mon, sugar. You've got on a brand-new pair of La Herencia's finest and the soles have never touched a dance floor."

Serena scooted her chair away from the table. "I'd love to dance." Deliberately, she looked across the table. "How about it, Rio?"

Ken and Nora laughed.

"Thought you were supposed to dance with the guy that brung you?" Cal said as Karl and Rosa got up and headed for the floor.

Serena shot him a look from beneath her lashes. "Don't worry, *Flash,* you'll get your turn."

"I better." He winked as she passed him on her way to meet Rio. He looked across the table. "C'mon, Maggie, let's show 'em how it's done."

Rio heard the invitation and glanced over his shoulder in time to see Cal grab Maggie's hand and pull her onto the dance floor.

Maggie.

Cal had called her Maggie, and it grated on Rio's nerves. Leave it to Cal. He had picked up on the nickname the minute he'd heard it; now they were all calling her Maggie, saying it suited her much better than Margaret. Rio didn't like that. The nickname was something only they shared, and hearing it on everyone else's lips didn't sit well at all.

Rio swung Serena into an easy two-step, moving them smoothly around the floor, but his heart wasn't in it. The woman in his arms was tall, willowy and graceful, but she wasn't the woman he wanted. The woman he wanted was across the floor in another man's arms.

They're just dancing, for crying out loud.

But did Cal have to hold her so close? Did she have to smile like she was having the time of her life?

My God, I'm jealous!

The revelation stunned Rio. He was jealous of Cal—of anybody—touching Maggie. Old friend or not, he wanted to walk across the dance floor, jerk Maggie out of Cal's arms and into his.

Maggie could feel Rio's eyes on her even from across the room. Shamelessly, the thought thrilled her. After the interruption on his back porch, she had found herself fantasizing about what might have happened if her parents hadn't shown up when they did.

"Hey."

"Wh-what?" she said, forcing her thoughts back to reality.

"I was about to offer a penny for your thoughts," Cal said. "But on second thought I think I'll save my money. You got stars in your eyes, girl. How long has this been going on between you and ol' Rio?"

"I don't know what you're talking about."

"Yeah, right. Pull my other leg. You two can't keep your eyes off each other."

"Cal McKinney, if you start teasing Rio and embarrass me, I swear I'll . . . I'll . . ."

"You'll what, sweet thing?"

"I'll sic your wife on you."

"Sounds kinky. Might be fun."

"Stop it," Maggie said, trying not to smile.

"Okay. I'll get serious. Are you?"

"Am I what?"

"Serious about Rio?"

"Cal," she warned.

"Okay, okay. I'll be good."

They danced quietly for a minute. "You could do a lot worse, Maggie. They don't come any better than Rio," Cal said, his voice completely serious.

"I know."

"Glad to hear it. Maybe you can talk him into staying in Texas where he belongs, instead of running off to Colorado. Hell, there's always room for a good stock contractor. He could make that place of his mama's pay off."

"Do you really think so, Cal?"

"Sugar, he could do right well for himself if he gave it half a chance."

An idea formed in Maggie's mind that would probably have made Rio furious if he had known about it. "Did you know he's been turned down for a loan to fix the place up?"

Cal drew Maggie back from his loose embrace. "The hell you say."

"Elena told me. He's using his savings, hoping he'll be able to recoup enough to buy a spread."

"Yeah, but in Colorado."

Cal was in a position to help Rio, and he'd do it without a second thought, but she knew Rio would never ask. His pride wouldn't let him, and if Rio ever found out what she was about to suggest, he would be furious. Risky business, she decided, but worth it if Rio could realize his dream. And if his dream were to be realized right here in Crystal Creek, Maggie for one wouldn't be a bit disappointed.

She looked up at Cal. "Maybe he wouldn't be so quick to leave Texas if someone he trusted could help him get the money. Maybe, if someone thought it was a good investment . . ."

Cal grinned, knowingly. "I always did say you were the smartest girl in school."

Maggie grinned back.

"And the bravest."

"You've been listening to the wrong people if you think I'm brave for being with Rio."

"Just the same, watch your back. Once in a while the talk can turn mean. I'd hate to see you and Rio lose out on something good just because some old biddies can't keep their mouths shut."

"Thanks, Cal."

"Any time, sugar."

The dance ended, and they headed back to the table, as did Rio and Serena, who knew good and well Rio's mind had been elsewhere. Maggie was just about to sit down, when Rio grabbed her hand. "Wanna dance?"

"I'd love to," she said and put her hand in his.

The band struck up George Strait's "A Fire I Can't Put Out" as Rio took her in his arms. They swayed to the easy rhythm, their bodies moving sensuously with the music's beat.

How long had it been since she had been held in a man's arms like this? Maggie wondered. *Too long.* Rio's embrace was fiercely protective and overwhelming seductive at the same time. With his left hand riding securely at the nip in her waist, he held her pressed against him, as if he had no plans to turn her loose until the end of the century. His right hand cradled hers to his chest, his thumb gently stroking her fingers. Delicious sensations moved across her body as if prompted by a misbegotten whirlwind, touching her here, there, everywhere, enticing, exciting, making her feel more alive than she had in oh, so long. Making her remember that she was a woman with needs.

She had dated a few times since she returned home, even been out dancing with one or two men, but she had never felt like this with any of them. All the desires, hungers she had thought dead, or at the very least, dormant in the presence of other men had sprung to life again. Was wanting Rio good or bad? Could she stop even if she wanted to?

How long had it been since a woman felt this good in his arms? Rio wondered. *Too long. Way too long.* Holding Maggie was like holding a piece of heaven. She was so soft, her body yielding to his perfectly, causing him to remember he was a man with needs. Needs that went far beyond the physical, although for the moment, Rio couldn't think much past the feel of her body pressed to his. Or the results. And he wasn't the only one. The way Maggie moved with him, the way she nestled in his arms told him she, too, was feeling more than the music.

He danced the way he did everything else—confidently. Responding to that confidence, Maggie laid her head on his shoulder, feeling safe, secure and intimately sheltered, despite the fact that they were in a room full of people.

Her action took him by surprise, and he almost drew back before he stopped himself. He'd had a lot of women put their head on his shoulder, but never like this. Not the way Maggie had just done, telling him more than words ever could that she trusted him totally, completely. Why was it that whenever she looked at him or touched him or did a hundred other little things, he felt no one had ever done it before? What was it about her that made him feel not quite so used up and worn out? When in his life had he ever known such peace, such hope, except when he was with her?

The song ended and they reluctantly parted. He escorted her back to the table, and discovered some of the joy had gone out of the evening. Not because he didn't enjoy the good company, but because the dangerous questions he'd been contemplating demanded answers regardless of his resolve to end the pretense. And with a knowledge born of Adam, Rio knew the answers would somehow change his life, change *him*.

A couple of hours and many tantalizing dances later, they said good-night to the other couples and drove back to Crystal Creek. Their conversation was pleasant, but sparse, both of them still struggling with their conflicting feelings. Yet, when Rio parked his truck in her parents' driveway and helped her out, neither wanted to end the evening.

"Would you like to sit for a while?" Maggie motioned toward the swing suspended from chains at the far end of the wide porch.

"Sure."

They settled onto the wooden swing, not too far apart, but not too close. Maggie held on to the chain at her end of the swing with one hand, the other resting primly in her lap. Rio leaned forward and rested his forearms on his knees.

"That was great fun," she said a moment later.

"If you don't count the number of times I stepped on your toes."

"You did not. Not once. You're smooth and powerful on a dance floor."

His head snapped around. Had he been too rough? "What do you mean, powerful?"

"I meant...well...powerful in the sense that you're confident."

"Oh," he said, relieved. "Some men would call that arrogance."

"Some women would call it sexy."

Maggie couldn't believe she had actually said what she did, but it was true. The kind of power Rio possessed had nothing to do with his size or his muscles and everything to do with his presence, with the way he made her feel when she was with him. And at the moment she was feeling...more than she should.

And she wasn't the only one. Even in the partial illumination from the lights inside the house, she could see Rio's eyes darken.

"Would you?" he asked, not altogether certain he was prepared for her answer.

There was no need to pretend, and she didn't even want to. "Yes."

Rio swallowed hard. God, she was something! All satin and softness and no pretense.

"I can't be the first woman to tell you that you're sexy?"

"Why not? It's true. I've been called good-lookin' a couple of times, though Lord knows why with this beat-up old face of mine. And my size has scared away a lot more women than it's ever attracted. Look at these," he said, holding out his hands before her. "Big enough to hold a twenty-pound ham in each one."

"Or a baby," she reminded him. *Or a woman's heart.* "Your hands are strong, but they're also gentle." As if to prove her statement, she reached up and took one of his hands in both of hers.

Rio knew they were treading on dangerous ground. If he was half the man he hoped he was, he should leave before things got serious. Like a serious kiss. Like seriously thinking about how good she would feel naked beneath him. Like seriously wanting her until he couldn't breathe. *Tell her now. Then go. While you've still got the chance, 'cause if you kiss her, you're a goner.*

Maggie knew how bold she had been, and part of her was shocked. Another part only recognized the wanting. And the wanting frightened her a little bit. Before, with Greg, the loving had always been fulfilling, but never...electric, never curl-your-toes wild. Not once had she entertained the kind of thoughts that skipped through her mind every time she came near Rio. The kind of thoughts her old Sunday school teacher would have deemed downright carnal. She could hear Mrs. Abernathy now, quoting Scripture, sermonizing so sternly even her father would have prickled. But she realized she wasn't ashamed. Not in the least. What she felt for Rio was right. More right than she'd ever thought possible.

Rio saw the desire in her eyes and knew he was done for. As his mouth found hers, he pulled her into his embrace.

Maggie's first thought was that her memory had failed her. Miserably. His kiss was nothing like she remembered and everything she wanted and more. She gave herself over to need. Hers. His. They were the same. With every breath, every heartbeat, she joined her mouth more deeply with his, needing, wanting. The sweet intensity of pleasure he created was as old as Eve and as new as her next breath.

A hunger, like nothing he had ever known, tore through Rio's body, into his heart and clear to his soul. It burned, consumed, then from the ashes gave birth to more hunger. She was like wildfire in his arms, and he toyed with the flames like a demented moth. He kissed her again and again. His body was shaking with need. Or was that hers? He wanted nothing more than to take her down right there on her parents' front porch and make love to her until they were both senseless.

But you can't, reason insisted. *This isn't some honky-tonk angel out for a one-night stand, even if her body does answer yours heat for heat, need for need. This is Maggie. And you have to get yourself under control... this... instant.*

"Maggie," he whispered, finally dragging his mouth from hers. "Oh, God, I'm so—"

"Please don't say you're sorry."

Surprised at her statement, he only stared.

"Life is too short for unnecessary apologies. You wanted to kiss me and I wanted to be kissed."

"Yes, but—"

"Rio, we haven't committed the unpardonable sin, nor do I expect—" her gaze met his "—to be showered with orange blossoms. We're adults. Healthy adults."

"You're something, you know that?"

"Because I'm honest?"

"No, because you're not afraid."

"Oh, I'm afraid all right."

"Of me?"

"No, of me. Or more to the point, of how you make me feel."

Just when he thought she couldn't surprise him any more, she did. "And how do you... feel?" He surprised himself with the question. Maybe some of Maggie's courage was rubbing off on him, because he had never before talked to a woman the way he was talking to her.

"Excited, a tad nervous. Scared. Aroused."

Rio almost lost what was left of his remaining control, which was damned little. This wasn't what he had intended, but Lord, she was making him forget all his intentions, good or otherwise. "Maggie, I..."

"Have I shocked you?"

"No," he lied. "It's just that I... Oh hell, Maggie, I've been trying to get up the nerve to say something all night, and now..."

"Now what?"

"Now I'm stuck between what I should do and what I wanna do."

"Exactly what is it you feel you should do?"

His gaze met hers. "Stay the hell away from you. For your own good. There's already too much talk. Any more and your reputation could be—"

"I'm not going to walk away from helping you, no matter how many tongues wag or how many stories are passed around. And that's final, so no more talk of 'my own good.' Now, what is it you want to do?"

"Kiss you again."

Maggie smiled, leaned forward and gently placed her mouth on his. Her kiss was tender, but certainly not tentative. In her own way she was telling him that *she* was having no difficulties between should and want. Her hand caressed his cheek as her lips lingered. "I enjoyed tonight, Rio," she said at last, then pulled away slightly before adding, "*All* of tonight. I think maybe we better leave it at that, for now. I don't know about you, but I'm not used to this much... excitement in one night." She rose from the swing and walked to the front door, where she turned and said a soft good-night, then went inside.

MAGGIE LEANED against the inside of the front door and listened to Rio drive away. Tonight had taken an unexpected turn, for both of them, she suspected. But not an unpleasant one. She sighed and a smile lifted the corners of her mouth. Not unpleasant at all.

"Have a nice time, dear?"

Maggie turned to find her mother at the foot of the stairs, watching her.

"Yes. I had a wonderful time. Are you just now going to bed?"

Eva's dainty right hand touched the collar of her velour robe. "Uh, no, I went to the kitchen for a glass of water."

Suddenly, her father stepped out of his study and into the foyer. "Thought I heard you come in, Margaret. Did you have a good time tonight?"

Maggie glanced from one parent to the other and knew precisely why they were both still up past their usual bedtime. "You know," she said, grinning, "you two are about as transparent as glass."

Her mother's eyes widened. "What do you mean, dear?"

"You were waiting up for me."

"Whatever gave you such an idea?" they protested simultaneously.

"Oh, don't pretend. Besides, I think it's kind of—" the grin curled into a full smile "—sweet."

Eva and Howard exchanged glances. It was a gesture that Maggie had come to recognize and even dread over the years. "What was that look that just passed between you?"

"What look?" Howard asked.

"The one that shows you two have more on your minds than making sure your little girl got home okay."

"Margaret..." her father began, in a tone of voice that he usually reserved for serious occasions.

"I knew it. First the look. Now the come-into-the-study voice. What's up?"

"Well," Eva said, trying to keep her gaze from continually darting to her husband to confirm his moral support, "we, uh, wanted to talk to you, dear."

This had all the earmarks of a lecture. "About?"

Howard reached for his wife's hand. "It's about Rio, sweetheart."

Maggie took a deep breath. "I see."

"It's not that we don't approve of Rio," Eva rushed to assure her.

"Not at all," Howard added. "You have every right to see whomever you wish."

"I take it this has something to do with the gossip making the rounds about Rio and me."

"Sweetheart, this is a small town. People talk." Her father's shoulders lifted in a helpless shrug. "I don't like it. I don't condone it. And Lord knows I try to prevent it whenever I can, but..."

"Are you asking me to stop seeing Rio?"

"No," he said, but not as firmly as Maggie had hoped.

"Then why are we even discussing this?"

"Because two people out of the congregation have come to your father—"

"Eva, I thought we agreed not to mention that episode."

"*We* didn't agree. I insisted that if we're going to treat Margaret like the mature adult she is, then she deserves all of the truth."

"Thank you, Mother."

At the sharpness in his daughter's voice, Howard Blake sighed and rubbed the bridge of his nose between his thumb and forefinger. "Now you're upset."

"Did you think I hadn't heard the rumors? Good heavens, this town *thrives* on gossip. How could I *not* have heard them?" Maggie stopped and took a deep breath. Confronting the same topic twice in a half hour had eclipsed the intimate moments she and Rio had shared, but even so, her parents didn't deserve her anger. She pushed away from the door and approached them at the foot of the stairs. "I'm sorry, Dad, but I've already had a similar conversation with Rio not thirty minutes ago."

"And how does he feel?"

"That he has to protect me by not seeing me anymore."

"And what did you say to him?"

She looked squarely at both her parents. "That I'm committed to helping him and Emily and nothing anyone can say will change my mind."

Eva arched an eyebrow at her husband. "What did I tell you?" As if the issue was now completely settled, she leaned over, kissed Maggie on the cheek and said, "I told your father you could handle this and I was right. Good night, dear."

Maggie's smile returned. "'Night, Mom. Sleep tight."

"You, too." With a wave, Eva Blake made her way upstairs to bed.

Howard, however, didn't make any move to join his wife. "Margaret," he said softly, reaching for her hand. "We love you and we only want what's best for you. I'm sorry if we sounded like overprotective—"

"You sounded like people who love me. And if I've neglected to mention it lately, I love you, too." She patted the hand holding hers. "Don't worry, Daddy. Your little girl can take of herself."

The frown eased from Howard's forehead. "Sometimes I wish you were my little girl again. Then I could make sure you don't get hurt. Again."

"You're talking about my crush on Rio all those years ago."

"I suppose."

"I'm not a teenager, Dad. I'm a grown woman. Teenagers get crushes. Grown women fall in love."

"Exactly," the good reverend replied.

ON THE DRIVE HOME Rio kept wondering how the tables had gotten turned. When it came to relationships, *he* was usually the one telling his partner not to expect too much, or telling himself he wasn't sorry when it ended. For years he had maintained that if he ever found a truly honest woman, he wouldn't let her go. Well, he'd found one, but he'd be damned if he knew what to do with her.

He had come back to Crystal Creek carrying the same chip on his shoulder that had been balanced there as long as he could remember. And for as long as he could remember, he had dared the world to knock it off. A few had tried using force and failed. And then, when he had least expected it, along came a five-foot-four-inch bit of sass and silk named Maggie Blake Conway, and with one kiss and the sweetest straight talk he had ever heard, she had sent that chip flying for parts unknown.

CHAPTER FIVE

THE RINGING of the phone roused Maggie the next morning. "Hello," she mumbled.

"Good morning." To Rio her voice sounded sleepy and sexy as all get-out, and for a few seconds he closed his eyes and indulged in a fantasy about lying in bed next to her listening to that voice only inches from his ear.

When she recognized her caller, Maggie was suddenly wide awake. "Good morning."

"The weather has turned so nice, I—I thought I'd take Emily on her first picnic this afternoon, and I wondered if...I thought maybe you might like to join us." He didn't want to talk about weather or picnics. What he wanted to tell her was how great she had felt in his arms last night and how much sweeter her lips were than he remembered, but he couldn't. He had never been good at expressing himself, and even if he had been, he wasn't sure he could have found the right words to tell Maggie how special their kisses had been, how...hopeful she made him feel. "You were coming by to check on her anyway, weren't you?" he asked when she didn't answer right away.

"Yes."

"And we need to talk about how to go about locating Emily's family."

"Yes, of course. Actually, I started checking her footprints yesterday. I should get some answers Monday."

"Good."

"Don't get your hopes up, Rio."

"Yeah. So, you—you think you might be interested in joining us?"

"Why not?" she said finally. "Saturdays in the fall are made for picnics, aren't they? What time?"

"Around one o'clock? Emily is awake and playful then."

"I wouldn't miss it, or her," Maggie said. *Or you,* she could have added. "What can I bring?"

"Just yourself." *What more could a man want?* he could have added.

"Sounds like my kind of picnic. See you at one."

Long after the conversation ended, Maggie recalled Rio's voice, particularly when he had said, "Just yourself." There had been both longing and reluctance in his tone, as if he were in the middle of some mental tug-of-war. She wondered if his feelings concerning their kisses were as ambiguous as hers.

Kissing Rio had started an emotional chain reaction she didn't know how to stop. Questions kept tumbling around in her mind like acrobats. What did the kiss mean? *What do you want it to mean?* What happens next? *What do you want to happen next?*

If she were honest with herself, she had to wonder what could ever come of her attraction to Rio. He wasn't interested in anything long-term. Not the ranch or a relationship.

And she wasn't interested in anything else.

Having known the stability of a good marriage, she wasn't willing to settle for anything less. But she didn't know what to do about the emotions that threatened to swamp her good sense whenever she was around Rio.

For a moment she had forgotten that they were only "seeing each other" in order to keep Emily's presence under wraps. For a moment she had forgotten they were only pretending. She knew she wasn't pretending when he kissed her. And neither was he.

No, Maggie thought, there was nothing phony about the way desire had coursed through her body like a Hill Country flash flood in early spring. Nothing fake about the burning need that had come from deep within her, leaping, glowing like a new flame climbing for air until finally, it burst into the open, a full-blown fire, hot and dangerous. No, it was real. So real, she couldn't remember having had those same feelings about Greg. So real, in fact, that all she could think about was spending the next few hours with the man who had made her feel like a love-struck girl of fourteen again. Suddenly, the hours between now and one o'clock seemed too many and too long.

SHE'S EARLY, Rio thought, when he heard Maggie's Suburban pull into the driveway. He walked to the kitchen window and watched her get out of her truck and start toward the house. She stopped for a moment, raised her face to the sun, took a deep breath, then continued walking. Dressed in jeans and sweatshirt, her hair pulled back on either side of her face and secured with combs, she looked very like that young girl he had kissed all those years ago. But last night had proved beyond the shadow of a doubt that she was a woman, all woman. And this morning had proved he was a bigger fool than he'd ever thought he could be.

He glanced down into the cup of thick, steaming coffee in his hand, as if its ebony depth might hold the answer to world peace. Or more appropriately, his peace, because he certainly had known precious little of the commodity since Maggie had left him sitting on her front porch last night. In the hours since she agreed to join him on the picnic, he had gone to the phone no fewer than three times to call her back and cancel, then changed his mind. He'd been wrong. He should have canceled.

His plan wasn't going to work.

Like a fool, he had convinced himself that the picnic was a great way to put their relationship back on a less personal basis after last night. And he'd been convinced, right up until the instant he looked up and saw her lift her face to the morning sun, until he saw the sun caress her skin and streak her hair with gold.

Until the pure sweetness of the moment had pierced his soul. That was when he'd realized just how big a fool he was, because he was trying to fool himself. He didn't want a less personal relationship with Maggie. He wanted more. And the more he wanted, the more she would be hurt, no matter how much she insisted otherwise.

Maggie knocked twice on the screen door. "Hello?"

"Coming," Rio said, more sharply than he'd intended.

"Did Emily keep you up all night?" she asked at his obviously less-than-sunny mood.

"No, I—uh. Sorry. You ready?"

She nodded. "Where's Elena?"

"In town."

At her quizzical look, he added, "One of her grandkids had a dentist appointment, and his parents had to work, so I told her to go ahead and take him."

Maggie propped a slender hand on her hip. "Now I see why I received the invitation. Needed a pinch hitter, huh?"

"No," Rio hurried to assure her. "I'm gonna take care of Emily today. You don't have to do a thing. Honest." He raised four fingers instead of the traditional three. "Scout's honor."

Maggie reached up and pushed his little finger down. "In some circles, that's considered blasphemy."

The contact of her hand on his acted like a sensual lightning rod, sending currents of awareness through both of them. Maggie was the first to pull away. She cleared her throat. "So, where have you stashed your star boarder?"

"In the bedroom sleeping." Rio's eyes never left her face. God, but she had a wonderful mouth. Today she was wearing some kind of lip gloss that tinted her lips the faintest shade of peach, and when she talked, the light caught the shine and made her mouth look wet. He could watch her mouth for hours. He could kiss it for a lot longer.

Ever so slightly, she stuck out her bottom lip in a pretend pout. "I'm disappointed."

For a heartbeat Rio thought he might slip right over the edge of sanity, reach for her and do all the things he had thought about doing to her last night. He told his mind to cool it, but his body wasn't so easy to convince.

"I was hoping she would be awake," Maggie added.

Rio turned and almost stomped across the kitchen. Not an easy feat, since he was uncomfortably hard. "She will be." With his back still to her, he poured himself more coffee.

What had gotten into him? Maggie wondered. One minute he was eating her up with his eyes, and the next, he put as much distance between them as he could. "I brought an old beach umbrella so she wouldn't get too much direct sun."

"Thanks."

She glanced at the kitchen table and noticed the picnic hamper, a thermos and folded blanket. "Can I help you load this stuff?"

He shook his head, took a deep breath and finally turned back to face her, his body now under control. "I'll get it."

"Rio," she said, seeing the frown on his face, "if you've changed your mind about this outing, it's all right with—"

Emily woke up crying.

"Would you mind seeing to her while I load up the truck?" Rio asked.

"Sure." A few minutes later Maggie emerged from the bedroom, carrying a dry and much happier Emily as Rio walked back in. "Shall I feed her before we go?"

"You don't have to. I'll do it."

"I'd like to do it, if you don't mind."

"No. I don't mind at all."

He watched her moving comfortably around his kitchen, preparing the bottle while holding the baby, talking sweetly to the child. The picture was disturbing. Disturbingly natural. Maybe too natural, Rio thought, listening to her hum softly, cradling the baby while she fed her. Maggie looked so right in this picture of domesticity. And Rio felt way too right. An internal message kept flashing, *This is the way it's supposed to be. Should be.* But could be was another matter altogether.

Maggie was almost through feeding Emily when they heard another truck pull up in the driveway. Rio looked outside. Cal and Serena were walking up to the porch. *Aw, hell. Just what I need. Gawkers.* "It's Cal and Serena."

He should have known Cal would be around sooner or later to get the straight skinny on the supposed courtship of Margaret Conway. And Serena, too. Especially after last night's shindig at the Lumber Yard. The two of them were so sappy over each other, they wanted to spread it around as thick as peanut butter, and Cal had made no bones about the fact that he considered the newest twosome in town a "likely prospect" for a good dose of sappy.

Emily! Rio thought, suddenly remembering his small, unofficial guest. "Oh, my God." He whipped around to face Maggie. "How are we going to explain Emily?"

Eyes wide, she opened her mouth to speak, but never got the chance.

Predictably, Cal didn't knock, but walked right on in. His hat pushed back on his head, a six-pack of Lone Star long necks tucked under one arm and a determined gleam in his eyes, he looked like a man with a mission. "We figured we'd find you two together." He stopped when he saw the baby in Maggie's arms. "What's this?" He glanced from Rio to Maggie. "Or should I say, whose is this?"

"Listen, Flash—"

"I swear, Cal McKinney, you're the world's worst tease." As a line of defense, Maggie wasn't certain the idea that had popped into her head could be considered a stroke of genius, but anything would be better than the direction of Cal's thoughts. "This is Emily, one of Elena's grandkids. Isn't she a doll? We're keeping an eye on her until Elena gets back from town."

"Oh, yeah, I forgot. She's got a herd of them, doesn't she? Say." Cal glanced around, completely forgetting about Emily. "You guys going somewhere?"

"On a picnic." Maggie and Rio exchanged glances, both relieved. "Hi, Serena," she said.

"Hi."

"Yeah. We were just about to leave when you showed up."

Cal cocked an eyebrow. "Taking the baby with you?"

"Sure," Maggie said, hoping she sounded convincing. "After spending my days working with kids from dysfunctional homes who've been forced to develop a get-even-or-get-out attitude, spending time with this little sweetie is like a tonic."

Cal made no comment, just looped his arm around Serena. "Looks like we're just in time. Catch, ace." Wearing a grin that redefined devilish, he tossed the six-pack to Rio. "Pop a couple of those, will ya?"

Cal never could take a hint, Rio thought, as he took two bottles of beer out of the pack and put the rest in the refrigerator. And it looked as if today wouldn't be the exception. Though grateful that Emily's presence hadn't become an issue, he still wished Cal would take his wife off somewhere and leave them alone. He handed Cal a beer. "Serena?" he asked, offering her the second bottle.

"No thanks." She arched an eyebrow at her husband. "I have a feeling I may turn out to be the designated driver."

Rio opened the cap on a tall amber bottle, leaned against the edge of the countertop and took his first swig of cold beer.

"So," Maggie said, juggling Emily from her arms to her shoulder while trying to set the bottle of milk on the table. "What brings the two of you out here?"

Serena watched Maggie holding the baby in her arms, and pain sliced into her heart, sharp and deep. She would never know the joy of holding her own child because of the disease she might be carrying in her body. A disease her child could inherit. Careful to hide her pain from Cal, Serena shrugged. "Ask my husband. He suddenly got this wild urge to come calling."

"Just being neighborly," Cal said.

Neighborly, my butt, Rio thought. He'd known Cal all his life and knew damned well the youngest McKinney son was up to something.

Cal took a long pull on his beer. "Sure had a hell of a good time last night. How 'bout you, Maggie?"

Maggie looked at Rio and her voice softened as she replied, "I had a wonderful time."

"Yeah, even got ol' Langley out on the dance floor. You know, I was beginning to think he'd gone plumb bashful in his old age. But I see he's still got a Cotton-eyed Joe or two left in him."

Serena gave Cal an affectionate jab to the ribs.

"Hey," her husband grunted.

"Hey, yourself," she replied, grinning up at him. "If I remember correctly, Rio isn't that much older than you are."

"It's not the age, darlin'," he insisted, giving Maggie a wink. "It's the mileage."

Rio had to grin. He wasn't really angry. A little teed off, perhaps, but only because of the momentary scare that too many questions would be asked about Emily. And because Cal and Serena had interrupted what he hoped would be a pleasant afternoon and a time for him and Maggie to get things straight between them. But no one could stay put off with Cal for very long. It wasn't Cal's nature to be mean or sharp-tongued. Of all the men Rio had known in his life, Cal was the one he trusted above all others.

"Am I supposed to be flattered that you drove all the way out here just to insult me?" Rio asked.

"Or impressed."

"Flash, I haven't been impressed with you since the time you dated both of the Williams sisters without either one of them knowing about the other." He saluted Cal with the long neck.

Hands on hips, Serena turned to Cal. "Now the truth comes out."

"Say, how 'bout showing me what you've done since you got back?" Cal said, sidestepping his wife's comment. "Yes sir, I'm fairly bustin' to see what you've done with the place."

"Chicken," Serena murmured sweetly.

"It's not the first time I've saved his butt," Rio said, moving toward the back door. "Doubt it will be the last."

"Miss me." Cal gave Serena a quick peck on the cheek and followed Rio out.

"Speaking of butts," Cal said when he and Rio were inside the barn. "I can see you've busted yours trying to get this place in shape."

"For all the good it'll do me."

"You still hell-bent on sellin'?"

Rio didn't answer immediately, and Cal took that as a positive sign.

"Don't have much choice."

"A man's always got a choice. Yes or no. Do or don't. Go or stay."

Rio leveled his gaze at Cal. "What's on your mind?"

"Horses."

"Horses?"

"And bulls. And calves."

"What's this, a stroll down memory lane, or are you thinking about going back on the circuit?"

Cal shook his head. "I'm done with getting my bones broken by some ornery bull with an attitude. No. I'm talking about stock contracting."

"Call me in Colorado in about a year."

"That's just it. I don't want to pay the long distance charges. I'd rather make a local call."

"What the hell are you talking about?"

"I'm talking about you turning this place your mother left you into a paying stock ranch. I'm talking about you staying where you belong."

"Well, you're talking crazy."

"Why?"

"Because."

"Oh, now there's an intelligent answer if I ever heard one."

"Look who's talking about staying where you belong. I seem to recall you were never one to pine for the old home place."

"That was before."

"Before what?"

"Serena."

There was nothing Rio could say to that. Until Serena Davis had walked into Cal's life one night in Wolverton, Rio had begun to think his friend might never grow up and settle down. A man would have to be blind not to see that Serena was good for Cal. Rio shrugged. "You got lucky."

"Damn straight. And so could you."

Rio's head snapped up. "If you're suggesting that Maggie and I—"

"Maggie? I'm talking about this ranch. Look, knot head, can't you get it through that thick skull of yours that you could have everything you want right here in Crystal Creek? Aren't you the one who always told me to straighten up and fly right, plan for the future, use my head for something other than to hold my hat? Well, now I'm telling you to do the same. You got a hell of a lot of potential here. Don't blow it."

Half-relieved that Cal didn't intend to press for a definition of his relationship with Maggie, and half-mad that he had stuck his nose in where he wasn't invited, Rio looked Cal straight in the eye and said, "You done?"

"Not quite. I want in."

"In where?"

"In business. I'm finally taking your advice and making an investment. I want to invest in your ranch."

You could have knocked Rio over with a feather. The last thing he had expected from Cal was an offer to become partners. "You're crazy."

"If I am, then I'm in good company. Ken wants a piece of the action, too. We talked about it last night on the way home, then again this morning. Slats ain't getting any younger and he wants to provide for Rory's college education. As for me, well..." He paused, then added, "Let's just say it's a hedge against inflation."

Stunned, Rio stared at his friend. "You *are* crazy."

"Like a fox. You and Slats are the two best horse-men this side of the Red River. I'd be crazy *not* to take this opportunity."

Suddenly comprehension dawned, and Rio thought he knew the reason for Cal's surprising offer. "No dice. I don't take handouts."

"I always knew you were hardheaded, but I didn't know you were stupid. This is business, ace. Good business."

"You've got a good business. Why would you want to take such a risk?"

Cal looked solemn for a moment before replying. "When Serena first came to me, she was already in business. La Herencia was hers, not mine. Don't get me wrong, it's good and gettin' better. I enjoy it. But maybe I want something that's mine. Hell, maybe I just want to show Daddy he was dead wrong about me for all those years. Whatever the reason, I think this can work, Rio. For all of us. So, here's the deal, ace. We put up the cash and you do the work. As soon as we hit break-even, we split the profits sixty-forty."

Thoughtful, Rio looked out the barn door at the ranch house. "This wasn't my plan."

"Yeah, but it's a damned good alternative."

He glanced at Cal. "I didn't come back to stay."

"I know, but sometimes a man has to take oppor-tunities where he finds them."

"I'm not sure I wanna stay." He glanced at the back of the house, thinking about Maggie. And Emily. "I'm not sure about a lot of things."

"I know that, too. Think about it. You've got the talent. Jeez, didn't you have the brains to switch from bull riding to working with stock while the rest of us were still getting tossed on our asses?"

Rio grinned in spite of himself. "Maybe that's where this harebrained idea came from. One too many times landing on your butt in the dirt."

"Who cares where it came from so long as it works? And it will work. I know it."

"We're talking a lot of money, Cal. And what makes you think we can get PRCA approval?"

"Why don't you stop being so damn stubborn and see this for what it is—a damn good opportunity for all of us *including* the Professional Rodeo Cowboys Association?"

They stood together for several minutes, neither speaking. Cal struggled, wanting to press the issue without bruising Rio's pride. Rio struggled with an emotion that was both pride and gratitude, wondering which would win out, not sure which he wanted to win out.

"I appreciate the offer, but—"

"Before you give me an answer, I got one more thing to say. Don't let pride stand in the way of something you know in your heart is worthwhile, Rio. Not my offer or anything else that life throws your way. You're listening to the voice of experience. If I'd hung on to my pride, I wouldn't have Serena, and believe me, no amount of pride could ever make up for that loss." Cal clapped him on the back. "Think about it, ace, and let me know." He turned to walk away, then turned back. "Oh, and by the way, now that I think about it, that stuff about potential and not blowing it applies to Maggie as well." Having delivered his final shot, Cal strolled away, leaving Rio alone.

When Cal stepped back inside the house, he was confronted with the vision of Serena holding little Emily, cooing softly to her, stroking her cheek. He stopped dead in his tracks. Watching his wife, seeing the longing in her eyes, was more than he could bear. It tore him apart to know, even though he accepted it completely, that they couldn't risk having children of their own. It wasn't fair that she should have to pour all her love onto him when she had so much to give. But then, life wasn't fair.

"Hey," he said, coming to stand behind Serena. He lifted a hand to touch her hair, then changed his mind for fear she might take it as a gesture of pity. "Maggie got you pinch-hitting, huh?"

"Only temporarily," Maggie said, reentering the kitchen with a blanket in her hand, which she folded, then stacked on top of the picnic hamper. She took Emily from Serena. "Where's Rio?"

"He'll be in shortly." Casually, Cal put his arm around his wife's shoulder. "We gotta be going."

Maggie put Emily on her shoulder. "You could join us. I'm sure there's plenty of food."

"No can do. We've got to stop over at the Hole in the Wall and check our inventory." Cal winked at Maggie. "Got to keep our customers happy."

"Maybe another time."

"Sure. C'mon, darlin'," he said, taking Serena's hand. "See ya, Maggie."

"See ya."

"Bye, Maggie," Serena said.

"Bye." She waved as the screen door closed behind them, then stared out at the barn. Why hadn't Rio come back? Had Cal talked to him about staying? Had he offered to help? More important, would Rio's pride allow him to accept?

Inside the barn, Rio leaned against one of the stalls, his thumbs hooked into the front pockets of his jeans. He hadn't expected Cal's offer. In fact, it had knocked the wind out of his sails for a moment or two.

He couldn't accept. Not because it wasn't a good deal. Far from it. Not because Cal and Ken would make lousy partners. They were probably the only two men on the planet he might even *consider* going into business with. He couldn't accept because... because...

Because what? It won't be all yours? Because you couldn't claim you built something out of nothing? You and you alone?

A man had his pride, Rio thought, no matter what Cal said.

Or is it because if you stay you'll have to face the past? All of it. If you stay you'll have to deal with your guilt and your shame. You'll have to live up to the image your mother clung to all those years you weren't here.

He shoved himself away from the stall. What the hell was he doing, raking himself over the hot bed of coals that was his past? A past he couldn't change. He wasn't going to take Cal up on his offer and that was that. Besides, even if he was interested in the offer, he couldn't do anything about it now. The most pressing piece of business was finding out where Emily came from, who her family was. Everything else took second place. He didn't have time to spend thinking about business. *So, McKinney will just have to wait for an answer.*

If he had thought about his rationale for more than two seconds, Rio would have realized he didn't want to give Cal an answer right away. He would have realized the offer was incredibly tempting no matter how much he protested otherwise, and if he thought about the offer for very long, he might run out of reasons *not* to take it.

And if he had thought about Cal's statement concerning Maggie for more than two seconds, he would have realized just how sweet those words were and just how much he hoped they were true.

"WELL, DID YOU do it?" Serena asked a short time later, back at the Double C. She had agreed with Cal's plan, but wasn't as certain of its success.

"Yeah."

"And?"

"And he didn't say no."

"Does that mean yes?"

"Same thing. Ol' Rio doesn't know it yet, but that's exactly what it means. If he was going to get his back up and let his pride make the decision, he would have done it today."

Serena noted the satisfied tone of Cal's voice and knew he was pleased as much for himself as for Rio. This venture was important to him. For a lot of reasons. "I hope J.T. isn't upset when he finds out you've invested in another ranch."

"This isn't ranching the way you think. Dad knows I would never get seriously involved in ranching other than the Double C, especially now."

"You mean since his heart attack?"

"Yeah. Of course, there was a time when he didn't think much of Rio."

"Because the two of you rodeoed together?" she asked.

"That, plus the fact he had a few misconceptions about Rio when we were kids, but he learned differently."

"What do you mean?"

"Just that while Rio and I were on the rodeo circuit together, Dad finally learned what I had known all along—it doesn't make any difference where a man's been—it's where he's going that counts."

Serena thought for a moment. "You're talking about the burden Rio carries because he's part Indian?"

"Half-breed is the term used in these parts, sugar. And on top of half-breed, illegitimate."

Serena's eyes widened. "Oh."

"Yeah, oh. And some folks still can't see past Rio's background."

"But you did."

"Never saw it in the first place. This is one of the best partnerships I've ever invested in."

"Are you sure you want to do this?" Serena asked.

"You mean the money?"

"No, becoming partners with Rio."

Cal laughed heartily. "Darlin', the day Rio Langley takes a partner will be followed closely by the Second Coming. He's a loner. Always has been. Always will be."

"But you just said—"

"I said loaning Rio the money to fix up the ranch was one of the best partnerships I ever invested in and it's true. Just depends on how you define the word, *partner,* darlin'."

"And how do you define it?"

"As someone who goes the extra mile for you. Someone who thinks loyalty and honesty are a way of life, not just some greeting-card sentiment. Someone who knows your faults and doesn't hold them against you. Someone you respect and who respects you. I've known Rio all my life. He's hauled my drunken butt out of more than a few bars and helped me fight my way out of a couple." Cal reached out and drew his wife into his embrace. "When the call came that Mom was going into the hospital for probably the last time, it was Rio who found me a ride on some crop duster's plane in the middle of the night in the middle of nowhere so I could make connections to Austin."

Serena looped her arms around Cal's waist, hooking her thumb in his belt loop as she leaned into his warm, hard body. "Now I understand why you called it the best partnership you've ever invested in."

"One of, not *the*," he said, gazing deep into her eyes. "You're *the* best partnership, sugar. You're my wife, lover, my *partner*."

"Thank you," she whispered, growing misty-eyed at the compliment.

"I only hope Rio will be as lucky."

Now it was Serena's turn to grin. "Judging from the way Margaret—excuse me—Maggie, seemed to be right at home, I think maybe he is and just doesn't know it."

"Yeah, that's something. The preacher's daughter and the outcast."

"Stranger things have happened. Too bad they have to put up with all the gossip and BS."

"I know, but it didn't seem to worry them today. They were certainly happy. And did you see the way they both looked at that baby?"

"Both of them were sort of goofy over that kid."

"And did you see the way they looked at each other?"

"You mean kind of like the way I'm looking at you now?"

A slow and incredibly sexy smile curved Serena's soft mouth. "Very much the way you're looking at me now."

Cal inclined his head enough to whisper in her ear. "What do you say I do more than look?" he asked, and was rewarded with a murmur that was both agreement and encouragement.

"I say you're a sweet talker, Cal McKinney. And I always was a sucker for sweet talkers."

"Speaking of sweet talking," he said, a serious tone in his voice, "you did your share today."

"When?"

"With Emily."

"Oh, that," Serena whispered.

He cupped her face in his hands, his thumbs gently stroking her jaw. "Loving you is a prideful thing, Serena. Every time I think about how lucky I am to have you, I nearly bust my buttons with pride. But you outdid yourself today. And I know it wasn't easy."

"Just because I'm afraid about having a child doesn't mean I have to ignore all the babies in the world. But you're right." Her eyes filled again. "It wasn't easy."

His hands moved down to caress her shoulders. "I've been thinking about that, about how you worry every month, even though we're careful. You know, if you're so afraid, and you'd feel safer, I could just have me one of those vasectomies." He grinned that sexy grin she loved so much. "Then all we'd have to worry about is where and how often."

Stunned at his offer, Serena looked into Cal's eyes, awed by the breadth and depth of his love for her. He had told her once that of the two of them, he was the one who knew how to live each day as it came, the one who knew how to squeeze every last sweet drop of life out of a day. And he had proved it again. "You keep having to teach me not to get stuck in the future, don't you?" she asked, tears clearly evident in her eyes.

"Yeah." He kissed the tip of her nose. "But you're gettin' the hang of it."

"I love you so much, Cal." It was a shame that people who only took her husband at face value were overlooking a loyal, compassionate man. That those who saw only laughter instead of a powerful life force glinting in his eyes missed a well of love so deep, so strong it could move mountains. "But I can't let you do that. It's too...too permanent. If something were to...to happen to me, you might want to remarry and have—"

"Look at me." When she did, she almost gasped at the intensity of his gaze. "I told you once that we'd build our future strong, out of love and nothing would tear it down. Well, I wasn't just talking to hear myself think out loud. And in case you didn't get it, the key word in that phrase is *we*."

"But doesn't a…one of those change you? I mean, I've heard that afterward some men don't feel—"

"Like a man?" Cal's grin grew wider and some of the intensity faded. "Hell darlin'. Just because of a little snip don't mean I'll be singing soprano in the choir. And as for manliness—" he winked "—I reckon I'll have enough steam left to keep both of us smiling for a while. Say forty or fifty years."

"I'm counting on it." She couldn't let him make such a sacrifice, of course, wouldn't let him, but oh, how she loved him for offering. "Don't make any rash decisions without consulting me, okay?"

"Whatever you say, darlin'." He kissed her soundly on the mouth.

Serena smiled against his lips, knowing she would keep on smiling as long as Cal was in her life, because he *was* her life.

CHAPTER SIX

SO FAR, I WOULDN'T CALL this picnic a roaring success, Maggie thought as she watched Rio stare off into space. Again. Beside them on the blanket, Emily slept peacefully in the dappled fall sunshine. As for Maggie, she could have been by herself for all the attention Rio had given her since he had returned from the barn a full half hour after Cal and Serena were gone.

They had driven to a place beside the Claro River and eaten in silence except for a minimum of conversation; pleasant enough but hardly what she had hoped for. Something was on his mind. Something worrisome enough to create the distance she had felt from the moment he walked back into the house. And on top of the worry etched in fine lines around his mouth and vibrating in the timbre of his voice, she caught a glimpse of pain in his eyes. Something was most definitely bothering him, and it appeared he wasn't going to tell her what it was without some prompting.

Should she ask? Maybe he would interpret her concern as interference. Maybe it was just none of her business. Rio was a grown man. He didn't need her to take care of him.

Or did he?

Watching him now, his forehead lined by a frown, she sensed he had taught himself not to depend on anyone else. *A real self-made man.* Only he had become an isolationist, keeping his own counsel, sharing nothing, not his joy or his pain. It wasn't natural. If Maggie had learned nothing else since losing her husband, she had learned that loneliness was a poor companion. She didn't want that for Rio. Her heart broke with the need to reach out to him, and she had to follow that need.

"It was nice of Cal and Serena to drop by." *Start slow and work your way up. The worst he can do is tell you it's none of your business.*

"Yeah."

"Cal's certainly changed since they married. He hasn't lost any of his charm, but there's a depth to him now that I've never seen before. I guess love can do that."

"I guess."

Maggie sighed. Lord, but the man was hard to reach. "Penny for your thoughts," she said, determined to chip away at his self-enforced solitude, only because she had the feeling he needed her to.

"Overpriced."

"I doubt it, from the frown on your face."

Now, he turned his head and met her gaze. "I'm sorry. Haven't been very good company, have I?"

"I'll live."

"You deserve better."

She reached across the blanket and touched his hand. "So do you. I don't like to see you..." She struggled for a word and finally settled on the single thread running through the frown, the distant stare and the timbre of his voice. "Hurting."

Rio glanced down at her slender, delicate fingers, lying against his work-roughened hands. When she touched him, everything changed.

It wasn't just that he wanted her, though God knew he did. Wanted her with a passion he hadn't even known he possessed. Almost as if he had stored up that passion over the years, just waiting for her to tap into its depths. When he looked at her, he wondered if he hadn't been waiting for her, waiting for a message from his own heart, since the moment of that first tender kiss.

Suddenly all his troublesome thoughts, all the pros and cons surrounding Cal's offer, all the defenses his pride was manufacturing seemed to coalesce into one powerful reality.

Maggie.

Without realizing it, she'd become a factor in his decision about accepting the offer. About staying in Crystal Creek. About the future.

Maggie, Maggie, Maggie. He was a fool to have let things go this far, yet he didn't seem to be able to stop the flood of his emotions. And now she saw right through him to the pain his pride had always insisted no one could uncover. How was he going to deal with this...this invasion of his heart? God, how was he going to walk away from her this time? Could he?

He slipped his hand from beneath hers, unable to bear touching her without wanting more. Absently plucking a long blade of Johnson grass from a clump beside the blanket, he tried to make his voice as nonchalant as possible when he spoke. "What makes you think I'm hurting?"

"Because it's what I see underneath that stoic expression you use to hide from the rest of the world. It's there for anyone to see. Anyone who cares enough to look."

And do you care? he wanted to ask, rolling the blade of grass back and forth between his thumb and finger. *Don't ask.* "You know," he said, hoping to change the subject, "when you were a kid, you were a little self-conscious and shy. Predictable."

She returned the smile, determined he should lose ground in his efforts to evade her. "You want predictable, buy a Timex."

Rio laughed. "The sweet little Maggie I know would never have said that."

"The sweet little Maggie you knew hadn't ever lost anyone she loved. Hadn't ever had to come face-to-face with the truth about herself."

Rio's laughter faded. "I'm sorry about your husband. I'm sorry you had to go through that."

"Greg's death was hard, and I don't mean just the fact that I lost my husband. The hardest part was finding myself. It's a funny thing about truth. When you're facing it, the pain is almost overwhelming. You would give almost anything not to have to go through it. But once you're on the other side, once you've been through the pain and survived, you're glad. It makes you stronger, gives you a much clearer view of the world. And of yourself."

She had thrown a wide loop around his attempt to change the subject and hauled him right back to his self-inflicted turmoil. And she wasn't about to turn him loose.

Maggie waited for him to say something. Anything. After several minutes of silence, she had almost given up hope.

"Cal and Ken have offered to back me if I want to turn Mama's land into a working stock ranch." *What the hell*, Rio thought. Maybe it was time he took a page out of her book and just said it, straight out.

The fact that he was talking was encouraging to Maggie. But the fact that he still thought of the ranch and land as Delora's didn't go unnoticed, and she suspected the reason he couldn't or wouldn't accept it as his was bound to affect his decision. As fearless as she had been a few moments earlier, her courage deserted her when it came to asking if he intended to stay. "Are you thinking they made the offer out of pity?"

"No." Despite his pride, he could admit to that much truth.

Maggie swallowed hard. She had to know. If he told Cal no, at least she would be out of her misery wondering if there could ever be a future for her and Rio. "Have you...made a decision?"

Maggie held her breath.

"No."

Relief whispered through her body.

"I can't give him an answer until I find Emily's folks. Right now that's got to be my priority."

"Of course." She didn't quite understand the reasoning behind his statement, unless it was simply to put off the inevitable, which could mean he had already decided and just hated to disappoint his two best friends. Phrases like "don't go borrowing trouble" and "hope springs eternal" skipped across her mind.

Rio tossed the now-mangled blade of grass aside. "You think something will turn up about the footprints?"

"There's always a possibility, but I'm not going to wait. Monday I'm going to start checking the blood types of all the baby girls born in area hospitals in the past three months."

"Then what?"

"We keep our fingers crossed."

IN HER ROOM at the Longhorn Motel, Tess Holloway gazed at the photo of Jeremy Westlake that she held tightly in her hands. She still loved him. Nothing would ever change that. But how many times had she

looked at his picture and remembered that awful
night when his father and hers had joined forces
against her? She could still recall it in such vivid,
painful detail. From the moment her father had come
to her room and told her that Mr. Westlake had asked
to see them both.

"C'mon girl, the man wants to see us." Lee Holloway had stood in the doorway of his daughter's room
and jerked a thumb over his shoulder in a gesture of
impatience.

"What for, Daddy?" She glanced at her watch.
"It's almost nine o'clock."

"Beats the hell outta me. I don't ask questions. I
just do what I'm told."

Despite his words, Tess had the feeling he knew
exactly what Mr. Westlake wanted, and if the gleam
in his eyes was any indication, not only knew, but
approved. *What's going on?* she wondered. Ever
since she and Jeremy had told their fathers that they
wanted to be married . . . and that Tess was pregnant,
both men had been unexpectedly reasonable and at
least somewhat supportive.

"Is Jeremy home?" Her eyes lit up, hoping Jeremy had returned early from a debate team function
in College Station.

"No."

Tess's heart sank. "Oh. Then I don't understand
why he wants to see me. Maybe whatever it is should
wait until Jeremy comes home."

"He said now."

Tess scampered off her bed, where she had spread out copies of several brides' magazines. "All right, I'm coming."

Now her heart beat faster. Something was terribly wrong. She could feel it. Why would John Westlake want to see her and her father, *without* Jeremy? What could be so urgent?

Suddenly the thought flashed through her mind that something might have happened to Jeremy. An accident!

"Is it Jeremy? Is he hurt—"

"Will you stop jabbering and come on? The man is waiting. You may think you're about to become the lady of the house, but I'm still a lowly chauffeur doing what I'm told." Lee Holloway hurried Tess out the door and down the hall.

Downstairs, John Westlake waited in his study.

"Tess," he said, motioning for her to take a chair opposite him.

"Is this about Jeremy, Mr. Westlake? Is he all right?"

"Depends on what you mean by all right, Tess."

She half rose from the chair, her hand fluttering to her throat and her eyes filling with tears. "There's been an accident—"

"No," Westlake assured her. "Nothing like that."

"Oh, thank God," she whispered, sinking back into the overstuffed chair. "Thank God."

Westlake cleared his throat. "It's clear that you care about my son."

"Yes. Very much."

John Westlake, power broker and one of the Texas state capitol's premier political movers and shakers, fixed his gaze on the young woman before him. "It's because you care that I asked to see you. It's because you care that I know you want only the best for Jeremy."

"Yes, of course."

"Then I have to tell you what Jeremy can't tell you, Tess. And as painful as this may be right now, if you really love my son the way you claim, then you'll do the right thing."

"I don't understand."

"I want you to end this pregnancy."

For a moment Tess thought she had heard him wrong. Then reality slowly seeped in and she knew that he was serious. Too shocked to speak, she glanced at her father. Lee Holloway refused to meet her gaze. *He knew! He knew!*

"Tess."

She whipped her gaze back to Jeremy's father.

"Do you understand what I'm asking of you?"

"Y-y-you can't ask me to do that," she whispered.

"Damn it, girl, don't go telling Mr. Westlake what he can ask and what he can't."

"Shut up, Holloway, and let me handle this."

"I can't, Mr. Westlake."

"Of course you can. It's done every day, Tess."

"Listen to him, girl." Another quelling look from Westlake sent Lee Holloway retreating.

"I know you love Jeremy and he thinks he loves you. For now, at least. But there will come a time when these feelings you think you have for each other won't be enough."

"What are you talking about?"

"I'm convinced that someday Jeremy would eventually grow to resent you and your baby if he is forced to give up the life he has been prepared for." When she started to speak, he waved her silent. "Jeremy has probably told you that he isn't interested in a life in politics. But he's lying to you and to himself. Jeremy has been groomed for a position of power all of his life. It's what he knows. And deep down, it's what he wants, no matter how rebellious he feels at the moment. And even if he does love you, that still doesn't change—"

"But he does love me."

"Possibly. But that doesn't alter the fact that I believe one day he will look at you and your child and see you both as a liability. You will be a millstone around his neck, the obstacle that keeps him from reaching his full potential and happiness."

"I don't believe you."

"Look around you, Tess. Can you see Jeremy giving up all this?"

"But why would he have to give it—"

"Because politicians have to have a spotless reputation. How would it look to voters for a candidate to have had an illegitimate child?"

"But we're getting married."

"One jump ahead of the obstetrician. People aren't fools."

"I don't want to talk to you anymore. I want to talk to Jeremy." Tess rose from her chair and turned toward the door.

"Sit your little butt back in that chair, girl," her father ordered. "You're too dumb to recognize a generous offer when it's in front of you."

"Holloway."

"Well, she is."

Tess turned back to John Westlake. "What's he talking about?"

"I'm recommending the best course of action for you, Tess, and I'm prepared to cover all your expenses. In fact, all your expenses for the next six months."

"Money? You think I want your money?"

Holloway stepped to her side and took hold of her arm. "Will you hush, girl!"

She stared at her father, stunned and hurt that he was so willing to be a part of this, this...unthinkable scheme! "You want me to kill my baby and I'm not going to do it. You hear me? Both of you! I won't!" She jerked herself free of her father's hold and ran toward the door.

"Tess!"

The command in John Westlake's voice was cold, hard. She stopped and turned to face him. "I won't change my mind, Mr. Westlake and when I tell Jeremy how you've—"

"He already knows."

Tess blinked. "What?"

"I didn't want to resort to this, but you leave me no choice, since you refuse to be reasonable." He reached inside his desk and withdrew an envelope. "This is a letter from Jeremy telling you almost word for word what I have been trying to tell you for the past few moments. He asked me to talk to you because, as much as it would hurt coming from me, it would be worse coming from him. That's why he left town, so he wouldn't have to face you."

"I told you all along you were dreaming too big," Holloway insisted. "Now you got no choice but to do as the man says. Least this way you get something out of the deal."

Tess barely heard her father's voice. She was staring at the note in John Westlake's hand. "Can...can I..."

Westlake walked straight to her and gave her the letter. She opened it and began to read. As she did, tears trailed down her pale cheeks, until finally she could scarcely make out Jeremy's signature at the bottom of the typed page. Oh, but she could feel. Pain. Rivers, oceans of pain pouring over her in icy waves.

It couldn't be true. But the words were there in black and white. How could she have believed Jeremy loved her if he could do something so cruel? How could she have loved him?

Suddenly the room grew dark and Tess thought she might faint, even hoped she would, but slowly the darkness receded and she was left with stark reality. Now she felt empty, hollow and utterly alone.

"I think it best if you leave before Jeremy returns. For your sake."

Tess looked at John Westlake and knew he cared less than nothing for her. Everything he had done today was for his son. Just as what she needed to do was for Jeremy, as well. If he didn't love her, didn't love their child, what was there left for her?

Now, months later, tears streaming down her face once more as she studied Jeremy's picture, she wondered how she could ever have allowed John Westlake and her father to browbeat her as they had that night. She had been weak, confused and so deeply hurt. Not that it had made any difference in the long run. She had refused the money, and left Jeremy a note, just as he had her. A note written in her hand, but conceived by her father and his. A note telling Jeremy that she had decided she was too young to become a mother and that she didn't want to be tied down to a baby... or to him.

And that she intended to have an abortion.

Tess clasped the photo to her breast, rocking gently, as if Emily were still in her arms. Dear Lord, had she ever actually thought she could go through with it? Looking back, she supposed so. She and her father had left that very night for Houston, and Lee Holloway was only too happy to take Westlake's money. But once Tess had time to think rationally, *without* pressure from her father and Jeremy's, she knew she couldn't do it.

They had been in Houston only two days when she'd told her father she intended to keep her baby. He'd exploded in a rage, saying her change of heart meant he would have to give up the money. He'd insisted she was stupid, even crazy and that if she didn't straighten up, he would call Mr. Westlake and they would force her to have the abortion. Only her love for Jeremy and her determination to keep his baby had given her the strength to run away from her father that night. Alone and lonely in a big city, she had been fortunate enough to get a job waiting tables in a small diner, until her advancing pregnancy had forced her to stop. Even then her luck had held and she'd found an unwed mother's home that had provisions for women with no money or family.

She sighed, staring down at the photograph, wishing things could have been different. Wishing she, Jeremy and Emily could have shared their lives. Now, the best she could hope for was to keep tabs on her baby from a distance.

She had called the child welfare people with a teary story that she was looking for her sister's baby. The sister, she had told them after describing Emily, was depressed, a little unbalanced, and had threatened to abandon the baby. To her relief, they informed her no child fitting that description was currently in the system. That meant Emily was still with Rio Langley.

So, she would stay in Crystal Creek and hope for a glimpse of her child. She would work at the coffee shop, live at the motel and wait until she knew Emily was safe and happy. It wasn't the life she had dreamed of or even hoped for, but it was all she had.

BY NOON MONDAY, Maggie had a computer printout of the names of all the babies sharing Emily's blood type born in Austin area hospitals in the past three months. Fifty-six names. Sighing, she rubbed the bridge of her nose between her thumb and index finger. This would require legwork. Lots of it. She prayed Rio had new soles on his boots, because by the time he tracked down every name on the list, he would need them.

By five o'clock Maggie had eliminated four of the names through some discreet phone calls. Her shoulders felt as if they had grapefruit-size knots in them, and she was more worried than ever that Rio's time would run out before he turned up Emily's mother. She knew she should call him and tell him. Warn him. Remind him time was running out. But she couldn't do it. Maggie knew she was being a coward, but she couldn't help herself. Tired and anxious as she was, the thought of facing Rio, of seeing the look of disappointment in his eyes, was too much. Not tonight, she decided. Bone-weary and soul-saddened, she slipped two files that needed attention into her briefcase and went home.

Because her parents were attending a meeting at the church, she ate alone, then tried to interest herself in a new mystery novel, and ended up watching a sitcom that didn't make her laugh. By the time her parents came home, she was exhausted from trying *not* to think about Rio and Emily. She kissed them goodnight and went to bed.

The phone rang at ten minutes before midnight.

"Hello?"

"Maggie?"

"Rio? Why are you calling at this time of—"

"It's Emily. I think she's sick."

In the background, Emily started to cry. Maggie sat bolt upright in her bed. "Is she running a fever?"

"Yeah. At least I think so. I don't have a thermometer." The strain in his voice made her heart beat faster.

"Have you called Dr. Purdy?"

"He's delivering a baby. I left word for him to call as soon as he got in. Maggie, can you—"

"I'll be there in fifteen minutes."

The distance between her parents' house and Rio's seemed like light-years instead of miles, and the time it took to get there felt like decades instead of minutes.

"How is she?" Maggie demanded of Rio as soon as she stepped inside the kitchen door. Rio's face was drawn with worry, his hair ruffled, undoubtedly from the many times he had run his fingers through the thick black waves.

"I don't know." To Rio, sweatshirt-clad Maggie looked like a guardian angel straight from heaven.

They hurried into the bedroom, which was lit by only one lamp on a nightstand. Maggie slung her purse on the bed, then bent over the portable crib Elena had borrowed from one of her children and touched her hand to Emily's cheek. Hot. And dry. Not a good sign, but she didn't say so for fear of upsetting Rio even more. Still, infants often ran fevers over a tummy ache or toothache, or for practically no reason at all. Certainly, Emily would bear watching, but for the moment, at least, the baby appeared to be restless but not in any pain.

She reached into her purse, removed a thermometer and shook it down. "Has she refused to eat?"

"No. She's got a great appetite. In fact, she ate some baby food around six, then took a whole bottle not an hour and a half ago." He brushed a finger across the soft cheek, and his stomach knotted. "She feels so warm."

"Has she thrown any of it back up?"

He shook his head, never taking his eyes from the baby.

"When was her last BM?"

That got Rio's attention. "What?"

"When was the last time she had a messy diaper?"

"I . . . I'm not sure—"

"Elena will know."

"Is *that* important?"

"Sometimes." The thermometer in hand, Maggie looked up at the worried man at her side. "Rio, I need to take her temperature and you might not want to stay to see it."

"Why?"

"Because it might look like I'm hurting her, but—"

"You won't."

"Of course not. Why don't you make us some coffee," she suggested.

He did as she asked, but reluctantly. In a few short minutes he was back in the bedroom.

"A hundred and three," Maggie announced, answering his unspoken question. She saw him flinch. "That's not outrageously high for an infant."

"It sounds outrageously high."

"Stay with her a second, will you? I'm going to call Elena."

When Maggie returned in about five minutes, she appeared much calmer, less concerned. "Elena thinks it's probably a tummy ache with a touch of constipation, but if the fever goes any higher, we should get her to Dr. Purdy, or if he's not available, to the emergency room."

All the color drained out of Rio's face. "Emergency room!"

"Oh, Lord, I'm sorry, I didn't mean to scare you. It's not as bad as it sounds, but often babies become dehydrated. There's only so much you can do at home."

"Jeez," he whispered.

Maggie sat down beside him. "Rio, listen to me. I'm no expert but I think she's going to be fine. And you know that if Elena thought it was anything serious, she would be out here so fast it would make both our heads spin. She told me she bought some acetaminophen for infant fevers, so, see? She even anticipated something like this might happen. We'll give Emily the drops and wait for a couple of hours. If she's not better, I promise we'll take her straight to Dr. Purdy."

"Sounds...reasonable."

Maggie patted his hand for a second or two, then disappeared into the kitchen. When she returned a moment later, she carried a bottle of acetaminophen elixir. "Right where Elena said it would be."

She set the bottle on a nearby table, withdrew an dropper of the cherry-flavored liquid, checked the amount, and squeezed some of the contents back into the bottle. Then she slid her hand beneath Emily's head, lifting it slightly. "C'mon, sweetie." Gently she squeezed the liquid into the baby's mouth. "This is going to make you feel so much better."

Emily took her medicine like a trooper, even smacking her rosebud mouth at the pleasant taste.

Maggie checked the clock on the nightstand beside the bed. "We'll keep an eye on her. Hopefully, she'll sleep." Glancing at Rio, she saw the worry lines around his mouth had deepened. "Would you like some coffee?"

He stared at Emily, who seemed to be comfortable for the time being. At least she wasn't crying the way she had been when he called Maggie. "Yeah, sure."

Rio was still gazing down at Emily a second later when Maggie called him into the kitchen. She held up an empty baby food jar of strained egg yolks that he'd left sitting on the counter. "Is this what you fed Emily around six o'clock?"

"Yeah. Elena usually feeds her cereal at that time. Says it helps her to sleep through the night."

"And egg yolks."

Rio shrugged, looking at her as if she were crazy. "I guess. It was in the pantry and she seemed like she was still hungry after the cereal. I figured cereal and eggs went together."

Maggie heaved a mammoth sigh. "I think I may have found the reason for Emily's fever."

Now he really was looking at her as if she had lost her mind. "What? Eggs?"

"Egg yolks, to be specific. And if she's got a rash, we've got our culprit." She headed for the bedroom and Rio followed.

"Maggie, why would something as simple as—"

"There," she said, lifting Emily's gown and pointing to the tiny stomach. The area of delicate baby skin just above the navel was covered in red dots. "She's allergic."

Shocked, Rio stared at the dots. "You mean those eggs caused that?"

"More than likely. It's not uncommon. That's why babies are usually introduced to foods one variety at a time, to see which ones trigger allergies and which don't."

"You mean, I did this to Emily by feeding her those damned egg yolks?"

"No," she assured him. "You didn't *do* anything *to* her. It would have happened no matter who fed her. I told you, this kind of reaction is not uncommon at all. And it's the reaction that caused the fever."

"Is she . . . is she gonna be all right?"

Maggie smiled. "Absolutely. By morning she'll probably be her sweet, cooing self again."

Rio was torn between relief and self-loathing. He scrubbed his stubbled face with his wide hands. "I didn't know, Maggie. I didn't know."

"How could you? I told you, this would have happened no matter who held the spoon. Don't beat yourself up over it. She's going to be fine."

Standing between the portable crib and the side of the bed, Rio looked down at Emily. "Looks like you're right."

Maggie glanced down, too. The baby was fast asleep, the soft light making her face appear even more angelic that usual. Maggie touched the little girl's cheek. "Feels cooler already. It's amazing how resilient they are."

Shaking with relief, Rio sat down on the bed. "Thanks, Maggie. Don't know what I would have done without you."

"I was happy to help." Now that the threat of danger had passed, she decided to ask him the question that had come to mind on the drive from her house to his. "Rio, why me instead of Elena?"

"What?"

"The logical person to call was Elena. Why did you call me?"

"I don't know," he said, a little surprised at her question. "The first thing that popped into my head was to get in touch with you."

Truthfully, his reaction was hardly surprising, because lately she was always on his mind. Or maybe it was because he felt as if Emily belonged to both of them and it was only right that Maggie should be there.

"I'm glad you called."

Instinctively, he reached for her hand. Holding it tight, he pulled her down beside him. "God, so am I. I don't know what I would have done without you here."

Side by side, their bodies touching, her hand still clasped in his, they stared at each other. Then slowly, as if it were the most natural thing in the world, Maggie put her head on Rio's shoulder and whispered, "I'll always be here if you need me."

A peacefulness flowed over him, soft as spring rain and as calm as dawn. Light-headed with joy after so much tension, he closed his eyes and savored the rightness of the moment. Seconds crawled by with only the sound of Emily's gentle breathing to accompany the beating of their hearts.

When Rio spoke at last, his voice was hushed, almost as if he didn't want anything above a whisper to disturb this time. "I was so scared."

"I know," she whispered back. "Me, too."

"Couldn't tell. You were wonderful. Does all that stuff just come natural to women?" His voice was a velvety night murmur.

"No. Lots of baby-sitting as a teenager. Working in the church nursery. Guess it's like riding a bicycle. You never forget."

"Lucky for me."

She smiled against his collar. "Why are we whispering?"

"Don't know."

Maggie lifted her head from his shoulder and looked into eyes as dark as the soft Texas night. She should go, she told herself. The crisis was past. She wasn't needed anymore. But she couldn't tear herself away from Rio's gaze or the delicious feeling of intimacy that settled around them like night mist.

"I—uh—never did get around to making that coffee," she said, still keeping her voice low.

In this light her green eyes were like dark emeralds that had a magic spell cast over them. Glowing with a deep fire, bewitching, drawing the beholder into their depths. "Hmm, coffee," he murmured, not really caring if he ever had another cup.

He was compromising her. He should tell her to go. There was no reason for her to remain, he told himself. No reason, but the most important one. He wanted her to stay. He needed her to stay.

"You...want some...?" she asked. Was that her voice sounding so breathy? she wondered. Was that her heartbeat sounding like a runaway train?

"Sure," he answered without thinking.

"I think that's..." At last Maggie cleared her throat and said in a normal voice. "I think that's a good idea." She slipped away from him and went into the kitchen.

Rio watched her walk away and suddenly felt bone-weary. And alone.

Maggie prolonged pouring the coffee, giving herself enough time to quiet her wildly beating heart. Finally, she put two mugs on a tray and returned to the bedroom. "Here you—"

Stretched out on the bed at a slightly awkward angle, as if he had barely had time to turn his head toward the pillow before toppling backward, Rio slept as peacefully as the baby in the crib. Maggie set the mugs on the nightstand and proceeded—with more than a little effort—to lift his legs onto the bed in order to make him more comfortable. He never stirred.

Maggie watched him sleep, his rugged face relaxed, appearing more youthful in the soft light. Just looking at him made her heart turn over. She felt so close to him. And it wasn't just the crisis they had shared. Something else had happened tonight. Something glorious and frightening and where-could-it-all-end wonderful.

She had done precisely the thing she had cautioned herself not to do. She had fallen in love all over again with Rio Langley.

CHAPTER SEVEN

MAGGIE WAS GONE when Rio woke up, and the first thought through his mind was how empty the house felt. Suddenly the sun streaming through the bedroom windows, or his mood for that matter, didn't seem so bright.

After checking on Emily, still snoozing peacefully, he wandered into the kitchen and discovered a note lying on the table.

Left a little before sunup. You and Emily both sleeping like babies. Call me.
Maggie.

The aroma of fresh coffee filled the air, and a pan of still warm biscuits sat on the counter. Standing there in yesterday's jeans, hopelessly rumpled shirt and stocking feet, Rio had a mental image of her moving around the kitchen in the hour before dawn, making the coffee, preparing the biscuits. Was that how it was with married people? There was something to be said for waking up to personal notes and home cooking. Not that he was entertaining the idea of marriage. It wasn't in his plan.

The screen door slammed shut, announcing Elena's arrival. Rio had been so deep in thought he hadn't heard her drive up.

"Good morning."

"Yeah," he responded, only now realizing the blackness of his mood was in direct proportion to how much he wished Maggie had still been there when he woke up. He missed her.

"How's Emily?"

"Fine. Fever's gone and she slept through most of the night."

Elena glanced at the pan of biscuits, then back to Rio's rumpled appearance. "How long did Maggie stay?"

Not long enough. Not nearly long enough. Then Rio realized the implication in Elena's question. "It's not what you're thinking."

"And just how do you know what I'm thinkin', sonny?"

"Well, I—"

"Well, you what?" Hands on her hips, Elena glared at him.

"Nothin'."

"Good. Now why don't you go shave off that black stubble that matches your mood so perfect, before you scare the baby half to death?"

Mumbling something about women being impossible, Rio headed for the bathroom.

Poor baby, Elena thought. *He's in deeper than he realizes. It's plain as a pig in a parlor.* And poor Maggie, Elena decided, more than a little pleased at the prospect of Rio and Maggie together. She'd certainly have her hands full. Having known and loved Rio most of his life, Elena knew only too well how stubborn he could be, particularly when he thought he was right. Mules with wooden heads could be more reasonable. And she suspected he was fighting his feelings for Maggie like a sinner at the gates of hell.

An hour later, shaved, fed and well into the sweaty job of moving sixty-pound bales of hay for the stalls, Rio had not called Maggie before starting work. He could call when he broke for lunch, he told himself. It was no big deal. Not like he was craving the sound of her voice or anything.

Like hell.

All right, so he was deliberately not calling. So what? Didn't mean a thing. He still thought it was best to keep their relationship as impersonal as possible, didn't he?

Fat chance, after last night.

Rio swung a bale up and stacked it atop three others, then with the back of his hand wiped the sweat from his forehead. He had never known the kind of icy, gut-twisting fear that had seized him when he realized Emily was sick. Instinctively, he had reached out for Maggie.

And she had come. And stayed. And promised, *I'll always be here if you need me.*

No one but his mother had ever done that for him. Maggie had, without a moment's hesitation and without expecting so much as a thank-you. Rio tried to remember what his life had been like before he returned home, but he couldn't. Such a short time ago, yet nothing seemed worth remembering before Maggie had come back into his life. And what would his life be like once he left Crystal Creek, left Maggie? When Rio tried to imagine that future, all he saw was emptiness. A cold, black emptiness.

Abruptly, he turned, walked out of the barn and made straight for the house. He had a driving need to hear the sound of Maggie's voice.

"Margaret Conway," she answered a few moments later.

"Hi."

Maggie smiled, not realizing until that moment how she had longed to hear the sound of his voice. "Hi."

"I got your note."

"You two were sleeping so soundly, I didn't have the heart to wake you."

"Thanks again. You got me through one of the worst nights of my life. I couldn't have made it without you."

"Oh, I'm not so sure of that."

"I am."

They fell silent for long seconds, until finally Maggie remembered the computer printout on her desk. "Rio, I received a list of names of babies born at approximately the same time as Emily and with her blood type. I've eliminated some, but there's still a lot to verify. Tracking down these babies and checking to be sure each child is with her parents won't be difficult, but it will take time.''

''I'll come by and pick up the list and get started before noon.''

''Rio,'' she hesitated, then said, ''All of this may be for nothing. We're running out of time.''

The fact that she'd said *we* and not *you* made him feel warm clear through to his soul. ''I know, but I've got to try, Maggie. See you in a little while.''

''I'll be waiting for you.''

But, in fact, she wasn't. When he got to her office, a receptionist handed him a large manila envelope, which he assumed contained the printout, and his second note of the day from Maggie. This one told him she had been called out of the office and would phone him later.

Later turned out to be that evening around seven.

''How did you make out?'' she asked him over the phone.

''Not too bad.'' He was more disappointed than he cared to admit that she had called instead of coming over. ''I worked my way through about two-thirds of the names, and I plan to stay with it for another hour or so.''

''Great. Any possibilities?''

''Three, as a matter of fact. One was put up for adoption, but I haven't been able to verify that for certain. Another was supposed to be put up for adoption but withdrawn right after she was born. And the third left the hospital with a grandmother because the parents intended to divorce. The first two were born to unwed mothers."

"Good possibilities, particularly the babies of the single mothers."

"Now what?"

"Well, if no more turn up from the list, we concentrate on these three. Account for their whereabouts if we can. The first one will be a snap because our computers keep track of all the adoptions in the county. The last case should be easy enough because the county clerk will have the names of all the pending divorce and custody cases. But the other one, the second one. may not be so easy."

"Why?"

"Sometimes when an unwed mother changes her mind at the last minute and decides to keep her baby, she gets a lot of flak from either her parents or the father. Sometimes these girls take off on their own to get away from the pressure."

Rio had an uncomfortable thought. "Do they ever give a false name at the hospital?"

"Occasionally."

"Great."

"Rio, don't get down. If we don't get any more than these three names, at least it's a place to start. We're not beaten by a long shot."

She was doing it again. Making him feel hopeful. "Yeah. Not by a long shot."

"I have to look in on one of my cases in Fredericksburg tomorrow morning. Why don't I meet you for lunch around eleven-thirty and we'll discuss our progress? How about eleven-thirty at the Longhorn?"

"Why don't you come out to the house? Elena's making stew and nobody does it better."

Maggie had an idea he was trying to protect her again and she wasn't having it. "Thanks, but if I come out to your place, I'll just spend too much time playing with Emily. The Longhorn will be fine. See you at eleven-thirty." She hung up before he could talk her into changing her mind.

TESS HOLLOWAY almost dropped the order of chicken-fried steak and french fries she was serving when she looked up and saw Rio Langley walk into the Longhorn. With him was an attractive woman Tess didn't recognize as anyone she'd seen before in the café. She watched Nora embrace the woman and smile at Rio. Rosa, too, acted as if she knew the woman. Tess's heart was hammering against her chest wall so loudly she wondered why they all didn't hear it.

"Rosa and I were just saying this morning what a great time we had the other night. We should do it again real soon."

"It was fun," Maggie said. "You and Rosa have obviously worked out a smooth transition," she added, directing the subject away from anything personal.

"Actually, the transition is complete. Nora is just here today helping me with inventory."

"And we better get back to it," Nora added.

Rosa handed them a couple of menus, saying, "I'll get Tess to take your order whenever you're ready."

"Thanks," Rio said, guiding Maggie toward a booth.

On the way they passed two women who were openly staring. Maggie looked directly at them, smiled and slipped her arm through Rio's.

"Maggie," he started as soon as they sat down.

"What did you find out?" Maggie launched right into the only subject she considered important.

The determined set of her mouth told him she had no intention of acknowledging the gossips. "You were right about the girl who changed her mind about adoption. She's going to be harder to track down than the others."

"Did you find anything?"

"She used the name Teresa Hall."

"Used? You think it was phony?"

"Yes. She listed herself as unemployed and the father unknown. She told the hospital that she had been working as a maid for an Austin family, but the work got too hard."

"Any idea of the family's name?"

"I'm working on it. Or I should say, Elena is working on it. She's claiming to be the girl's aunt, desperate to find her. The hospital clerk promised to check with the maternity nurses on both shifts and call Elena back this afternoon."

Maggie's eyes lit up. "That's terrific. I may put you to work for the county."

Rio shook his head. "No thanks. Don't think my nerves could stand it. I'd rather face a rodeo arena full of bulls any day."

She reached across the table and touched his hand. "You've done a great job, but I don't want you to get your hopes too high. This may turn out to be a dead end."

"Maybe. But I've got a feeling this will lead to something solid."

She saw the hope in his eyes and didn't have the heart to dampen it further. If the young woman turned out to be Emily's mother and if they could find her, there was still no guarantee she would want her baby back. "I hope you're right."

Rio turned his hand over until her fingertips rested in his palm. Gently, his thumb stroked across her fingers. "I hope so too."

"Can I take your order?"

They both looked up at the young waitress.

"Hello," Maggie said, offering a warm smile. "You must be new."

"Yes, ma'am."

She snapped her fingers. "I remember Rosa mentioning she had hired someone. Tess, isn't it?"

"Yes ma'am. T-Tess Holloway."

"Well, Tess, what's the plate lunch special today?"

"Uh," the girl said nervously, licking her lips. "Meat loaf, parslied new potatoes and green beans. You get your choice of corn bread or rolls. Coffee or tea."

"Sounds fine. I'll take corn bread and iced tea."

Rio took Maggie's menu, stacked it with his and handed them back to Tess. "Make it two."

"Comin' right—" In the middle of taking down the order, the point snapped off Tess's pencil. She prayed they didn't see how her hand was shaking. "Right up."

She served them their food, then went back three times to see if they needed more tea, in hopes of catching bits of their conversation and maybe a scrap of information about Emily. But she heard nothing. By the time they got up to leave, Tess was a nervous wreck. While Rio paid Rosa for the meals and the woman talked to Nora, Tess worked her way toward the cash register, refilling coffee cups for other customers. She still hoped to overhear some mention of Emily.

"Don't forget," the woman said to Rosa, "Teresa's regular appointment was changed from Monday to Tuesday of next week. Her therapist is still out sick."

"Thanks for reminding me. I can't tell you how much the therapy has helped her. And I can't tell you how grateful I am for your help. Are all welfare caseworkers as dedicated as you are?"

The sound of breaking glass suddenly drew their attention.

Tess stood, eyes wide, staring at Maggie, the remains of a shattered coffeepot at her feet, a dark circle of wet liquid on the skirt of her uniform.

"Tess!" Nora hurried over to inspect the damage, with Rosa right behind her. "What happened?"

"I—uh—" Tess jerked her gaze away from Maggie's face. "I—uh—it slipped out of my hand. I'm so sor . . . sorry, Ms. Walters. You can take it out of my pay."

"Nonsense. It was an accident." Rosa looked up as Rio and Maggie headed toward the door. "Y'all take care."

Rio walked Maggie to her car. "Are you coming by to see Emily later?"

"If that's all right with you."

It was more than all right, but Rio simply said, "Sure."

"Around seven?"

"Fine." As he helped her into her car, then watched her drive away, Rio mentally calculated how many hours remained between now and seven o'clock. How many long hours.

BY THE TIME Tess had cleaned up the broken coffee urn, they were gone. By the time she had a minute to herself after the lunch crowd, she was close to tears. All her planning was for nothing. That woman with Rio Langley was a social worker!

Emily, her precious little baby girl, was probably in a foster home right now. She couldn't stand the thought of her child with people who weren't family. Tess had to know for sure.

"Ms. Walters," Tess said, as the last of the lunch crowd left, "could I use the phone in the office to call about an ad for a used car I saw in the newspaper?"

"Help yourself."

"Thanks." Tess hated lying to her boss, but she couldn't tell the truth. And she couldn't make her feet move fast enough to get to the telephone and check to see if her fictitious sister's baby was now in the Claro County welfare system.

"WELL, YOU'RE ALL SET." Elena, purse in hand and ready to leave, held the screen door open as Rio stepped inside. "Emily's had her dinner and she's in the swing. I wound it up real good. Your supper's warmin' in the oven, and there's iced tea in the fridge."

"Thanks." He brushed dust from his jeans.

"I got bread dough risin' on the counter overnight. Don't lift the cup towel or it'll fall."

"Yes, ma'am."

"And stay out of those blackberries." She shook her finger at him. "I'm gonna use them in a cobbler tomorrow."

"Yes, ma'am," Rio said obediently.

Frowning, Elena looked at her watch. "That woman from the hospital ain't ever called. I figured she wasn't gonna call since it's six o'clock. Maybe I better stay for a mite longer just in case."

"You're probably right. She probably won't call this late."

The phone rang. They exchanged glances, and then Elena hurried to pick up the receiver.

"Hello. Yes, Ms. Littlefield." Vigorously, Elena nodded her head, indicating this was indeed the call they had been waiting for. "I'd just about given up on you callin' today. Is that so? Well, I know how that goes, best-laid plans and all. Yes, of course, I'm still interested in the information." There was a long pause while Elena listened, nodding occasionally. Then suddenly she frowned. "And where is that? Uh-huh. How do you spell that? Well, thanks ever so much, Ms. Littlefield. I sure do appreciate everything you've done. Yeah, thanks again. Bye."

"What did she say?"

"Gimme a pencil and some paper so I can write this down 'fore I forget it."

Rio jerked open a drawer, scratched around for a pencil and came up with a ballpoint pen. He looked around for something to write on and had to settle for a used envelope from the gas company. "Did she have a name?"

Elena scribbled something on the flap of the envelope. "No, but she did find out the girl callin' herself Teresa Hall was going to a kinda boardin' house for single mothers after she left the hospital. Here." She handed him the envelope. "Something called Agape House."

It wasn't much, Rio thought, but it was better than nothing. At least it was one more piece to the puzzle.

"Well," Elena said. "You gonna just stand there, or are you gonna call this place and see what the deal is?"

"They may not answer my questions. I wish Maggie were already here."

"I am," Maggie said from the doorway. "What's going on?"

"We got a lead on the mother that kept her baby," Elena answered."

Maggie's eyes lit up. "What is it? A name?"

"Not the mother's name." Rio handed her the envelope. "The name of a house where she might have gone after she left the hospital."

Maggie glanced at the name. "I know this place. It's a privately-run combination home for unwed mothers and halfway house. Girls can work or go back to school, and the home provides day-care for a limited number of children."

"Would they talk to you, do you think?" Elena asked.

"All I can do is try."

"How soon?" As far as Rio was concerned, an hour was too long to wait, but he knew it wasn't within his control.

She looked at him, a twinkle sparkling in her green eyes. "How long will it take to drive to Austin?"

"You mean, today? Now?"

"I've met the director of the house and the benefactor who originally provided the endowment to start the project. Maybe I could persuade her to see us."

"Can't you just call?"

Understandably Rio was anxious, but Maggie knew how to proceed.

"I think it would be better if we could talk to her in person. Less official that way. And if I'm convincing enough, we might even be able to do it tonight."

"Well, don't just stand there," Elena ordered. "Get to it. I'll stay with Emily."

Maggie wasn't quite convincing enough. She called for an appointment and discovered they wouldn't be able to see the director until the following afternoon.

"Don't fret." Elena patted Maggie's shoulder. "Whatever there is to find out'll still be there tomorrow."

"I know. It's just... disappointing."

Elena sighed. "Reckon I best be goin'. I'll see you two tomorrow."

"Good night, Elena." The women exchanged glances, acknowledging the fact that Rio had been silent since Maggie had hung up from talking with

Agape House. Elena tilted her head in Rio's direction as if to say, "He needs you." Maggie nodded hers in understanding.

Once they were alone, she turned to him. "I'm sorry."

"Not your fault. You did all you could."

"I just wish we could have gone tonight."

"Like Elena says, it'll still be there tomorrow." Emily started to fret, her swing obviously having wound down. "Duty calls."

Maggie followed him into the bedroom and was immediately greeted with a toothless smile from Emily. "Hi, sweetie. Look at you. Swinging like such a big girl." The baby was dressed in a soft pink romper and tiny sneakers with an aqua shirt and matching socks. "I swear she grows an inch every day."

"Hey," Rio said, glad to have something other than disappointment to think about. "You want to see her latest trick?"

"Oh, Rio, you make her sound like a trained puppy."

"Watch this." He lifted Emily out of the swing and placed her tummy down on the tester bed. She kicked her feet and arms like a pantomime of a swimmer.

"Some trick."

"Wait. Just wait. You'll see."

The two adults stood at the side of the bed watching the child as if any minute they expected her to jump through a hoop. For her part, Emily stared back for a moment, then decided the pattern in the quilt covering the bed was infinitely more interesting. She gurgled and oohed at the calico prints in a Texas Star pattern. Then suddenly she lifted her head, looked at Maggie and Rio... and rolled over from her stomach to her back.

Maggie squealed. "Did you see that? She rolled over. All by herself."

"I know. She did it for the first time this afternoon. You could've knocked me over with a feather."

"Did Elena see her do it?"

"Yeah. She stood there with her hands on her hips and said, 'Bout time, lazybones.' But I could see she was tickled."

Gently, Maggie sat down on the bed, then stretched out so that her head was close to Emily's. "What a smart girl you are." Emily smiled from ear to ear and cooed. "Yes, you are," Maggie cooed back. "Smart and sweet and pretty." At the sound of the softly encouraging voice, Emily grinned even more and pumped her little legs in excitement.

Watching them practically nose to nose, auburn waves next to golden curls, Rio thought they just might be the two most beautiful females in the world.

In his world.

As often happened, the truth came blazing forth unexpected. Perhaps that was why, at first, Rio didn't realize the admission he had just made to himself. Didn't realize he had all but waved a white flag in the losing battle against his feelings for both of them. Understanding came slowly but certainly of how important these two wonderful females had become to him.

But a short while later, something happened that he couldn't ignore, something Rio knew he would never forget.

Arms folded across his chest, he leaned against the frame of the bathroom door and watched Maggie giving Emily a bath, their heads again close together, only now the smaller one was covered in shampoo. Resting in the crook of Maggie's arm, Emily splashed playfully while Maggie rinsed out the shampoo with clear water from a cup.

"Now you're squeaky clean," she announced, as Emily blinked water from her eyes, unperturbed. "We'll get you nice and dry and into a comfy gown and you'll sleep so-o-o well." Carefully, Maggie lifted the little slick-as-a-seal body onto the towel spread across her knees, then began toweling the baby. Barefoot, the front of her dress damp from the bathing, no woman had ever looked more beautiful than she.

"Hard to say which one of you is the wettest," he said from the doorway.

Maggie glanced up, smiling. "Can't expect a girl to take a decent bath without splashing, can you? Don't worry about the water on the floor. I'll clean it up later after she goes down."

"Much later. I heated up the supper that Elena left. As soon as Emily goes to bed, we're gonna eat. I'm starved."

"Me too. Here. Hold her while I pop the drain cover."

Maggie rose with Emily in her arms. Rio reached for the baby, but before they could make the transfer, Maggie's bare foot slipped on a spot of water. He caught them both to him in a quick save.

"Rio," Maggie gasped.

"I've got you." As his powerful arms locked them to him, his gaze met Maggie's.

Rio stood there, his arms full of Maggie and Emily, and suddenly it was as if time stopped, framed by this single, startling moment. The sensation of belonging, of rightness, was so strong it almost took his breath away. The air was still, yet charged with a kind of invisible electricity that surrounded them, bound them together. He could *feel* the aura of energy wrapped around them.

Maggie couldn't pull her gaze from Rio's. She felt suspended in midair, weightless, yet inexorably bound to him, almost as if they were no longer separate, but one.

Rio had never put much stock into the spiritual heritage his mother had told him was his birthright as a Kiowa. But now, embracing so much love, strength and beauty, he saw and felt, perhaps for the first time, the bond his mother had spoken of, the bond his mother had tried to make him understand would one day show him the only truth worth seeing. A bond of souls that were fated to be together. A truth that would change his life.

He had no idea how long they stood embracing. It could have been seconds or hours. All he knew was that he didn't want to lose that feeling of completeness, of being part of someone else and her being part of him. Only when Emily began to squirm did he reluctantly release them.

Maggie blinked as if coming out of a trance. "Rio?"

"You..." His mouth was dry and his hands were shaking. "You almost fell."

"Th-thanks for saving me."

"I think it's the other way around." Before she could question his response, he took Emily into the bedroom and started dressing her for bed. Maggie followed, but stopped short of offering to help. The fact of the matter was, her hands were shaking so badly she couldn't have helped if she had offered.

What in the world happened? Was the house hit by lightning? Did a tornado touch down, then vanish?

The same force of nature that could shake her the way the past few seconds had was the force inevitably pulling her and Rio together. And Maggie knew it. Standing in the middle of the tiny bathroom, she *knew* her life was, and perhaps always had been, bound to Rio's. She no longer questioned whatever it was between them. It was love. Even if Rio didn't realize or recognize it as such. Even if, God forbid, they never laid eyes on each after this very moment, Maggie knew they shared a powerful bond of love.

She sat down beside him on the bed as he leaned over and placed Emily in the portable crib. They watched her drift off to sleep, her sweet-smelling, rosebud cheek snuggled against a downy blanket. Neither spoke, both hesitant to talk about what had just happened, but content to be together.

Then Rio looked at Maggie and saw his own feelings mirrored in her green eyes. It was more than he expected and not enough.

He had been alone—deep inside himself where it counted most—all his life, yet in the span of a few short days he had found himself reaching out for the warmth Maggie offered with everything she did and said. A smile, a touch, a soft word. And now she was here beside him with longing in her eyes.

All the reasons he shouldn't kiss her, touch her, came pouring into his consciousness like flood waters over a riverbank. But instead of drowning, Rio swam against the tide, propelled by a desire more deeply seated even than self-preservation.

The desire to love and be loved.

Maggie waited for his kiss, waited, knowing it would seal their special bond, once and forever. The inevitability of the moment didn't frighten her. Didn't raise any questions. For her, the questions had all been answered, no matter what happened tomorrow or the next day or the next year. She loved Rio. Nothing had changed that. Nothing would.

He touched her hair, smoothing several strands back from her face. "Are you still afraid?" There was no need to explain his question. Both knew. As it had the night before, an intimacy settled around them, compelling whispers and soft voices.

She shook her head.

"You should be."

"Why? Because what I feel is so strong?"

He shook his head. "Because we don't know where it will—" He almost said "end," but changed his mind. "Take us."

"Doesn't matter."

"It should."

"I'm going to remove that word from your vocabulary."

"Maggie—"

She silenced him with a fingertip to his lips. "I want to be with you, Rio. Just be with you. I want to hold you and have you hold me." She wanted him to understand she needed time, they both needed time, to deal with the strength and depth of their feelings. "I'm not ready to take the next step. I'm not ready to make love to you. Nor am I asking for deathless promises. Can't we just see where this takes us? Can't we just enjoy the feelings? It's been so long, and it feels so good."

She wound her arm around his neck. He slipped his arm around her shoulder and leaned her back onto the bed even as his mouth crushed hers.

She tasted heat and desire and something else. She tasted a need, a longing so deep it was fathomless. The same need she had tasted with that very first kiss

so long ago, only now she could answer need for
need. She pressed her body to his, claiming the heat
as he slanted his mouth over hers, first one way, then
another, until she felt consumed, devoured.

Rio thought he could hear her heart beating,
drumming out the rhythm of need, and he resisted—
barely—the urge to fit his hand over her breast and
feel the pulse. He wanted her wrapped around him in
the most intimate way possible. He wanted to take
her—take them both—to the edge of ecstasy and beyond, until physically, they would share the same kind
of experience they had shared spiritually tonight.

But now was too soon. Rio knew, would have
known even without Maggie telling him, she wasn't
ready to make love. They needed time to be with each
other. Time to trust that the whirlpool of emotions
they were immersed in wouldn't drown them. Holding her, kissing her felt so good he hated to stop, but
knew he must.

"Maggie," he whispered, finally dragging his
mouth from hers. "Sweet Maggie."

She sighed and snuggled her head to his shoulder.
"It's been so long, Rio."

"For me, too."

She tilted her head back far enough to look at his
face. "What do you mean?"

"Just that it's been a while since I've been with a
woman like you. No, I take that back. It's been a
while since I've been with a woman. I've never been
with anyone like you." He gazed into her eyes. "I

can't say I've lived like a monk, but I can say no woman has ever made me feel the way you do. Or did, for that matter.''

She rested her hand on his chest, and a slender finger toyed with one of the snaps on his shirt pocket. "This might sound crazy, but I'm glad nothing ever came of the crush I had on you."

"You are?" He couldn't keep the disappointment from his voice.

Maggie placed a feather-light kiss on his chin. "Hmmm. We weren't ready for each other then. We had to experience all the things we've been through to become the people we are now. We had to grow up."

"Think so?"

"Yes. I could never have acted on my feelings for you if I hadn't known what it is to lose something fine and wonderful. And I don't think you could have made the decision to try and find Emily's mother if you hadn't lost yours."

"My mother's people would say we finally found the right path to walk, one that was cut for us before time began. That we had gained wisdom."

"I don't feel very wise at the moment. I just feel incredibly, deliciously warm and good."

"You look incredibly, deliciously good."

Seeing the sparks of desire spring to life in his eyes again, Maggie decided that lingering on the bed was less than wise. "I think maybe I should go home."

"I think maybe that's—" He gave her a crooked little grin. "I won't say it's a good idea. But maybe the right idea."

"I suppose," she agreed halfheartedly as she pushed herself up and slid toward the edge of the bed.

Rio grabbed her arm. "Kiss me good night. One kiss."

"Then I guess I better make it count," she said, moving back into his embrace, as if it were the most natural place in the world for her to be.

CHAPTER EIGHT

SITTING in the cane-bottom chair, a booted foot resting on the rail of the back porch, and a steaming cup of coffee in one hand, Rio watched the new day being born and wondered how many times he had seen the sunrise from this very spot. Thousands, maybe. Even as a child, rather than lie in bed on a Saturday morning, he'd preferred to sit on this porch and watch the sun come up. It never failed to stir his spirit, and if he were a man given to poetry, which he wasn't, he could have said it was like experiencing a rebirth, an awakening that had nothing to do with daylight or dark. Sunrise meant another chance to correct yesterday's mistakes and fulfill today's dreams. It meant a second chance.

That's the miracle Maggie's brought me. A second chance.

Miracle was the perfect word to describe Maggie, he thought, sipping the hot coffee. How else did he explain a woman like Maggie, a woman of grace and beauty, a lady from the ground up, giving a worn-out cowboy like him the time of day, much less a hope for a future without loneliness?

Whoa, cowboy. Aren't you jumping the gun?

Was he? Was he assuming too much, too soon? Did he want her so badly that he assumed she felt the same things he did? Could he be mistaken?

No, Rio decided, not after last night. Last night *had* changed everything. For both of them. Maggie knew it, too. He'd seen it in her eyes, felt it in her touch, tasted it in her kiss. Whatever had passed between them in that brief but revealing embrace couldn't be denied or ignored. No, his feelings for Maggie were too strong now. The question was not what he felt, but what he intended to do about his feelings.

The one thing Rio did know was that his conversation with Cal about becoming a stock contractor played a part in the answer to his question. Regardless of how insistent he had been about hanging on to his pride and not taking the offer, the more he thought about himself and Maggie together, the more he thought about Cal's offer.

So, this wasn't Colorado. It wasn't even close. So what? Did he have to live his life away from Texas, away from the past, in order to be happy? Until recently, he had always thought so. Until Maggie.

The more they were together, the more Rio knew a decision to walk away from her would be like cutting himself in half. He would probably never be whole again. Strange, he thought, coming back here was supposed to have been a snap. Just get rid of the property and say adios. After all, he'd said his goodbyes years ago. Then why hadn't he done what he'd come to town to do and hit the road?

The answer was simple: Maggie.

"Maggie, Maggie, Maggie," Rio whispered to the new day.

He had some decisions to make.

Emily chose that moment to announce her first demands of the morning: a dry diaper and food. Rio set his cup on the porch rail and headed for the bedroom. "Comin', sunshine."

He scooped Emily out of the crib, his big hands holding her up so that they were at eye level.

"Good morning, sunshine." Emily smiled, enjoying the deep timbre of the now-familiar voice. "Time for chow, huh?" Following the usual routine, the diaper change was closely followed by a full tummy and then ... playtime.

Rio made funny faces and noises and Emily laughed.

Emily "talked" and Rio pretended to understand every word.

Rio played "this little piggy went to market," and Emily squealed in delight.

For Rio these minutes—as few as fifteen, or as many as forty-five between the time Emily woke and the time Elena arrived—were a rare gift. With the exception of Maggie's daily visits, these were the best minutes of the day. Amazing, he thought, how he had gone from being terrified of being alone with the baby to actually enjoying their time together. So much so that, even though Emily had been a part of his life for only a few days, he couldn't remember what his life had been like without her.

I could say the same about Maggie, he thought, knowing both statements were true. Two females. Both beautiful, both soft and sweet, both more dear to him than his own life. *Maybe, for once, your luck has turned, cowboy.* Sprawled across the big tester bed, propped up on one elbow with Emily beside him kicking happily, Rio decided maybe he was right.

Elena found them like that when she arrived a few minutes later. Hands on her hips, she looked at them and made a tsking sound. "What am I gonna do with you two?"

Rio scooped Emily up and carried her into the kitchen, where Elena was making a fresh pot of coffee. "You can feed this one." He pointed a finger to his own chest. "As for this one—" he situated Emily in her swing "—she's in great shape."

Elena watched as Rio grinned down at the baby. She could see how close he and Emily had become, and she knew how hard it was going to be for Rio when they were separated. The separation was inevitable, and she sensed Rio tended to put it out of his mind because he didn't want to think about it.

Elena handed him a cup of coffee. "I'm sure gonna miss her when she's gone."

Rio whipped his head around and stared at her, knowing the reminder was deliberate. He swallowed hard. "Yeah." Then he added brusquely, "Guess I better get to that section of fence that needs mending."

"I reckon so."

Wearing a scowl on his face, Rio downed half of the coffee and left the house.

His mood had improved only marginally by the time he came back to the house for the noon meal.

"Has Maggie called?" he asked, the second he hung his hat on one of the pegs mounted to the wall just inside the kitchen door.

"Not yet. How many pork chops you want? Two or three?" Elena asked, dishing up helpings of black-eyed peas and turnip greens.

Rio started for the bathroom to wash his hands, rolling up his sleeves as he went. "Make it one. I'm not real hungry."

A few minutes later he came back into the kitchen with not only clean hands but a clean shirt and his best boots. Elena gave him the once over as she set a plate of piping-hot food in front of him. "You gonna tend to those two calves this afternoon dressed like that?"

"Took care of 'em before I came in. But I need the vet—what's his name?"

"Manny Hernandez."

"Yeah, I need him out here to look at one of them." He stopped slathering butter on his corn bread. "You think you could call him for me?"

"Sure. Where you goin'?"

"The Double C."

"Fine time to go visitin'."

"This isn't a social call. It's business."

"Business?"

"Cal and Ken, they—uh—sorta think I'd make a decent stock contractor."

Elena smiled, satisfied he was going to talk business with Cal, pleased with herself and proud of Rio. "You be back for supper?"

He shrugged his shoulders. "Depends on whether or not Maggie calls and what she has to say when she does."

"She gonna talk to those shelter people?"

Rio checked his watch. Maggie was supposed to have an appointment with the director of the shelter sometime after lunch. Even though he had insisted on going along, Maggie had decided it might be best if she went alone, promising to call him the minute she could. He suspected she was reluctant to have him accompany her because she feared this would be another dead end. "Hopefully, within an hour or so, she'll have answers to some of our questions. Maybe even the mother's name."

"Don't get your hopes up, sonny."

Despite the well-intentioned warning, his hopes *were* up. He had a feeling today was going to be the day everything started to fall into place.

"ABOUT TIME you showed your ugly face around here." Ken Slattery walked out of the Double C barn about the same time Rio stepped out of his truck and closed the door. The two men shook hands.

"Yeah, well, you know how it is. I've been busy."

"So Cal tells me." Ken thought he had a good idea why Rio had come. He also thought his friend was a bit nervous despite the fact that he held himself ramrod straight. "How about something to wash the dust outta your throat?"

"Sounds good."

"Lettie Mae usually keeps a pitcher of lemonade on hand. Hits the spot 'long about this time of day, and I'll bet I can sweet-talk her outta a couple of glasses."

"My money's on you," Rio said, as he watched Ken walk toward the kitchen of the big house.

Rio had been at the Double C many times, but he never ceased to be impressed. When he was a child and young man, this house had represented everything the good life was supposed to be. The McKinneys were one of the most prosperous families in Claro County, but they had never given the impression money mattered more than people. Rio had grown up believing that the house, the land and the McKinneys themselves were the ideal of wealth and success. His own dreams of success had changed over the years, but his view of J. T. McKinney and his family had never changed. And even though he knew there had been a period when Cal's father had not been his greatest supporter, Rio respected the man for all he had accomplished and the way he treated his family.

Ken came out of the kitchen, crossed the yard and handed Rio a frosty glass of cold lemonade. "Here's to you."

"The same." Rio raised his glass in a salute, then tipped his head back and took a long drink.

"So, what's on your mind?"

"Your offer," Rio said point-blank. Ken nodded.

"I have to tell you I thought Cal was crazy when he first mentioned it."

"And now?"

Rio stared into his half-empty glass for a moment before meeting Ken's gaze. "You sure you wanna throw in with me?"

"Wouldn't have included myself in the offer otherwise. You've known me long enough to know that."

"Yeah. Guess so. But you know we're not talking nickels and dimes. The going price for a good buckin' horse is seventy-five hundred dollars and a seasoned bull can run nearly fifteen grand. And that's not countin' trucks, feed, vet bills and enough hands to keep it all running smooth."

"I've thought about all that. So has Cal."

"And stock contracting is competitive as hell. Even though there's more than seven hundred pro rodeos a year, there's close to a hundred contractors out there going head to head for business. You sure you want to take that kind of chance?"

"Sounds like you're trying to talk me outta this investment."

"No. Just want you to know what you're up against."

"Can I ask you something, Rio?"

"Shoot."

"What do you want? If you could have anything, what would it be?"

"A place of my own," Rio answered without hesitation and almost added, *some place to belong*.

Ken nodded again. "A man needs something he can call his. Something he can be proud of. Not that I'm not proud to be workin' at the Double C. I am. The McKinneys are like family, but I have to think about more than myself now. Nora and Rory deserve the kind of security they've never had, and I want to be the man to give it to them. That's why...I want to make this work." When Rio didn't comment, Ken looked him in the eyes. "If you're wondering how I feel about this deal, let me tell you straight out. You're good with stock, Rio. One of the best I've ever seen. A sight better than Cal and damned near as good as J.T. I'd trust you with any horse on the place. But all of that don't mean a tinker's damn if your heart's not here."

"What do you mean? This is my home."

"And you've been gone for more than twelve years. A man can do just so much roaming around. Sooner or later he's got to put down roots. You ready for that? 'Cause if you're not, we're all wasting our time. Think about it hard, Rio. Cal and I are only putting in money. You're the one who will have to do most of the work. And the worryin'.''

Rio straightened his shoulders slightly. "I'm no stranger to hard work.''

"But a man works hardest when he's got more at stake than money.'' When Rio frowned, Ken added, "Like proving something to himself. Or the love of a woman. Or both.''

"And if I decide not—''

"You've already decided to take the offer, or you wouldn't be here," Ken said flatly.

Rio knew Ken was right. Somewhere in the jumbled mess that passed for his brain, he had decided before he ever left his place to take Cal and Ken up on their deal.

"Which is it for you, Rio? Proving yourself or the woman?''

The fact that Ken said *the* and not *a* woman told Rio he already knew the answer. But Rio needed to hear himself say the words. Speak the commitment.

"Both," Rio said and felt more hopeful than he had in years.

RIO CALLED Maggie's office twice before leaving the Double C and was told the first time that she was on an outside appointment, and the second that she would not be back for the rest of the day. In his gut, Rio knew something was wrong, and on the drive back to his place he dreamed up at least a half dozen reasons why Maggie had decided not to return to her office. Or call him. He thought of at least that many scenarios resulting from her meeting with the director of the shelter: the mother they were looking for was alive and well *with* her baby; the woman they had come to see at the shelter and the mother they sought were not one and the same; the mother at the shelter had given up her baby for adoption, and there was documentation for proof.

But none of the scenarios included driving into his driveway and finding Maggie's car parked there.

"I decided to come over instead of calling," she said as soon as he walked into the house.

He hadn't realized until that very moment how glad he was to see her, how much he needed to see her, and not just for news of Emily's parentage, but for himself. And the fact that she was here, now, confirmed everything Ken had said, confirmed everything Rio felt.

"We called, but you'd already left the Double C," Elena said. "Want some iced tea?"

Never taking his eyes from Maggie's face, Rio shook his head.

"Well—" Elena wiped her hands on her apron "—reckon that's my cue to go make sure Emily is sound asleep." She glanced from Maggie to Rio and knew they hadn't heard a word, nor did they care, so she left quietly.

Rio took off his hat. "How are you?"

"Fine. How are you?" Maggie gnawed her bottom lip. Last night she'd thought their relationship had turned a corner, but now they both sounded so formal, so distant. She needed him close. And he would need her close, especially when she told him that, even though she had a name, they weren't a lot closer to finding Emily's mother.

Rio broke his stare long enough to hang his hat on the peg, then turned and walked straight to her. "God, I'm glad you're here," he whispered as he reached for her.

She went into his arms with a sigh of relief. "So am I." Her arms slipped around his waist and she held him. "So am I."

"How are you? Really?"

"Better, now that you're holding me."

He held her tighter. "Your office said you were gone for the day. I was getting concerned."

"I'm sorry if I worried you, but I had two outside appointments today, plus my interview at the shelter, and time got away from me."

"Did you see the director of the shelter?"

"Yes."

At the hesitation in her voice, Rio drew back and looked at her. "Something's wrong."

"No...and yes. I didn't get bad news. On the other hand, I can't say the news is exactly earth-shattering."

They sat down at the kitchen table, and before she could say a word, he took both her hands in his. "Maggie, whatever you found out—good or bad—I know you've done your best. No one could have done more, and I want you to know how grateful I am."

"I did get in to see the director at the shelter. She remembered me from a seminar on child abuse last year, so getting her cooperation wasn't difficult. She confirmed that a girl by the name of Teresa Hall was in the shelter for almost two weeks."

"Was?"

Maggie nodded. "The girl left without any notice and didn't leave any forwarding address. Their records didn't show a next of kin."

"Damn. Another dead end."

"Not ... not exactly."

"What does that mean?"

"The director told me that part of the requirement for staying at the shelter includes answering some questions pertaining to the mother's medical history and the baby's. They also ask for the name of the baby's father or a next of kin in case of emergency."

"Makes sense."

"Teresa Hall's only relative was her father, but she didn't know where he was. She did give the baby's father's name."

"That's great. If we can't find the mother, maybe we can find him."

"It's just a name, Rio. And it could be as false as the one she used. No address. This guy could be anywhere in the country."

"But it's a place to start, Maggie."

She smiled, unwilling to snatch away even this tiny bit of hope. "You're right."

"So?"

"The name Teresa Hall put down as Emily's father was Jeremy Westlake."

CHAPTER NINE

"WHAT DID YOU SAY?"

"The name Teresa Hall gave as the baby's father was—"

"Jeremy Westlake," he finished with her.

Maggie's eyes widened. "You know him?"

For a moment Rio thought she was joking, but then he realized she would never joke about this. "You're sure the name was Westlake?"

She held on to the hands that held hers. "Positive."

"No mistake."

"Not unless Teresa Hall lied. Rio, what is it? You look so..." *Shocked* was the only word to describe the expression on his face.

Rio rose from the table, walked to the window and gazed out as if he were absorbed in the beautiful fall day outside. But when he turned back to Maggie, his eyes were hard, his mouth set. "I thought you were gonna tell me Emily had inherited some God-awful disease or something, but this..."

Maggie went to him. "Rio, I don't understand. Do you know this Jeremy Westlake?"

He shook his head. "Never laid eyes on him."

"But . . . then you know of him?"

"Yeah. I know of him. And his father."

"His father?" Something was dreadfully wrong, but she was at a loss as to what. "I still don't—"

"John Westlake of the Terrytown Westlakes, of the power and influence Westlakes, of the rich and snooty Westlakes—"

"Rio, what are you talking about?"

He grabbed her by the shoulders, almost shaking her. "I'm talking about the man who shoves his little mistakes clear out of sight. I'm talking about the man who seduced my mother, then set her aside like last week's newspaper. I'm talking about John Hardin Westlake. My father."

Maggie couldn't have prevented her mouth from falling open if she tried. "Y-your father!"

"That's right," he all but spit out.

"If he's your father, then that means . . ." The full realization of what she was thinking, of what she had almost said, stunned her. "Oh, dear Lord," she gasped.

Rio released his grip on her shoulders. "This is one mess that even the Lord might not tackle."

"I—I had no idea."

"How could you? My mother, Elena and I are the only people who knew. And, of course, my father."

He spoke the words with such venom and anger that Maggie felt the urge to step back. "But . . . are you certain this Jeremy Westlake is connected to your...to John Westlake?''

"It's ironic." He shook his head. "Jeremy is part of the reason I left Crystal Creek all those years ago.''

Maggie took him by the hand and led him back to the table. "Tell me," she said softly.

He gazed into her eyes and saw no censure, only encouragement, only love. He felt her strength, felt it flow from her body to his, from her heart to his.

Rio's gaze drifted beyond her, almost as if he were looking into his past. "When I was five, my mother told me why I didn't have a father like the other kids. Not who, but why. From then on, it wasn't a topic for discussion. But in a way he was there, almost like an invisible third person in our lives. We worked hard for what we had, and we never had much. But a few times, when things got down-to-the-last-can-of-beans tough—like when our old truck laid down and died, or a tornado took part of the roof off—money would miraculously appear. She told me she got loans from the bank, but I knew she wasn't telling the truth. The only times in my life that I ever knew her to lie.''

He took a deep breath, then continued. "When it came time to think about college, I figured it was a lost cause. We couldn't afford it, and my grades weren't good enough for a scholarship. Then one day, my mother told me she had been saving since I was a baby and I was going to college. That's when I put it all together; that's when I knew for sure that my *fa-*

ther had been the source of our miracle money over the years."

The hand lying on the table balled into a fist. "And I hated him for it. The son of a bitch didn't have the balls to face us, to face his responsibility. He couldn't spare any time for us, only money to ease his conscience."

He paused for several minutes. Maggie didn't press him, knowing he needed to get it out of his system in his own way. Finally, his gaze again focused on her face. "When I was a senior, I cut class one day, drove into Austin and got a copy of my birth certificate. That's how I got his name. I started digging for information. Wasn't hard. Westlake is some big deal kinda citizen. Thinking about it now, I guess I wanted to have it out with him. Man to man. And maybe, somewhere in the back of my mind, I hoped when we finally talked, he would accept me."

Rio clenched and unclenched his fist. Without thinking, Maggie reached out and touched his hand. Instantly, Rio relaxed his hand, and their fingers intertwined.

"Then I found out about... about his other son. Westlake had a legitimate son to carry his name. I knew he would never recognize me as his. And I knew the longer I stayed here, the stronger my hate would grow. So... I said to hell with John Westlake, and to hell with the past. I never looked back—until my mother died."

He was spent, wrung out, his emotions raw and just below the surface. He had reached into the darkness of his past and dragged all the ugliness, the scars, the pain out into the light. He had faced it, perhaps for the first time as an adult. Now she understood fully why hanging on to Emily was so important to him, why making every effort to find the young mother had become almost an obsession. No one deserved to go through the kind of pain he had known as a child, and if it was within his power to save even one child from such a fate, he would do whatever it took to accomplish it. She had never known a more courageous man.

Tears slid down her cheeks and dropped onto their entwined fingers. Rio looked down, then lifted his eyes to Maggie's. "I..." He swallowed hard. "Don't cry for me. I don't want your pity."

Through her tears Maggie saw him fighting the emotion that welled in his own eyes. "How about my love?" She touched her hand to his cheek. "Because that's what I'm offering you. All my love."

Rio stared at her, his heart suddenly filled to bursting with tenderness, yearning, passion and the hundreds of emotions he had always dismissed because he had never experienced their depths. Well, he was experiencing them now, and he knew nothing in life would ever be as sweet as this moment. "Maggie," he whispered. "I...I—"

"My love is a gift. You don't have to say anything or do anything. You don't even have to return it. But don't expect me to take it back. I couldn't if I wanted to, and I don't. I just want to love you, Rio. And if you can't love me back now, then I'll—"

Before she could finish, he was out of his chair and she was in his arms. For a heartbeat he molded her to him, then his hands fisted in her hair. "Can't love you back?" he breathed against her neck as he tilted her head back. "My God, don't you know?" He lifted his head and stared into her beloved face. "Sweet Maggie. I can't do anything *but* love you. You're in my dreams, in my heart, and I hope in my life from now on." He kissed her mouth, nipping gently at the corners as if he were sipping a sweet nectar. "I tried to stay away. For your sake."

"I didn't want you to stay away."

"Me either. Not now. Not anymore. God, you taste so good."

Her arms went around his neck. "Oh Rio, Rio."

He kissed her long, deep and hard, pouring all his emotion into the kiss, willing her to know how very much he loved her, wanted her, treasured her.

"Well, I figured you two had enough time to . . ." In the kitchen doorway, Elena stopped short. "Oops."

Rio ended the kiss, but kept Maggie in his arms. "It's all right, Elena."

"I didn't mean to interrupt. I'll just come back—"

"No," Maggie said, smiling. "Really, it's all right."

"Besides, you need to know what's happened." Still in Rio's embrace, Maggie felt him tense.

Now it was Elena's turn to smile. "I reckon a blind man could see what's happened. You two finally got around to seein' what I've known—"

"Elena, I wasn't talking about Maggie and me. This has to do with the Westlakes."

At the mention of the name, Elena went pale. "W- what about 'em?"

"Maggie got the name of the baby's father from the shelter where Emily and her mother went after they left the hospital. The name is Jeremy West- lake."

"Sweet Lord," Elena whispered as she slid into one of the kitchen chairs. "If that ain't one for the books."

"I didn't understand why Rio was so shocked at hearing the name, but then he told me about..." She glanced at Rio and he nodded as if to say, go ahead. "Then he told me about his father."

Elena, her eyes filled with tears, looked from Rio to Maggie. "He told you everythin'?"

"Yes."

"Good," she said, sniffing, pulling a hankie from her apron and wiping her nose. "That secret's been locked up too long. Delora refused to talk about it. I always thought she woulda been better off if she had. Rio too." She blew her nose. "So what are you gonna do about this turn of events?"

"I'm not sure," he said.

"Well, one thing for sure. Now we know why little Emily landed on your doorstep."

Rio released Maggie reluctantly and she returned to her chair at the table. "Why do you say that, Elena?"

"Think about the note Rio found with her. 'Look after her like she was your own family,'" she paraphrased. "Don't that tell you somethin'? 'Cause it's sure as hell plain to me."

Maggie turned to Rio. "Whoever left Emily knew that you were related to her father."

"Bull's-eye," Elena said.

Rio looked doubtful. "But no one knew but you, Mother and me and Westlake. And I can damn well guarantee he didn't go spilling his guts to anyone."

"What about the boy, Jeremy?" Maggie asked. "Maybe he knew and he told the mother?"

"Don't think so. He knew nothing about me, and Westlake sure went to a lotta trouble to make sure it stayed that way."

"Well, somebody told that young woman, and she came lookin' to leave her baby with you."

"Elena's right, Rio. I mean, a baby fathered by your half brother ending up on your doorstep? It can't be coincidental."

"Maybe the girl lied," Elena threw in.

"Possible, but why would she lie to the shelter people?"

"The director talked to the woman who interviewed Emily's mother. At first she didn't want to

give them a name, but when told she couldn't stay at
the shelter without the name of someone who might
care for the child if anything happened to her, she
gave them the name to use only in case of an emergency," Maggie said. "I don't think she would have
taken a chance with something as important to her as
her baby. I think she was telling the truth about Jeremy Westlake."

"We still don't know who told her about Rio and
the Westlakes."

"When we find out how she knew, maybe then
we'll know who she is."

"And where she is," Rio added.

Maggie sighed in frustration. "But how do we go
about finding out?"

Rio glanced from Elena to Maggie. "We have to
start with the only clue we've got. Jeremy Westlake."

Elena walked over to Rio and put a hand on his
shoulder. "You're not thinkin' about talkin' to him,
are you, sonny?"

"Don't know any other way to find out if there's
even a possibility that he's the father, do you?"

"You're askin' for a lotta grief. I hate to see you
tackle the Westlakes head-on."

"Not all of them. Just the boy."

"How you gonna do that without lockin' horns
with the old man?"

"I'm not sure. I do know the kid goes to school at
U.T."

"That University of Texas is a right big place. How you gonna find one measly kid outta thousands?"

"With my help." Maggie rose from the table and stepped close to Rio. "I can find out. Through the computer. Child Protective Services *is* part of a statewide system that has access to almost all state agencies. I can't access confidential information, but I'll bet I could at least get some information from the registrar's office."

Rio captured her face in his broad hands, and held it lovingly. "What would I do without you?"

She placed both of her hands on his. "I hope you never find out."

"You're running a big risk, you know that?"

"Yes and I'll do it gladly, only..."

"Only what?"

"I'm concerned about what will happen when you have to confront Jeremy Westlake."

He frowned. "Confront? You saying you think we might wind up in some kind of fight?"

"I'm not worried about anything physical, but Rio, this is your *half brother.* Whether you like it or not, the two of you are related."

"We're strangers."

"You won't be after this. How are you going to feel if the meeting goes badly? More important, how are you going to feel if it doesn't?"

"I don't get your drift," he said, puzzled.

Gently, Maggie laid her hand on his chest. "Rio, have you ever stopped to consider what might happen if you meet this boy and you like him? And he likes you? Have you thought about how all of this might turn out? Are you certain you want to go through with this? Maybe it would be wiser—"

"No. I haven't thought about it, but it doesn't make any difference if I think this—" he couldn't quite bring himself to say brother, even half brother "—this kid is the greatest thing since sliced bread. I'm determined to find Emily's mother and I'd meet with the devil himself if I thought it would help."

"Just the same, I'm afraid you're in for more pain."

He pulled her against him and held her tight. "Doesn't matter. As long as I know you'll be here when I get back."

THE CAMPUS of the University of Texas sprawled over 350 acres, and teemed with students all year round. Even at 7:45 a.m., throngs of students hurried everywhere. Standing outside the political science building, Rio waited, holding in his hand a sheet of information, faxed to Maggie's office, that gave Jeremy Westlake's vital statistics as required by the university. In the upper-right-hand corner was a remarkably good facsimile of a photograph.

Rio stared at the picture. The eyes that stared back at him could have been his own. The boy's hair was lighter, his cheekbones not quite as high, but then he didn't have Rio's native American ancestry. What he did have was a similarly shaped face. Despite Rio's wish to the contrary, there was definitely a family resemblance. *Some family.*

Now that he was here, waiting to meet the kid, he wasn't sure of the best way to go about making contact. Did he just walk up and introduce himself, then say, "And by the way, did you know you and I have the same father?" *Too blunt.* Maybe he could ask the kid if he knew a girl by the name of Teresa Hall? *He might lie.* That was a possibility no matter what approach he used, Rio realized. Then where would they be? Square one.

At that moment two young men with backpacks came out of the building, walking toward the spot where Rio stood, following the sidewalk around to the right. They were both about the same age and height. Each had light brown hair. *Damn! Could be either one.* He had to make a decision. Quick. *Bite the bullet and do it.*

"Westlake," Rio called out. One of the boys stopped and turned in Rio's direction.

He walked up to the young man. "You Jeremy Westlake?"

"Yeah. Do I know you?"

"No, but I'm looking for a friend of yours and thought you might know where she is."

"Who you looking for?"

"Teresa Hall."

Rio watched the boy's face carefully for any sign of recognition, and for a second he thought there was a glint of... something, but then it was gone.

"Wh-who?"

"Teresa Hall," Rio said distinctly.

The boy stared as if he were trying to make a connection, then finally shook his head. "Sorry. Don't know her." Jeremy turned to walk away.

"Hold it." Either the kid was one helluva good liar or he was telling the truth.

"I'd love to help, but I've got another class—"

"Then you better plan on cutting."

Now it was Jeremy's turn to give Rio a good hard look. The guy was rude, but he was also one big cowboy. Too big, Jeremy decided, to tangle with. "Look mister, I told you I don't know any girl by the name of Teresa Hall. For a minute I thought you said something clsc. There's thousands of girls running around U.T. You can't expect me to know them all. I'm good—" the kid grinned "—but I'm not that good." He turned and started walking away.

Smartass little son of a bitch. Rio had an urge to jerk the kid up by the collar and teach him a lesson in manners. "Not even if this one is the mother of your child?"

Jeremy stopped dead in his tracks. Slowly, he faced the tall cowboy. "What the hell are you talking about?"

"About a girl who had a baby out of wedlock. Ring any bells, kid?" Rio figured the boy would probably laugh at the old-fashioned term, but he didn't care. *And so help me, if he gives me any guff about liber-*

*ated women and this being the nineties, I'll knock him
clean into next week.*

Jeremy's heart skipped a beat, and thoughts of Tess
crowded his mind before he could push them aside.
His father was right, he had to get over her. "What
are you, this girl's brother, out for revenge?"

Rio almost laughed out loud at the irony of the
question. "I asked you if that rang any bells?"

Jeremy glanced away. "No."

"You're lying."

"Now just a damned minute—"

"No. You wait." Rio gave in to his urge. He
grabbed the kid's shirt, and hauled him around until
they were face-to-face. "I came here to get some answers, and by God, I'm not leaving until I do." He
glanced around, looking for some place less public,
and settled on the shelter of a massive pecan tree. He
practically dragged Jeremy Westlake the dozen or so
feet to its shade.

"Hey, knock it off or I'll call the campus cops."

"Shut up." Rio slung Jeremy against the pecan
tree's trunk, slamming the backpack into his shoulders. "A young girl with her newborn baby went to a
shelter for unwed mothers, and she gave your name
as the baby's father. Now I'll ask you just once more.
Do you know Teresa Hall?"

His eyes wide with shock, Jeremy stuttered, "M-
me?"

"That's right, Romeo. Now answer me."

"N-no. I never met anyone by that name. I swear."

Rio wanted to believe he was lying. Something deep inside himself, something ugly, wanted to hate this young man. But he couldn't. And like it or not, he thought the kid was telling the truth. He released Jeremy's shirt and took a step back.

"Listen, uh." Jeremy cleared his throat, relieved. "You say this girl named me as the father?"

"Yeah."

"What did she look like?"

"I told you—" Jeremy flinched at the edge on the big man's voice. "We're trying to find the mother. She left the baby on my doorstep."

"Jeez," Jeremy breathed. No wonder the guy was running around trying to find the father. The cowboy had calmed down, and for an instant Jeremy almost felt sorry for him. "Sorry I can't help you."

"Yeah."

Jeremy backed up, fully intending to walk away and never look back, but something about the way the cowboy was staring made him stop. "Can I ask *you* a question?"

Rio nodded his head.

"Who the hell are you?"

"Rio Langley." He waited for some sign that Jeremy recognized the name Langley. None came.

"Well, if this baby belongs to a stranger, Mr. Langley, do you mind telling me why you felt you had to jump my ass personally, like you needed to get even with me or something?"

Rio looked into Jeremy Westlake's eyes and knew it was now or not at all. Either he told the kid who and what he was or he never told him.

"Because..."

"Because what? I think I've got a right to know after the way you pounced on me."

"Yeah. You're right. I came at you like a bull outta the chute. So I wouldn't blame you if you don't believe what I'm about to say any more than I believed you. At first."

Now what? Jeremy thought.

"I don't know any other way to say this than straight out." Rio took a deep breath. "You and I are...your father and mine...they're the same. The only difference is, I was an embarrassing mistake John Westlake didn't want anyone to know about."

Jeremy's eyes went as round as silver dollars, then narrowed to slits. "When you grabbed me I thought you were crazy. Now I see you're crazy like a fox. What is this? Some kind of hokey little blackmail scheme?"

"It's true."

"Well, Mr. Langley, or whatever your name is, it won't work. My father... *my* father—" he poked his finger to his chest for emphasis "—won't pay you a nickel. So, you can go peddle your story to some sleazy tabloid for all I care. Just get the hell out of my sight." Then, he turned, taking wide steps away from this wild man.

"Ask him," Rio said, still keeping his voice calm. "Ask your father if it's true. Ask him if the name Delora Langley means anything."

Jeremy whipped around. "Wh-who did you say?"

"Delora Langley. My mother."

Jeremy shook his head, but Rio could see recognition in his eyes. He might never have met Delora Langley, but he sure as hell knew her name.

"She worked for your family." Rio's voice tightened as he talked and he had to concentrate on not balling his hands into fists of frustration. "When Westlake found out I was on the way, he kicked her out. Oh, he sent money whenever he had an attack of conscience. Otherwise..." Deliberately forcing his voice to a cold, steady calm, Rio said, "The great John Hardin Westlake couldn't be bothered with an illegitimate son."

"Lying bastard."

"You got the bastard part right."

"My father will take you to court for spreading these lies. And to think I almost felt sorry for you a minute ago. Get away from me. You're nothing but trash."

Rio knew he was wasting his breath. The kid didn't believe him. He was going to defend his worthless father no matter what. Suddenly all Rio wanted was to go home and hold Maggie in his arms.

"You're a real piece of work, kid. A Westlake all right. Every selfish inch of you."

Rio turned his back on Jeremy Westlake and walked away.

THE DRIVE HOME was one of the longest Rio had ever made. By the time he pulled into his driveway, he finally understood what people meant when they said someone carried the weight of the world on his shoulders. At the moment his felt as if they were burdened by at least two extra tons. The only thing that lightened the load was the sight of Maggie's car parked at the back end of the driveway.

When he stepped inside and hung his hat on a peg, she was there, waiting, just as she had been last night. And in almost a replay of last night, they stared at each other for a long moment.

Then they were in each other's arms.

"I couldn't wait for you to call."

"Glad you didn't," he breathed into her hair.

"Was it bad?" She leaned back, then brushed a lock of hair from his forehead.

"I've had better days meeting the business end of a bull," Rio confided.

"Did you tell him who you were?"

"He didn't believe me. Can't blame him under the circumstances."

"And what about the girl giving his name as Emily's father?"

"He denied ever knowing anybody named Teresa Hall."

"You believe him?"

"About that? Yeah." Rio raked his hands through his hair. "He thought I had come to blackmail him. To sell my story to the tabloids. His father must have convinced him the Westlakes were so high-and-mighty and great that everyone wanted a piece of them. And he called me trash. For God's sake, Maggie. What has John Hardin Westlake done to his son?"

What indeed, Maggie thought, seeing the anguish on Rio's face. What had he done to both his sons?

And she had to be the one to bring him more bad news. Maggie would rather have cut out her tongue than have to cause him further pain, but it was out of her hands. Time had run out for Emily, even though she had promised not to say anything until tomorrow. But even if she wanted to give Rio more time, she couldn't. One of the other caseworkers had accidentally come across several unofficial requests for information concerning Emily, and Maggie had been forced to make the case official today.

Maggie fought tears, knowing the situation was hopeless and too painful to bear.

But she had no choice.

"Rio... I—I have to talk to you."

"In a minute." He pulled her back into his embrace. "You feel so good."

"Rio... please?"

More than the word *please*, the tone of her voice compelled him to release her. "What's wrong?"

"I... I... I have to take Emily."

His lips silently formed the word *no* but before he could find his voice, Maggie placed her fingertip to his mouth. "I don't want to. I'd give my life not to have to. But it's out of my hands. One of the other caseworkers saw a request for information on Emily, and I *had* to officially put her into the system."

"Who made the request?"

"I'm not—"

"Could it have been Emily's mother?"

"The caseworker said the caller didn't identify herself."

"Her? That means it *could* have been the mother."

"Rio, don't you see? It doesn't make any difference who called. I still have to take Emily."

"When?" was all he asked.

"Late tomorrow afternoon," she whispered.

Maggie had seen defeat on the faces of homeless mothers and children. She had seen it on the faces of parents desperately trying to get help for a sick child. But she had never witnessed the kind of anguish she now saw in the eyes of the man she loved. And she was powerless to help. The only thing she could do was pour out her love for him and hope it eased the pain. The one thing she feared most of all was that he might shut her out.

She knew how hard it had been for him to let her into his life, into his heart, after having been alone and a loner all his life. She prayed he didn't withdraw from her now.

"Does Elena know?"

"Yes. She took Emily for a walk down by the grape arbor. She said she wanted some time with her."

He nodded solemnly. "Think I'll walk down there." He started out the door, then stopped and turned back to her. "You want...you want to come?"

She wanted to shout *yes, yes,* but in her heart she knew it would be better if he had the baby to himself for a while. To tell her goodbye. "No. You go ahead. But..."

"Yeah."

"I'll be back in the morning. Early."

"No need."

"Yes, there is a need." She didn't even try to keep the anger from her voice. He *was* retreating again. Away from the pain. Away from her. "My need to be with you when...when Emily..." With the last word, all the anger fell away, replaced by a desperate ache to take him in her arms. Knowing such action would be difficult for him to handle at that moment, she settled for touching his cheek softly. Ever so softly. "I wish there was some other way." She closed her eyes and whispered, "Dear Lord, if there was any other way..." When she opened her eyes a tear slid down her cheek. "I don't want you to be hurt."

"I've been hurt before."

"Yes. But not like this."

She was right and Rio knew it. And there wasn't a damned thing he could do to stop the pain that was only hours away. Hours, hell! Already his gut was tied in knots, and a strange tightness squeezing his heart warned it was only going to get worse.

After Maggie left a few minutes later, he wanted to go after her and beg her to stay with him. Stay with him and Emily. All night. He needed to hold her, needed to feel close to her. But he didn't. Instead, he devoted his last hours with Emily to playing, tickling.

And rocking her to sleep.

Even Elena, always the first to say he was spoiling the baby, didn't object when he sat down in the old rocker with Emily in his arms. She had simply kissed the baby, then Rio, and left crying. Long after Emily was sleeping securely in her crib, Rio continued to sit in the rocker, gazing down at the sweet little face.

He had known from the first that she was only on loan to him, but that didn't make it hurt less. For the first time in his life, Rio wanted to believe in prayer.

So, the man who hadn't spent time on his knees except possibly in the process of picking himself or one of his rodeo buddies up off a barroom floor slipped silently out of the rocker, and went down on one knee beside the crib.

Rio had no idea how long he knelt beside Emily's bed. He only knew when he finally crawled into the old tester bed, he dreamed of another child. A hoped-to-be child. This one, with auburn curls and soft green eyes, was the image of her mother and the center of her father's heart.

He was still lost in the image when a loud knock sounded on his door. Rio looked at the clock. Three a.m. "Who in hell?" he mumbled, staggering across the kitchen floor. He jerked open the door and blinked twice, wondering if he was still dreaming.

"Can I come in?"

Rio moved back, opening the door wider, and Jeremy Westlake stepped inside.

CHAPTER TEN

THE LAST PERSON Rio ever expected to see standing in his kitchen was Jeremy Westlake, but there he was, hands in his pockets, looking like a lost puppy.

Rio scrubbed his face with his hands. "Where did you come from? I didn't hear a car drive up."

"I, uh, parked down the road," Jeremy answered, hesitant to admit the reason stemmed from lack of courage. He had spent a full thirty minutes walking around his car, rehearsing what he intended to say.

"How did you find me?"

Jeremy shrugged, not meeting Rio's gaze. "Wasn't hard. A guy at the Texaco station at the edge of town told me how to find the house." Jeremy glanced around. "Nice house."

"My mother's."

"Uh, yeah. I'd, uh, like to talk to her if you wouldn't mind."

"You're too late," Rio said flatly. "She passed away almost a month ago."

Jeremy's head snapped up. "Oh. Jeez, I'm... sorry."

Tired and heartsick about Emily's leaving, Rio was in no mood for this unexpected late-night visit. "You didn't come all the way out here to offer your condolences. What's on your mind?"

"I, uh, got to thinking about some of the stuff you told me."

"And?"

"And I had a talk with my father, if you could call it that. He did most of the talking." Jeremy motioned to a chair. "Mind if I sit down?"

"Suit yourself." Rio pulled a chair away from the table, flipped it around and straddled it in one smooth motion. "Whatever you thought was so all-fired important you had to come knocking on my door in the middle of the night, it better be good. Spit it out, then get movin'."

In the process of pulling out his own chair, Jeremy stopped. His hand fell away from the back of the chair, and he straightened his shoulders and looked Rio square in the face. "After the things I said to you this morning, you've got every right to tell me to go to hell or call the cops. Or both. But before you do, I owe you an apology. That's why I'm here. That and..."

"Go on."

"To tell you that I know you're telling the truth."

"About?" For some reason Rio couldn't explain, he wasn't willing to let the kid off with partial statements and assumptions.

"About my... *our* father." His spurt of courage gone, Jeremy sat down hard in the chair.

So, Rio thought, *at last it's all out in the open.* He should have felt elated, even vindicated, but somehow he didn't. All he felt was pity for the boy sitting across from him. *I've had years to come to terms with the truth. This kid's had maybe a few hours.* Rio sighed. "You want some coffee?" he offered, knowing there was some left from the pot made for supper. "I can heat it up."

"No, thanks. After today, the last thing I need is more stimulation."

Rio nodded and waited, instinctively knowing the boy had more to say.

"We had an argument. A real doozer. He, uh, denied it. Said you were probably sent by some of his political enemies. And for a couple of seconds I almost believed him."

"You wanted to believe him."

"Yeah, I guess you're right."

"What changed your mind?"

"Your name. I never mentioned it, just described you as tall and big, but I didn't tell him your name. Then he slipped and called you Rio. That's when I knew you were telling the truth and he was lying. I told him so."

Rio snorted. "I'm sure that went over big."

"He went crazy. Started yelling at me, asking me if I was on drugs or drunk. Wanted to know who put me up to this. I tried to leave, but he grabbed me and told me I wasn't going anywhere without his permission. I've never seen him so out of control."

And for a man like John Westlake, Rio thought, nothing could be worse than being out of control.

"He hit you?"

"No! He wouldn't ever..." A long sigh slipped from Jeremy. "At least I don't think he would ever take a swing at me." Jeremy raked both his hands through his hair. "After today, I'm not sure about anything, except that I owe you an apology, and I hope you'll accept it."

The world Jeremy Westlake thought was safe, secure and balanced had turned upside down today, and he was having a hard time dealing with it. *Welcome to the real world, kid.*

"No shame in an honest mistake."

Jeremy's gaze met Rio's. "How long have you known?"

"About the fact that I was a bastard? Or—"

"I'm sorry. When I called you that this morning, I didn't know... I never would have—"

"Don't worry about it, kid. I don't. And haven't in a lotta years."

"How many?"

"My mother told me when I was five, but I didn't have the name of the man until I was a senior in high school."

Jeremy was quiet for long moments, then his face tightened and he doubled up his fist and hit the tabletop. "How could he do that to you? How could any man know he's got a son and just ignore him? I don't understand. I'll never understand. And I don't think I'll ever forgive him."

"You will."

"Have you?"

"It's different with me. He was never part of my life. I never missed him," Rio lied.

"Damn him!" Jeremy hit the table again.

"Take it easy. You'll wake up Emily."

Immediately, the boy's fists relaxed. "Sorry. Emily? That your wife?"

"No, the baby I told you about."

"Oh, yeah." Jeremy ducked his head. "I, uh...there's something else I better tell you."

Rio sat up straight. "You change your mind about that, too?"

"No. I never met Teresa Hall..." He glanced away.

"But?"

"I got a girl pregnant. But she had an abortion," he said in a rush, as if to assure Rio he hadn't lied. "We were supposed to get married. Then she left a note saying she'd decided she didn't want to be a mother and that she was going to, you know, get rid of it."

Despite the fact that Jeremy's voice was calm, Rio could tell he still carried around a lot of pain over the incident. *So the kid hasn't lived life on a silver platter. So some girl dumped him. She probably lied about the baby hoping to get money from his old man. So life sucks. So what?*

"Maybe it was for the best." *Hell, I don't know what to say to the kid. What am I? His shrink?*

Jeremy shook his head. "I thought she really loved me."

What now? The kid gonna break down and cry on my shoulder?

"I believed her. Guess you think that makes me a jerk?"

"No. It makes you just like everybody else."

"Have you ever been in love, Mr. Langley?"

"Under the circumstances, don't you think you should call me Rio? And yes, I have been."

"Did you . . . did you get over it?"

"No. I can honestly say I never did." *And never will.* An image of Maggie's sweet face swam across Rio's mind, and he smiled. *Not in this life or the next.*

"Mr. Langley . . . Rio?"

Jeremy's voice snapped Rio out of his thoughts. "Yeah?"

"I have absolutely no right to ask a favor of you, but I'd appreciate it if you would see your way clear to let me stay here until morning. I'm not asking to stay in the house," he rushed to assure Rio. "I'll sleep in my car. It's just...I don't want to go back while my father's at home. You see, I've decided to move out."

"Don't make any snap judgments or decisions, kid. It's rough out here with the working class. Better think twice before you give up a college education and an easy life."

"I'm not giving up my education. Lots of students work and attend classes," Jeremy said, determination edging his voice.

Rio pushed himself up and away from the chair. "Maybe you *better* sleep on it, kid. But not in a damned car. I've got an extra bed. Down the hall, second room on your right."

Jeremy scrambled to his feet and extended his hand. "Thanks."

They shook hands briefly. "Well, good night, and thanks again."

"Yeah."

For several minutes after the kid had gone down the short hallway and closed the bedroom door behind him, Rio stood in the silent kitchen, wondering how he was going to explain Jeremy Westlake's presence to Elena. *Hell, what am I saying? I'm not sure I can explain to myself.* Tomorrow morning was going to be... Suddenly he remembered exactly what tomorrow morning was going to be.

It was going to be hell.

WHEN MAGGIE PULLED in behind Rio's truck, the sun was barely peeking over the horizon, rosy pink and a thousand shades of gold. She turned off the engine and stared out through the windshield. Sunrise was one of her favorite times of day, usually leaving her breathless and incredibly hopeful. Today, watching the glow of a new day, she felt only a deep sadness. Today, she had to be part of a hurtful separation that would be a long time healing. Days ago—it seemed like weeks in retrospect—she had described to her father the unique bonding that had taken place between Rio and little Emily. What she hadn't known at the time was that she would become a part of that intimacy and come to love the child as much as Rio. And now she would not only be a part of the separation process, her heart would break right along with Rio's.

Knowing Elena didn't arrive for at least another half hour, Maggie planned on preparing breakfast in hopes that she, Rio and Emily could spend some precious time together. With a weary sigh, she got out of her car and headed toward the back door.

The aroma of bacon frying tweaked her nose even before her hand was on the doorknob. *He probably didn't get any more sleep than I did. Oh, Rio, I wish things could have turned out the way you wanted them to. For your sake as well as Emily's.* Expecting to find Rio in the kitchen, she came to an abrupt halt when she found instead a young man, shirtless, shoeless and holding a sizzling frying pan.

At the sound of the back door closing, Jeremy looked up. "Hi," he said. "Uh, I guess you're looking for Rio." *Who certainly has attractive friends,* he thought.

"Y-yes. Who are you?" But even before he answered, Maggie jumped to the correct conclusion. She didn't have to strain her eyes to see the young man's resemblance to Rio.

"I'm Jeremy Westlake. Sorry I can't shake your hand but I've got mine full." Holding a fork in one hand, he motioned to the pan of sizzling a bacon and another pan containing scrambled eggs.

"Margaret Conway. Where's—"

"Good morning."

She turned at the sound of Rio's voice, to find him standing in the doorway, holding Emily. For a moment the presence of Jeremy Westlake, or anyone else in the world for that matter, was forgotten as her gaze met Rio's.

If she had thought her heart was broken before, she had been gravely mistaken. Because now it was shattering into tiny pieces. Seeing the two of them together, Emily snuggled against Rio's broad chest, was almost more than she could take. Tears burned her eyes, and her throat tightened. Maggie smiled, unable to trust so frail an instrument as her voice.

Rio studied her, knowing she was fighting tears, knowing this day would be as painful for her as it was for him. And there wasn't one damned thing he could do to stop the pain any more than he could stop Emily from being taken away. Slowly, he walked over to Maggie and kissed her lightly, quickly on the lips. Anything more might have opened emotional floodgates that neither could close.

Jeremy watched the way Rio and the woman looked at each other and needed no explanation of what was between them. The emotion, the bond was so powerful he could actually feel it, as though it were an invisible force field. An exclusive force field, he realized, with only room enough for two. Make that three. The infant in Rio's arms was definitely included.

"I guess that's the baby, huh?"

Jeremy's question broke the spell and both Rio and Maggie turned to look at him. "The one you told me about."

"Yeah," Rio said. "Maggie Conway, this is—"

"We introduced ourselves," Maggie said, still not sure what to make of the young Westlake's presence.

"After she got over the shock of finding me in your kitchen," Jeremy was quick to add.

"He showed up early this morning—"

"Three a.m. to be exact."

Maggie glanced from one to the other. "Why?"

"Uh, well—"

"Maggie knows everything, Jeremy."

"Oh."

"Why don't you dish up that chow and I'll fill Maggie in."

Fifteen minutes later Maggie had been brought up-to-date on everything that had happened since Rio and Jeremy's encounter the morning before. What still shocked her was the apparent ease with which Rio accepted the young man who was both stranger and family.

"Rio's right, you know," Maggie said, commenting on the statement Rio had made to Jeremy about thinking twice before leaving home. "Working and going to school at the same time isn't a bed of roses. Perhaps when you and your father have had a chance to cool down, you can work—"

"You miss the point, Ms. Conway. I don't want to work it out with my father. Not now, at least. And it's going to be a long time before I can get past what he's done. Forgiving and forgetting won't happen overnight."

"It rarely does. Still, he *is* your father and—"

"Rio's gotten along without him all these years. So can I."

"Hold it, kid." Rio put down the forkful of eggs that was halfway to his mouth. "I'm no yardstick to measure yourself by. You've got choices I didn't have. And you've damned sure got a sight more to lose than I did. Remember, anything you decide today, you've gotta sleep with tonight."

"Up until yesterday I might have agreed with you, but now I'm not so sure. What good is a relationship when there's no trust? Even if you still care about someone, it's hard to get past the lies."

"You talking about your father or your girlfriend, the one who took off?"

"Mostly my girl. I still love her, but if she walked through that door right now and asked me to forgive her..." Jeremy shook his head. "I don't know. Knowing she could abort my baby like that tore me up inside." He looked over at Emily, still held in Rio's strong arms. "How could anybody willingly hurt anything so innocent?" His gaze met Rio's. "Could

I . . . would you mind if I held her? I'll be supercareful."

Maggie saw the hesitation in Rio's eyes. He hadn't relinquished his possession of the baby for a moment, not even to her. All through breakfast he had eaten with one hand and held Emily with the other. Maggie understood his need to keep her with him as long as possible, and she was on the verge of explaining to Jeremy when Rio very cautiously handed the baby to him.

"Keep one hand under her bottom and the other under her head," Rio instructed.

"Jeez, she's so little. And soft." The younger man's hands were not nearly as wide as Rio's, and he struggled to keep the baby from wobbling. Finally, he settled Emily in the crook of one arm, his other hand on her little rump. "Hey there, little girl." He stared down into her tiny face. "Wow, look at those eyes. She's—" He glanced up to find the other two watching him intently. "Something."

Rio's eyes were fastened on Emily, and Maggie watched as his jaw tensed. Before she could reach out and touch his hand in a gesture of comfort, he got up from the table and walked out the back door.

"Did I say something wrong? Maybe I shouldn't have—"

"It's not you, Jeremy. He's not himself today. In a few hours, Child Protective Services will be here to pick up Emily. Rio has tried for a week to locate the baby's mother with no results. He had hoped, well . . ."

"No wonder he looked funny when I asked to hold her. I better go apologize and give her back."

"No, wait," Maggie said as he rose from his chair. "I think it would be better if we gave him a little time to sort of get himself together."

"Sure." Jeremy sat back down.

At that moment they heard another car pull up outside. "That will be Elena," Maggie said.

"Elena?"

She smiled, anticipating the look on the older woman's face when she walked in and saw Jeremy. "An old friend of Rio's. Sort of like an aunt, you might say."

Sure enough, the back door opened, Elena stepped inside and came to a dead stop. "Good Lord have mercy!" she exclaimed, catching sight of Jeremy. "What's that boy gone and done?"

"Elena Morales, this is Jeremy Westlake—"

"I knew it! I told him yesterday he was askin' for grief. Now just look what he's gone and done. Nothin' good's gonna come from this, you mark my words. Where's sonny?"

"I think he may be in the barn, and Elena . . ." Maggie said when the other woman turned toward the door, obviously intent on following Rio, "he knows what he's doing. He's okay."

Elena gave Jeremy a quick and near-lethal glance. "He better be." She turned on her heel and headed for the barn.

When Elena returned ten minutes later, along with Rio, she was calmer, even subdued.

"Where's Emily?" Rio asked the instant he walked through the door.

Maggie was at the sink, washing the breakfast dishes. Jeremy was drying. She wiped her hands on the apron tied around her slim waist. "I put her down for her morning nap."

"I'll check on her," he said softly.

"Rio—"

"Elena." Maggie reached out and put a hand on her arm. "Let him do this his way."

She covered Maggie's hand with hers. "I reckon he's got to."

In the interval between the time Elena followed Rio to the barn and then returned, Jeremy had donned a shirt and combed his hair. "Can I get you a cup of coffee, ma'am?"

"I'll pour my own." Elena glared at him, then begrudgingly added, "Thank you."

"Yes, ma'am."

"Don't ma'am me, boy. I'm not your ma."

"Yes m—, Ms. Morales."

Elena cut him a hard look. "Accordin' to Rio, you're aimin' to take on the world all by yourself."

"Well, that's not exactly—"

"Don't sound to me like you got the sense God gave a goose, boy."

Jeremy flushed. "I've got enough sense to know when I'm not wanted." He started for the door, only to have Rio step in front of him.

"Calm down."

Jeremy looked down at his feet, embarrassed at his flare of temper. "She's right. You've got enough to deal with today without me hanging around. Maggie told me about Emily." A look of intense pain flashed across Rio's eyes for an instant, then it was gone, but not before Jeremy saw it. "I'm sorry, man. It was bad enough to lose a baby the way I did, but having one for a while, *then* losing it... You've got more guts than I do."

"What's he talkin' about?" Elena wanted to know.

"It's personal," Maggie said in Jeremy's defense.

He smiled his thanks, but said, "I got a girl pregnant, Ms. Morales, and she had an abortion. Tess was always so sweet I never dreamed she would do anything like that."

"Tess?"

"Yeah. That was her name—Tess Holloway. Her dad was our chauffeur. That's how we met and fell in love. At least *I* fell in love with her."

Maggie stepped closer to Jeremy. "What did you say her name was?"

"Tess Holloway."

Maggie and Elena exchanged knowing glances. "Slender, about my height?"

"Yes."

"Short blond hair?" Elena asked.

"No. It was almost to her waist. She wore it that way so the weight would help control the natural curl. Why do you ask?"

"She coulda cut it," Elena surmised.

"Possible," Maggie agreed.

Rio moved closer to Maggie. "What are you two talking about?"

"The waitress at the Longhorn. You remember. She waited on us the other day."

Rio shook his head. "The one who dropped the coffeepot," she reminded him without success. "She told me her name was Tess Holloway."

"When?" Jeremy jumped into the conversation.

"Yesterday. No, the day before. Or the one before that. I'm not sure."

"She got hired on about a week ago," Elena informed them. "Rosa Walters told me she was a hard worker."

"A week ago? About the same time Emily showed up," Rio said, his thoughts beginning to parallel Maggie's and Elena's.

Jeremy turned to Rio. "What does the baby have to do—"

"It's almost too good to be true," Maggie said, her voice laced with excitement.

"Slow down. Both of you," Rio suddenly commanded, the coldness in his voice effectively puncturing any bubbles of excitement. "You're letting your imagination run away like a wild mustang. What's the point of speculating? Dammit, this is hard enough."

"Oh, sweetheart," Maggie whispered, reaching out to touch his face. "I'm sorry. But don't you see the connection?"

"No. You were right the first time. It's too good to be true."

"Will someone please tell me what the hell is going on?" Jeremy exclaimed.

Hands on her hips, Elena turned to Jeremy. "Keep your breeches on, boy. You're 'bout to find out."

"TESS, DID YOU TAKE that elderly couple's order? Looks like they've been waiting a while."

"Yes, Ms. Walters. Cook's working on it now."

"Thanks. And I thought we agreed you were going to call me Rosa?"

"Yes, ma'am . . . I mean Rosa."

The new owner of the Longhorn Coffee Shop smiled. "Much better." She heaved a deep sigh. "Well, now that we've got a breather between the breakfast and lunch runs, will you go back and ask Cook if he intends to do catfish or meat loaf for the lunch special?" Then Rosa snapped her fingers and added, "Oh, and would you check the walk-in cooler and see how many strawberries are left? I don't want to put strawberry shortcake on the menu if we don't have enough."

"Okay." Tess pushed open the swinging doors leading to the kitchen and sailed through, out of sight.

At that moment Rio pulled up in front of the Longhorn and shut off the truck's engine. Jeremy immediately jerked open the door.

"Hold it, kid." Rio reached across Maggie, seated in the middle, and put his hand on Jeremy's shoulder. "Now, we've told you all we know and what we think. But we're not sure if this is the right girl, so don't go bustin' in there like a bull in a china closet, you hear me?" Jeremy nodded.

Maggie was quick to agree. "And even if she *is* the right girl . . ." Both men looked at her. "She may not appreciate the fact that we've tracked her down. She may not want anything to do with any of us."

"Not my Tess."

"She may not be your Tess," Maggie reminded Jeremy. "All that I'm saying is to go slow, all right?"

"Okay." Jeremy was out of his side of the truck and waiting for them at the café's front door.

"Well, hi there," Rosa greeted them. "Y'all need breakfast?"

Rio glanced around. "Just coffee for three, thanks, Rosa."

They settled in a booth, Jeremy craning his neck to look for the girl called Tess.

Rosa brought three cups of coffee. "Can I get you anything else?"

"Rosa, does that waitress still work for you? The girl that accidentally dropped that coffeepot the other day?"

Rosa smiled. "Tess. Sure. She's in the back."

Jeremy's heart nearly shot out of his chest. He had told himself a hundred times on the ride into town that he didn't care if this girl was Tess or not. He'd told himself that Maggie's and Elena's conclusions were dead wrong. That even if it was his Tess working at the café, it didn't change things between them. She had lied to him, and that was that. But no matter how hard he tried to convince himself that he could handle seeing her again, he couldn't extinguish the tiny flame of hope that burned in his heart.

"Could we speak to her?"

"Is something wrong?"

"No," Maggie assured her. "We just want to ask her a question."

"Sure." Rosa turned toward the kitchen. "Tess!"

"Yes, ma'am," said a voice from the other side of the swinging doors. "Cook said catfish today and meat loaf tomorrow." Tess stepped into view, her head down, reading from a piece of paper. "And we've got six quarts of straw..." She raised her head and halted in midsentence.

Jeremy rose from the booth and stepped forward. "Tess?"

"Jeremy!" Her hands flew to her mouth, and the paper fluttered to the floor.

Rio and Maggie rose from the booth and stood behind Jeremy.

"Oh, no," Tess cried, seeing the looks on their faces. "Oh, no." They knew. Everything was ruined. All her plans. All her hopes for Emily.

"Tess," Jeremy whispered. "Is it really you?"

"Oh, Jeremy." By now fat teardrops were sliding down her cheeks.

"What's going on here?" Rosa said, coming to stand beside Tess.

Jeremy ignored the question, in fact, ignored everything and everyone except Tess. "I've got to talk to you."

She shook her head. "I—it's no good." Her gaze went to Maggie, silently begging for help. "I'm sorry. There was just no other way. I'm sorry."

"Maggie? Rio? Who is this young man?" Rosa asked.

"A friend of Tess's," Maggie said. "Could we use that booth in the far corner to talk to Tess for a minute?"

Rosa looked doubtful, but she trusted Maggie and Rio. "I guess so." She touched the girl's arm. "I'll be at the cash register if you need me."

As the four of them walked to the booth, Maggie positioned herself so that she and Tess would be on one side of the booth, Rio and Jeremy on the other. She had no idea how this confrontation would turn out, but she suspected that they hadn't seen the last of Tess Holloway's tears.

"Tess—" Jeremy began, but Maggie waved him quiet.

The girl sat with her head down, her hands folded nervously in her lap. "Tess," Maggie began. "No one is mad at you. We just need to know the truth."

Tess lifted her tear-stained face. "About Emily?"

Out of the corner of her eye, Maggie saw a muscle tighten in Rio's jaw. "Are you Emily's mother?" she asked.

Tess glanced from Maggie to Jeremy to Rio, her eyes wide, fearful. Then she looked straight at Jeremy. "Y-yes."

For several seconds no one spoke, no one moved. Now that they had the answer to the all-important question, no one knew what to do next.

Stunned, Jeremy stared at Tess, his mind trying to process her single-word answer. An answer that had changed everything in an instant. He swallowed hard, remembering holding the baby—his baby—in his arms. It was his baby. It had to be.

"E-Emily's in a foster home, isn't she?" Tess said, regret coloring her voice.

"She's right where you left her." Rio's voice was cold, accusatory. Maggie almost sighed in relief. He hadn't made a sound since they first saw Tess, and she had begun to worry over his silence.

"You didn't give her to the welfare people?"

Rio shook his head. "Why?" was all he asked, but no one at the table needed more, especially not Tess.

She wiped at the tears running down her pale cheeks. "I couldn't keep her. I tried, but I just couldn't. No job, nowhere to go—"

"You could have come to me," Jeremy said quietly. "She is mine, isn't she?"

For the first time since they had entered the café, Maggie thought she saw a hint of happiness in the girl's eyes. "Yes, oh yes, Jeremy. She's yours." Then the hint faded. "But I couldn't come to you after... after what I'd done. After the way I'd left."

"Why did you leave? I told you we would be married. Why, Tess? I don't understand."

"I—I...they told me it was for the best. They told me I'd ruin any chance you had for becoming somebody important in Austin."

"Who?" Gently, Maggie touched Tess's arm. "Who told you that?"

"My father." She looked into Jeremy's eyes. "And yours."

"Mine?"

"Easy," Rio cautioned, seeing the kid double his hands into fists.

"What did my father say to you?

"Th-that you had been raised to have a career in politics. That even though you *thought* we were...we were in love, it wouldn't last. And...and one day you would look at me and hate me...and the baby, because we kept you from what you really wanted."

"And you believed him? My God, Tess. Why didn't you come to me?"

She stared at him, pain etched into her young face. "You were gone! They told me *you* didn't want to see me, that you left and asked them to take care of the *situation*. That's why you left the letter."

All of the color drained from Jeremy's face. "The debate trip. Dad insisted that I go. Now I know why. And what letter are you talking about?"

"The one you left with your father telling me t-to... to take what they offered and have the abortion."

"Oh, Tess." He reached across the table and held her hand. "I didn't know. I didn't know."

"Y-you didn't send them to talk to me?" she asked, almost afraid to hope. "And the letter?"

"No. I never wrote any letter. Was it typed or in my handwriting?"

"Typed, I think. And the money. Did you know about the money?"

"What money?"

"The ten thousand dollars your father gave mine for the... you know, hospital. I didn't take it, Jeremy," she rushed to assure him. "I couldn't. But my father did. And when I decided to keep the baby, he..."

"Where's your father?" Rio asked, his own hands itching to slam into something hard, preferably John Westlake's face.

"I don't know. After Emily was born, I ran away because I was afraid he would tell Mr. Westlake and they would make me give her up. Then I... I had to give her up anyway. But I tried to keep track of her. I even called the welfare people to see if Mr. Langley had turned her in."

Everything the girl said made sense, as far as it went, but Maggie still had some questions. "Tess, why did you come looking for Rio?"

"Oh, I wasn't looking for Mr. Langley, I was looking for his mother. Mrs. Rowley—she's cooked for the Westlakes since before Jeremy was born— loved to gossip. She told me about Rio's mother and how Mr. Westlake kicked her out, and how she and Mrs. Langley still exchanged Christmas cards. That's how I found out where you live, where your mother lived. Only when I got to Crystal Creek, she was... Anyway, I was so scared, until I overheard you talking in the café one afternoon about how you had learned the hard way how important family was and that you would give anything just to have some family. That's when I decided that Emily would be in good hands with you. I mean, she wouldn't ever know her daddy, but she could know her..." Tess suddenly stopped, her gaze darting from Jeremy to Rio.

"It's okay, Tess." Jeremy squeezed her hand. "All the lies are out in the open now. I know that Rio and I are related."

"You do? How?"

"It's a long story," Rio said, gazing at Maggie, "that didn't start out happy, and for a while I thought was going to end the same way. Then I learned that sometimes you have to give up something to get a lot more.'' Wasn't he living proof? He had given up Emily and gotten Maggie. And as it turned out, in a way he had gotten Emily back as well. ''But right now I think there's a little girl who would like to see her mama.''

If Rio lived to be one hundred, he would never forget the look of sheer joy on Tess Holloway's tear-stained face.

CHAPTER ELEVEN

TESS, JEREMY, Rio and Maggie had driven back to the ranch and been greeted by a very anxious Elena, who took one look at their faces and smiled. Since then, the house and everyone in it, including Emily, had taken on an almost festive air. A few minutes earlier, Rio had caught Jeremy and Tess stealing a quick kiss in the hall. The truth was out; Jeremy and Tess were together and Emily had her parents. Everything was as it should be.

Everything except Rio. He couldn't claim the same peace the others seemed to have. Something still churned in his gut, gnawing at him, denying him peace. And that something had to do with John Westlake. In his heart, Rio knew there would be no peace for him until he finished with Westlake. But he said nothing to the others.

No need to throw a damper on their happiness, he thought, from his familiar vantage point on the porch. The front legs of the chair were tilted precariously and a bottle of beer dangled from his fingers. Elena and Tess were giving Emily her bath, and laughter, soft and feminine, drifted through the house and out into the fall night.

"Tess and I are going to get married," Jeremy said from the doorway.

The news was not unexpected, considering the two young people hadn't been able to keep their eyes, much less their hands, off each other since they had resolved their problems. "How are you gonna provide for a wife and child?" Rio didn't like the coldness in his voice, but neither did he feel willing to do anything about it.

"Probably not very well for a while. Elena has offered to keep Emily so Tess can go on working at the Longhorn. I'm going to try to stay in school full-time, work part-time as long as I can. When that doesn't work, I'll switch and do school part-time and get a full-time job. We won't have much, but we're both willing to sacrifice as long as we can be together."

The legs of the chair came down hard on the wooden-planked floor. "So, that's it. You ride off into the sunset and live happily ever after."

"Doubt it will be that easy. As a matter of fact, it'll probably be damned hard." Jeremy couldn't account for the touch of sarcasm he detected in his brother's voice. *His brother.* Half brother, to be precise, but Jeremy wasn't interested in precision. As an only child he had dreamed of siblings, and now that he had a brother, he wasn't about to start quibbling about halves versus wholes. It saddened him to realize Rio didn't share his feelings, but maybe, in time, they could learn to be friends. Jeremy would settle for friends.

"You don't know what hard is, kid. You haven't got the faintest idea."

"But you do."

"Damned right. And if I was any kind of a—" Once again, he had stopped short of saying the word *brother* "—straight shooter, I'd tell you to get out while the getting's good."

"I don't believe you."

"You should."

"Why? Because you're older? Wiser?"

Rio snorted. "Not so's you'd notice."

"So you've got fourteen years and some hard knocks on me. That doesn't mean you can tell me how to live my life any more than the old man could."

"And you're not even ticked off about it, are you?"

"What?"

"The old man has manipulated your entire life, and you're just gonna blow it off 'cause you've got Tess and Emily, and that's all that matters."

"Yeah. Tess and Emily *are* all that matters. What's with you?"

"What's with me," Rio spit out. "You have to ask that after everything that's happened? He lied to you, kid. He lied *about* me. And all of it, so he could have his way, so he could live the life he wanted without any inconvenience. He never cared who got hurt in the long run. Not my mother, or you or Tess. For

God's sake, he didn't even care about a little unborn baby! Doesn't that make you rip-roaring, tear-up-the-town mad?''

At that exact moment Maggie stepped out onto the porch. "What's going on?"

"Ask him," Jeremy said and stormed past her.

"Rio?"

He shook his head. "Nothin'. It's nothin'." The churning in his gut he now recognized clearly as good old-fashioned rage. He was mad. Damn mad. Fighting mad. But not at Jeremy.

It wasn't the manipulation of Jeremy's life that stoked his anger. It was the fact that he, Rio Langley, self-proclaimed loner, had allowed the same thing to happen to him, on a different level. At least Jeremy had the advantage of recognizing the manipulation when he saw it. He, on the other hand, had lived his entire life based on the premise that he was his own man, beholden to no one, answering to no one. But the truth—the gut-wrenching, god-awful, bitter truth—was that everything he had done, all the decisions he had made in his life up to this very moment had been influenced by his feelings about one man.

John Hardin Westlake.

It wasn't Jeremy who was rip-roaring, tear-up-the-town mad, but Rio. It wasn't Jeremy who was filled with rage and the blood lust for revenge, but Rio.

Revenge.

The word congealed in the pit of his stomach, cold, thick and heavy. Dear God, was that what gnawed at his insides like a cancer? Was that what had compelled him to forge a life without the warmth of a woman?

Rio had never considered himself a vengeful man. And now to come face-to-face with the realization that he had lived the better part of his life with the idea of revenge smoldering in the back of his mind didn't sit well. Not well at all. Suddenly all the rage he had denied for years ripped at him, clawing for freedom like a vicious, imprisoned tiger. He broke out in a cold sweat.

"Rio?" Maggie said softly. "Please. You're scaring me."

He turned to find her staring up at him, her green eyes filled with concern. Rio pulled her roughly into his arms. "Maggie, Maggie," he breathed as his mouth sought hers.

The kiss was greedy, ravenous. What she tasted on his mouth wasn't desire or a desperate need. What she tasted was something darker, something deeper than mere need. She tasted fear. Shocked at the unexpected roughness, Maggie started to pull away, but stopped herself.

He was afraid. Of what? Of whom? Then as suddenly as the question had come, the answer came, too. Rio was frightened of himself, of his own feelings. Feelings he had kept bottled up for years, possibly all his life. The events of the past two days had popped the cork on all those emotions he had kept tucked away in some dark corner for all these years. Now they were prowling like a starved cat.

Rio gasped for air as he tore his mouth from hers. "Oh, God, what am I doing?"

"It's all right," she whispered.

"Did I hurt you?"

"No, but I'm worried that you're hurting yourself."

"What are you talking about?"

"The anger I felt when you kissed me."

"I'm sorry. I never meant—"

"Don't do this, Rio," she begged. "Don't shut yourself off from me. I thought we were past all of that."

"Past what? I told you, it's nothin'."

Maggie pulled away from him. "You're wrong. It's everything if it comes between us."

He pulled her back into his arms. "Nothing is going to come between us." Didn't she know that without her he was lost?

"The anger is coming between us, right now."

"I'm not mad!" He almost shoved her away from him, his voice filling the darkness, slicing across the still night air like a razor.

"Yes, you are."

He whipped around to face her, and suddenly the angry tiger inside him sprang free. "Don't try to tell me how I feel. You don't know how I feel." He took a deep breath. "No one knows..."

"What don't I know, Rio?"

"That I hate him. I've always hated him."

"John Westlake?"

"*Yes!*"

At last, Maggie thought. Maybe now he would be free of the anger. She wanted him to talk, wanted him to get it all out of his system.

"I hate him for all the times he wasn't around. And all the times he was." Rio tapped a finger to his temple. "Here." He tapped a finger to his chest. "And here. I hate him because I've carried him around with me for years, telling myself he didn't matter that much—" he snapped his fingers "—in my life. He never had. He never would."

"And he doesn't."

"But he does, Maggie. He's always mattered because I couldn't turn myself loose from him until now. Seeing him through Jeremy's eyes, seeing what he's done to that boy, made me realize how much and for how long I've let the hate twist and turn inside me. It made me see that he's influenced my life more than I wanted to admit. Even coming back home, trying to make this worthless ranch work, trying to rescue Emily, all of it was because I've let that son of a bitch affect my life. It made me see that I ran away from him when I was a kid, and I've been running ever since."

"Maybe you came back because you were tired of running."

"What?"

"Maybe you came back to finish what you started twelve years ago. So stop looking back. Finish what you started. Go talk to him, Rio. Face-to-face. And maybe you'll be free of him."

Rio released a long, heavy sigh. "What good would that do? All I can expect is more lies. It's too late, Maggie. Twelve years too late."

"No, it's not," she said vehemently. "Don't you see? You're doing it again. Telling yourself it's no good *because of him.* If you don't face him now, Rio, you'll be doing the same thing you did all those years ago. You'll be running away." She stepped closer, gazing up at him with all the love in her heart shining in her eyes.

"I love you, Rio. Nothing you do will ever change that. But you need to do this for yourself. No one else. Sometimes you have to draw a line through your past or deny yourself a future."

THE FOLLOWING MORNING when the butler opened the door to the Westlake mansion, Rio didn't wait for an invitation, but brushed past the servant and into the marbled foyer. He didn't even bother removing his hat.

"You can't come in here," the butler insisted.

"I'm in, and I wanna see your boss."

"Do you have an appointment?"

"No."

"Then I'm sorry, sir. I'm afraid I'll have to ask you to leave."

Rio folded his arms across his chest, shook his head, then glanced up the wide staircase to the second floor. "Is he upstairs?"

"Mr. Westlake is preparing to go to his office, but—"

"Tell him that Rio Langley is here to see him. And tell him if he doesn't come down, I'm coming up."

"I'm sorry, sir—"

"Just do it. Now."

The butler looked at the tall, broad-shouldered cowboy with his dusty boots and belligerent attitude and decided to let his employer handle this one. He wasn't paid enough to risk a broken nose, or worse. "One moment, sir." The servant turned and climbed the stairs.

Rio wiped damp palms on the seat of his jeans and waited. *Easy, cowboy. You're sweatin' like a two-dollar Saturday night hooker in Sunday morning service.*

Most of the anger he'd experienced last night had disappeared. Instead, he was going through the same kind of anxiety he used to feel when he had a bad dream as a child and his mother tried to reassure him by showing him there were no monsters in the closet. Those few tense seconds, waiting between the time she opened the door and turned on the light, were hell. Just like now.

In an effort to keep his mind occupied, Rio glanced around the expensively furnished lower floor. From where he stood in the foyer, he could see an expan-

sive living room decorated in the kind of heavy floral
fabrics and dark woods he'd seen pictured in magazines. In the opposite direction from the living room
was a small library. Floor-to-ceiling shelves, loaded
with every imaginable kind of book. The entire house
looked expensive and overdone. And cold.

Accustomed to the simplicity of natural wood and
plain cotton window curtains, Rio was uncomfortable. Not in an intimidated sort of way, but in the way
an ill-fitting coat feels confining. He couldn't wait to
draw a breath of fresh Hill Country air again.

"You wanted to see me."

Rio's heart jumped. He looked up and for the first
time in his life stared into the face of the man who had
sired him.

Standing at the bottom of the staircase directly
across the foyer, John Westlake stared back at the son
he had never claimed.

Westlake was shorter than his elder son by almost
a foot. He had thinning gray hair and a paunch. The
suit he wore was undoubtedly custom-made, and the
shoes probably cost more than Rio had made rodeo-
ing in a month.

Otherwise, he looked . . . ordinary.

Incredibly ordinary.

He's just a man, Rio thought, more than slightly
amazed. He wasn't sure exactly what he had expected, but he supposed someone more distin-
guished-looking, or with a more influential air,
or . . . just more. But Westlake didn't fit any of the

images he had conjured up over the years. If Rio hadn't had firsthand knowledge of how ruthless this man could be, he could easily have described him as a middle-aged, overweight businessman, much like thousands of other Austin businessmen.

Suddenly a strange peace settled over Rio, and the anxiety vanished. *There really aren't any monsters in the closet.* Just as in his childhood nightmares, the monsters were all in his mind. The thought that he might have continued his self-imposed life of isolation if he hadn't returned home to Crystal Creek sent a shudder through him. No, not just home. Home to Maggie.

Maggie. Sweet Maggie. She had helped him come to this moment. She was the difference. The turning point in his life.

And he was free. He could look at this man and not hate him. In fact, now he could look at the man and feel nothing, because that was exactly what John Westlake was to him. Nothing. Facing him, Rio realized that all the things he had thought he needed so desperately to say now seemed meaningless.

"I said, did you want to see me?"

Calmly, more calmly that he would ever have thought possible, Rio slid his hands into the hip pockets of his jeans and said honestly, "Not particularly."

"Then why are you here?"

"To tell you that Jeremy is staying with me temporarily."

For a second, Rio thought he caught a flash of panic in the other man's eyes, but it passed so quickly he wasn't certain.

"So," Westlake said coldly. "That's why you came? To gloat over some victory you think you've won? Did you think you could turn Jeremy against me by filling his head full of lies about me?" Westlake straightened his shoulders and adjusted his tie. "I admitted to my mistake with your mother—"

Rio pulled his hands out of his pockets. "Her name was Delora."

"And I assured him that you'd had everything you needed over the years. This entire affair has been blown completely out of proportion."

"I don't think Jeremy sees it that way."

"Then he's acting very foolishly."

"Jeremy's a lot of things. Young, inexperienced. But he's no fool. He proved that when he walked away from you."

"Ah," Westlake responded, smiling. "Now I see what this is all about. Revenge. You're simply using Jeremy to get back at me for not legitimizing you, is that it?" For the first time he looked Rio up and down. "I should have expected something like this. Do you have a particular sum in mind?"

"I don't want your money." Rio glanced down at his boots, more to hide his pity than his anger, then back at Westlake. "You may find this hard to believe, but money's not the most important thing in the world. At least not to me, and I believe not to Jeremy. Not anymore.''

"And I suppose you want me to believe he's going to give up living like this, driving nice cars and having ample spending money, for a newfound relationship with his *brother?*'' When Rio didn't respond immediately, Westlake said, "All right, all right, I'll concede that for the moment you have some influence over Jeremy. And I'm willing to compensate you, but I warn you, don't push me too far.'' He reached inside his breast pocket and removed a checkbook.

Rio took a good hard look at John Westlake, and all he saw was a man throwing away joy and happiness with both hands. He would probably die a lonely old man without ever knowing what he'd done. Sad, Rio thought. Thank God, no such end awaited him.

"You haven't got anything I want,'' Rio said.

And it was true.

John Westlake didn't have anything he wanted or needed. Everything he needed, or ever would need, was waiting for him in Crystal Creek.

He turned to leave, then stopped and turned back. "I never thought the day would come when I'd feel sorry for you, but I do.''

"I don't need your pity, and you'll change your mind about the money.''

"I won't be back. And I wouldn't look for Jeremy any time soon if I were you. He's gonna be real busy with Tess and the baby.'' At the look of surprise on

Westlake's face, Rio couldn't help but smile. "Yeah, that's right. All your hard work for nothin'. They're together, and they're gonna stay together 'cause they've got something more important than money or power or fancy houses. Her name's Emily, and she's three months old. Think about that, Westlake."

Rio turned and walked away. He didn't look back.

"YOU'RE GONNA wear a hole in that rug if you don't stop pacin'," Elena insisted.

"I'm down to my last nerve, and it's frayed. If I stand still, I'll go nuts."

"Reckon you don't want another cup of coffee then."

Maggie cut Elena a look, only to discover she was smiling. "How can you sit there calmly darning a sock when he's with ... *that man?*"

"You're the one told him to go."

"Oh, please don't remind me. What do you think has happened?"

"I got no crystal ball."

"Now *you're* making me crazy." Frustrated, Maggie gnawed on her bottom lip. "What was that? Did you hear his truck drive in?"

"Maggie," Elena said, looking her straight in the eye, "stop blamin' yourself and stop fidgetin'."

She ceased pacing, walked to the window and lifted the curtain to look out. "I do blame myself, Elena. If I hadn't pushed him, he never would have gone."

"Then it's a good thing you pushed."

"How can you say that?"

"'Cause it was time. Had to come to this. Lord knows, it's been brewin' long enough."

"That's not what you said yesterday," Maggie reminded her. "What changed your mind?"

"That kid. He's Rio made over, I tell ya. Knowin' he stood up to his daddy, then came lookin' for Rio, made me think twice. Sometimes dreadin' the trouble is worse than anything that comes of it."

"I just wish I knew what was happening. For all we know the two of them could be punching each other out this very minute."

"Wouldn't bet against Rio."

"Westlake might have him arrested!"

Elena rose from her chair. The half-darned sock dangled from one hand as she pointed a finger at Maggie. "If you don't stop frettin', I'm fixin' to tie you to a chair. Now sit down before you faint dead away."

Maggie sat, but if possible, her nerves were more raw than before. "How can you be so calm?" She felt as if her life were coming apart, as if *she* were coming apart, unraveling like a loose ball of yarn.

"Keep myself busy."

"How can you—" Maggie looked closer at the sock Elena was darning. "So you're not worried, huh?"

"Not a bit."

"You're not even a teeny—" she measured a sliver of space between her thumb and index finger "—weeny bit concerned?"

"Nope."

"Then tell me why you're darning a brown sock with red thread."

Elena looked at her, then the sock. "Damnation. That boy's gonna drive me to an early grave."

Maggie tried not to smile and failed. "Did Jeremy say what time he and Tess would be back?"

"They took Emily in to show 'er off to Rosa Walters, and I suspect, anybody else that'll stand still. Then Jeremy had to drive to that college for somethin' or other. I reckon they'll turn up around supper time."

Neither said a word for several minutes, and Maggie thought about how quiet the house seemed without the baby around. "I'm going to miss Emily," she said.

"I reckon we all will."

"Did Jeremy say anything to you about where he and Tess are going to live?"

"They're gonna stay in her room at the Longhorn till they figger out what to do. Don't think he's got much skill, and with times hard like they are, he'll be lucky to find a job. But I've got an idea that might—"

There was a noise outside, and Maggie jumped out of her chair. "What was that?"

Elena stopped darning. "Sounds like Rio's truck."

They waited, both wanting to run to the door but neither daring to.

"You okay, sonny?" Elena asked a second after Rio stepped inside.

"Yeah."

She gave him the once-over, satisfied herself that he was telling the truth and nodded. "Then I'll leave you to Maggie."

"Are you really all right?" she whispered after Elena left the room. Rio nodded. He was looking at her so strangely, as if he hadn't seen her in days instead of hours.

"And...what about Mr. Westlake? Is he all right?" She couldn't completely rid herself of visions of the man lying in a bloody heap.

A slow grin spread across Rio's face. "The last time I saw him, he was standing upright. Not a mark on him."

Maggie didn't realize she had been holding her breath until then. "Good. I've been going out of my mind, imagining all kinds of scenarios that ended with you in jail."

"I'm not going anywhere."

The ring of confidence in his voice made her even more curious about what had happened between him and John Westlake. "Can you... do you want to tell me what happened?"

The grin faded as Rio pondered the question for a minute. "Not now," he said, so matter-of-factly she could have been asking him if he wanted a cup of coffee. "Later, I'll tell you everything, but for now there's something much more important on my mind."

The man who had gone to confront his past no longer existed. In his place stood a confident man, at peace with himself. She had no idea what had happened to bring about this peace, but for the time being, she didn't even care. He was here and he was all right. That was all that mattered. "I understand."

"Yeah, you do. You always have. C'mere, Maggie."

He was still staring at her with that strange look on his face, part wistful longing, part... Her eyes widened. *Part desire.* She rose from her chair and went to stand in front of him. "Rio—"

"Shh." His fingertip touched her lips, then his hand slid around to capture her nape. He pulled her close. "I wanna tell you what's on my mind." His thumb stroked the side of her neck, making her want to close her eyes and revel in the delicious sensation. "Know what I remember most about that first kiss sitting on your parents' front porch?

He wrapped his other hand around her waist and pulled her even closer. "No," she whispered.

"I thought you had the softest lips I'd ever kissed. And I'd already kissed my fair share of girls." He widened his stance and shifted his weight ever so slightly. Just enough to cause her body to fit intimately to his.

"You had a reputation."

"I was a hell-raiser from the get go and you were the preacher's daughter." He ran his hand up and down her arm. "I never thought I was good enough for you."

His touch was heaven. "Even preachers' daughters like to be kissed."

"So I've discovered."

"Did you know I was in love with you even then?"

He dipped his head and brushed her lips with his. "If I had known what it meant to be loved by you, I never would have left." He threaded all ten fingers in her hair and tilted her head back so that she couldn't look anywhere but his eyes. "Maybe I would have learned then what I learned today. That I don't want to run away from anything. I want to run *to* something. To you. Sweet Maggie. Will you marry me?"

CHAPTER TWELVE

"So, what do you think, Mrs. Langley?"

"I think, Mr. Langley, that our wedding day was about as perfect as we could ever hope for."

Rio gazed into his wife's beautiful green eyes. "And it's not over yet."

"Hmm." She smiled and nestled her head on his chest.

They were standing together, watching the sunset shoot a blaze of colors from gold to deep purple across the Texas sky.

"It *was* a perfect day, wasn't it?"

Rio chuckled, and Maggie felt the vibration against her ear. "If you don't count the fact that Rory Jones nearly fell into the well wearing his Sunday suit, and Cal got a ticket driving with Serena like a bat outta hell from Austin, and showed up only fifteen minutes before the ceremony started. And don't forget your father forgetting the words for the first time in— how many years did your mother say?"

"More than twenty. Poor Dad. But you'll have to admit it was perfect the way it turned out."

Rio planted a kiss on the top of her head. "As long as it turned out that you and I are married in the eyes of God and the state of Texas, then yeah, it turned out perfect."

Small and informal, the ceremony, with Maggie's father presiding and her mother playing the piano, had been a celebration of love and family. Besides the Blakes, Elena, Jeremy, Tess and Emily, Cal and Serena, Ken and Nora and a handful of friends had witnessed their vows.

Everything had gone off as planned, with the exception of the good reverend stumbling over forgotten words, and a few tears, plus one major and very important last-minute change.

Maggie turned in Rio's arms so that she could see his face. "Tell me something. What made you switch best men at the last minute and ask Jeremy? Cal was a good sport about stepping aside, but I must confess it was a surprise."

Rio thought for a long time before answering. "This morning he was playing with Emily in the yard. Tess joined them, and I watched the three of them together, and realized that they were my family, at least a large part of it. It just seemed right that he should be the one standing beside me when I took you to love and to cherish."

"I'm glad."

"At first I wasn't sure he could cut it."

"You mean being your best man?"

"That. But mostly I mean about working here, living here."

"Well, I have to admit I was a little shocked when Elena offered to have her old trailer house moved out here, and parked on that small meadow on the west side of the barn so they could be close."

"Yeah. I was sure as hell antsy about having all this...*family* around. Having him and Tess and Emily within walking distance could have been a disaster."

"But it hasn't been."

"No. In fact, it's been anything but. I think that's mostly due to the kid's attitude. You know, he's worked alongside me for the past month, finalizing the details for the stock contracting business while we wait for approval from the Professional Rodeo Cowboys Association. The kid's a quick study, and he's got a better feel for ranch work than I expected."

"That's because he's got the best teacher in the world. The best example of how to be a loving, caring, hardworking man."

"Whatever I am, whatever I've done or will do counts for nothing without you." Rio pulled her close, closer. "You know how much I love you, Maggie?"

"I think so."

He shook his head. "You know how long I've waited for this day? This night?"

Maggie's heartbeat rocketed to a wild rhythm, and her body flushed hot, cold, then hotter still. "Yes," she whispered as his hands stroked up and down her arms. The dress she had chosen for her wedding was a simple sheath style with a portrait neckline made of delicate aqua lace over aqua silk, except for the sleeves, which were lace only. So sheer that she could feel the heat of Rio's touch through the flimsy fabric.

"And I don't know about you—" he kissed her lightly at a corner of her mouth, as if tasting her was the only thing worth doing in the entire world "—but I'm tired of waiting." Despite the statement he nibbled at her bottom lip as if it were the appetizer for a full-course meal meant to be savored for hours.

"Yes."

"I've dreamed of having you in my arms—" he placed little just-a-taste-here, just-a-taste-there kisses along her cheek and up to her ear "—in my bed, for so long."

Maggie arched her neck and turned her head to give him free access as she reveled in the sensual sampling excursion. "Oh, yes."

"Maggie. Sweet Maggie."

"Rio, Rio..."

Suddenly he felt her stiffen in his arms. "Maggie?"

She cleared her throat. "Sweetheart, I think..."

"What?" he murmured against the curve of her neck.

"Don't look now," she said a little breathlessly. "But that large part of your family is coming up the steps."

Rio lifted his head and looked out the screen door. Sure enough, Tess and Jeremy, holding Emily, were walking up to the back porch.

"Hi," they said in unison when they saw the newlyweds.

"Hi," Maggie answered, her heart still beating wildly, her body still trembling from her husband's touch. "Come on in."

Rio shot her a quelling look, but she couldn't just ignore the couple standing on the porch.

Rio nearly groaned out loud at the interruption. As much as he enjoyed seeing Tess, Jeremy and especially little Emily, at the moment he could cheerfully wish they would all vanish off the face of the earth.

"Uh, we thought...well," Jeremy stammered when they stepped inside.

Tess jumped in to rescue her suddenly tongue-tied husband. "We wanted to get you something. We thought about some champagne—"

"But we remembered you don't drink, Maggie."

"We tried to think of something special because, well...if it wasn't for y'all, me and Jeremy and Emily wouldn't be together, and there's just not enough money in the world to repay that debt.''

''We kept coming up with ideas, and then tossing them out for one reason or another, mostly because of our limited budget. Then Tess thought of something.'' Jeremy shrugged. ''It's not like a real wedding gift, but well...'' He put his free arm around Tess and cleared his throat. ''We'd be proud if both of you would do us the honor of becoming Emily's godparents.''

Maggie reached for Rio's hand. With her other hand she wiped at a tear. She gazed up at her husband, silently asking if his answer was the same as hers. It was. Smiling, she said, ''That's the nicest wedding gift anyone could receive. Thank you both, and yes, we'll be thrilled to be Emily's godparents.''

''We appreciate you asking,'' Rio added, his voice tight with emotion.

''We, uh... We know you all are busy, but, uh... could I talk with you a minute, Rio?''

''Sure.'' He turned to Maggie and answered the ''what's up?'' look in her eyes with a ''beats me'' shrug, then followed Jeremy out into the balmy fall evening.

Standing under the star-filled Texas sky, Rio waited for the kid to say whatever was on his mind. Finally, Jeremy began, ''I wanted to thank you for everything you've done for Tess and me. And Emily.''

When Rio started to dismiss the compliment, Jeremy raised his hand. "No. I owe you. And it's important for me to tell you," he insisted, his voice and expression tense.

"I, uh, did something today you may not like, but I thought it had to be done. I've thought a lot about my dad and why he did what he did to you. I don't understand it. I never will, but you were right when you said I couldn't cut him out of my life. I went to see him this morning."

So, Rio thought, that accounted for the kid's mysterious two-hour disappearance while all the frantic wedding preparations were going on. He hadn't thought much about it at the time because he, too, had decided to find something to keep himself busy, and out of the women's way.

"I told him you were getting married." Jeremy glanced down at his boots. "I also told him I was changing my major from law to agriculture—" he lifted his gaze to Rio's "—and if he intended to yank my college fund money that was fine with me. The money would make things easier, but I can make it on my own."

"And?"

"He said the money was mine. He didn't care what I did with it."

"I'm surprised."

"So was I. I figured he would tell me to shift for myself now that I'm not playing his game, but..."

"But what?"

"He seemed different. Sort of quiet and...old. He looked real old, Rio. Funny," Jeremy said. "I never thought of him that way until today. He was always so forceful and compelling that I guess I thought he would live forever."

"You feeling sorry for him? You thinking of going back?"

"No!" came the quick reply. "No. But for the first time I saw him as a man, and not just my father. I gave him one of those pictures we had taken of Emily at K-Mart the other day. He tried to act like he didn't care, but I saw him glance at the photo before he stuffed it into his pocket."

"Don't expect miracles, kid."

"I don't expect anything from him. I only wanted to make *my*—" he pointed his finger to his chest "—peace. I had to do it for me, not for him."

Rio nodded, understanding completely. They stood, not speaking for several moments.

"You think I made a mistake?" Jeremy asked.

"Going to see the old man?"

"No. Changing my major. It'll mean another year, maybe two in order to graduate, but it's what I want to do."

Rio shrugged noncommittally, but secretly he was pleased. More than pleased. "It's your life, kid."

"Yeah, I know. And that's why I wanted to talk to you." He took a deep breath, and plunged right into the topic that had been on his mind for days. "I'm going for a degree in farm and ranch management, and I...I want to work on the ranch. I know I'm green, but I'm learning, and I swear to you, Rio, I've never felt as good about anything as I have working with the stock...and working with you. And I might as well get the rest of it off my chest," he added quickly, looking directly at Rio.

"Today...today was..." He cleared his throat again. "Well, I wanted to say thanks for asking me to stand up for you today. I wish I'd the nerve to ask you to do that for me when Tess and I went to that Justice of the Peace last month and got married, but I was afraid you'd..." Jeremy swallowed hard. "Well, what I'm trying to say is that Tess and I owe you a lot, and I just wanted you to know how grateful we are. Especially me. My only regret is that I didn't find out you were my brother years ago."

Thunderstruck, Rio couldn't find words to express what he was feeling. He decided that if he tried he would probably end up sounding like a barroom poet after one too many. So, he simply held out his hand. When Jeremy clasped it in a firm handshake, Rio could feel the new calluses caused by hard work.

Yeah, the kid was going to do all right. "Thanks, Jeremy," Rio said solemnly. Gratefully.

Jeremy grinned. "You know, that's the first time you haven't called me 'kid.' I think we're making progress."

Rio grinned back, knowing that after tonight he would never call him "kid" again. They held the handshake for a second or two longer than usual, then broke away.

"Well, uh, I guess your bride is wondering where you are."

"Yeah. I guess so."

"Thanks again. For *everything*." A wealth of emotion was conveyed in the single word.

"You earned it."

The two men, both accepting their pasts, and eager for their futures, walked back into the house.

Maggie was playing with Emily when they entered. "Everything okay?" she asked, handing the baby to her mother.

Rio jerked his head toward Jeremy. "My brother's decided he wants to be a rancher. What do you think of that?"

Tess and Jeremy exchanged looks, then smiled at each other. Tess went to stand beside her husband.

Maggie hadn't taken her eyes off Rio since he had addressed Jeremy as "brother." "I—I..." She fought tears. "I think that's wonderful." Then she moved closer to Rio. She gazed up at him and whispered, "I think you're wonderful."

They stared into each other's eyes, heedless of the other couple until finally Tess said, "I think we've worn out our welcome."

"Yeah," Jeremy agreed, grinning. "I think we better go."

"What?" Maggie pulled her eyes away from Rio. "Oh, yes. Good night."

"'Night," Rio echoed as the threesome left. He turned to his bride. "I thought they'd never leave."

"Neither did I."

"Now, let's see." Rio dipped his head for more kisses. "Where were we before they showed up?"

"I think you were about to make love to me."

He released a deep sigh as he hauled her into a fierce embrace. "You can count on it."

"Hmm," she murmured, giving him a quick, soft kiss. "Will you give me a moment before you come to bed?"

Rio swallowed hard, and nodded as she slipped out of his arms and walked toward the bedroom.

My wife, he thought, and smiled to himself. Who would ever have thought he could be so lucky? *A woman who loves me. A shot at a real future. What more could a man want?*

Nothing. He had it all. Including a family he hadn't even counted on a few months ago. *Yeah. You got it all, cowboy.*

Then why was he as nervous as a long-tailed cat in a room full of rocking chairs?

For the first time in Rio's life he had all the happiness any man could want, and more. He wasn't used to this much joy, but from now on he intended to get used to it because he had a feeling there was more to come.

Nervously, he glanced at his watch. Only five minutes had passed, but it seemed like twenty. "Maggie?" he said. When she didn't answer he walked toward the bedroom. "Maggie?" Slowly, Rio opened the bedroom door and came to an abrupt halt.

The room was bathed in a soft glow from candles placed in front of the mirror of the antique dressing table, on the windowsill, and on the night tables beside the bed. He had never seen anything so downright beautiful in his life. . . .

Except Maggie.

Dressed in an aqua silk floor-length gown the identical shade of her wedding dress, she stood next to the bed waiting for him. The candlelight danced over her auburn hair like fairies in a ring and touched her skin with a soft, warm glow. She held out her arms for him, and Rio thought his heart was going to stop beating right then and there.

At the sight of her, Rio's eyes darkened. He came toward her, stopped only inches away and simply stared. "Y-you...you're so beautiful." The words were pitifully inadequate to describe his feelings, but even if he had been a poet, he doubted he could ever have found words sufficient to describe her beauty. She looked like an angel, all softness and light. His angel. His hand shook as he touched her cheek.

"I love you so much, Maggie. I need you."

Maggie's breath quickened. She stepped closer, bringing her body into tantalizing contact with his. "And I need you. I love you. More than I ever thought possible. Almost more than my heart can hold."

His hand slid to her bare shoulder, and she could feel the trembling. "I want you so much I'm shaking."

She smiled, lifted her hands to his chest so that he could feel her similar response. "I know the feeling."

He drew in an unsteady breath. "For the first time in my life, I feel awkward."

"It's just you and me. The way it was always supposed to be."

"You're so gorgeous. I can't believe you're mine."

"All yours." She looked up, and caught a glimpse of uncertainty in his eyes. "And you're mine, Rio. Now and forever. Nothing will ever change that."

"God, I hope not."

"You can count on it."

"I've lived my whole life by the rule of a drifter—don't hold on to nothin' too long because nothin' lasts forever."

"We will. I promise you, we will," she said, understanding his need for reassurance. His need to know that he would never have to drift again, be alone again. Ever. And she understood that she had the power to make him believe her. She intended to exercise that power.

After tonight there would be no need for assurances because he would know beyond the shadow of a doubt how much she loved him. After tonight there would be no need ever to wonder if she was ashamed of what they had found together. Because he'd know that love, real love, was shameless in its truth and forever in its heart.

The world compressed to only the two of them. This moment. This heartbeat.

Standing in front of him, Maggie began to unbutton his shirt. "You and I are forever, Rio." She worked her way down until she got to the last button, the one directly above his belt buckle. Then she spread her fingers wide, gathered a handful of fabric in each hand, and slowly pulled his shirt out of his pants.

She finished unbuttoning the shirt, spread the front open, and pushed it off his shoulders and down his arms.

The air in Rio's lungs was suddenly in short supply and his body reacted in an extremely predictable manner.

"I'm going to love you," she whispered, stringing a line of kisses across his bare chest, "for a long, long time. All of you." She lifted her head, stepped back, then slowly walked around to stand behind him, silk whispering, her body brushing his as she moved. "The good and the bad." She placed her hands on his back, sliding them upward over his shoulders until her fingers were buried in his long, thick hair. "Your strengths, and your weaknesses."

Rio was dying by degrees and it was pure heaven.

Maggie's hands trailed down his shoulders and back, stopping at his waist, then up again, then down again, her fingertips stroking his skin, stroking his need.

Then her hands stopped, and she kissed a spot on his back just above his waist. Then another and another. Kisses. Dozens, maybe even hundreds of kisses. Soft, hard. Quick, slow. Tiny kisses where her lips barely caressed his skin and lingering kisses where she flicked her tongue over his heated flesh.

He couldn't breathe, couldn't think of anything but what she was doing to him, and how much he wanted her never to stop and yet how much he wanted her to stop so he could do the same things to her. His hands curled into fists at his sides and his entire body was drawn tight as a bow. Then she stopped and he almost screamed for her to continue.

When he would have turned to her, she stopped him with a soft, breathy command. "Wait."

The gentle rasp of silk moving over her body filled the quiet room. A second later, the aqua gown was pooled on the floor beside their feet.

She was... Rio swallowed, or tried to swallow. He couldn't. His mouth was dry and his heart was beating so fast he was sure he would die.

And then—oh, sweet heaven—then she leaned forward, pressing her warm, naked body to his as she slipped her arms around his waist. Slowly, deliberately, she swayed back and forth, the tips of her breasts stroking his skin as lightning strokes the sky with electricity right before a storm.

Rio gasped, then groaned, his heart nearly shooting out of his body and, if possible, its rhythm redoubling. But when—again slowly, deliberately—she walked around to face him, Rio thought his heart might actually stop.

She stood close enough to be able to touch him, yet far enough away so that he could see every soft, sweet inch of her. She was as God had created her. Perfect. His.

And then he knew. He understood. Everything she was doing, every sensation she was creating was designed to let him know not only how much she wanted him, but *how* she wanted him. Unconditionally. Unashamedly. There were no barriers to her love. No boundaries.

"I love you. Completely. Forever."

He couldn't stand another second of the sweet torture of not touching her. He pulled her into his arms and held her to him, her breasts plumping against his bare chest. But it wasn't enough. It didn't satisfy all the nights without her, all the lonely nights. "And I'll love you just as much, just as long."

He kissed her then the way he had waited to kiss her all day, maybe all his life. Long, deep and hard.

And as he lowered her to the bed, she welcomed his kiss. Gloried in it. Nothing in life was certain except this... this love. This bond. This most intimate of commitments.

No longer content for her to be the aggressor, Rio shed his own clothes and took full charge.

He was a graceful, powerful male. He did not intend to overpower, yet he did, in the same way males had been dominating females since the first coupling—by the sheer strength of his need to mate, to claim and her need to be mated, to be claimed. And she gloried in the power, in the claiming, as had Eve and every woman since.

He worshiped her with his mouth, his hands, his body, telling her in the language of passion how much he loved her. And Maggie answered back, sweetly, hotly, matching him kiss for kiss, touch for touch, passion for passion. Everywhere his lips touched, she burned. Every time her hands stroked, he whispered encouragement. They lost themselves in each other, becoming single-minded in their need for each other.

And then he took her and she gave herself in the timeless ritual of mating, the timeless joining of souls. She filled the well of loneliness he had always known even as he filled her body. He accepted her gift of love and hope even as she accepted his body. And when the end came, it was like soaring from the mountain-top, racing with the wind, flying to the moon—all the wonderful things love songs since the first note had promised. And it was more because the soaring, racing, flying pleasure—sweet, blissful, soul-shattering pleasure—was theirs alone.

And then there was peace. A peace like nothing either had ever felt before because it, too, was theirs alone.

Outside their bedroom window, stars sparkled like diamonds scattered across black velvet, and a breeze mingled with their sighs in the soft Hill Country night.